A SUNSHINE BAY DUET

LOVE'S FRESH START AND COME HOME TO LOVE

JEANINE LAUREN

LOVE'S FRESH START

For Amin, with love

"Why did I say I'd do this?" Sylvia Tremblay muttered as she readjusted her scarf to better protect her neck from the chilly spring breeze. She peered up at the steel-grey clouds that covered Sunshine Bay and hoped it wouldn't rain.

Because the doctor insisted that you try walking, the taskmaster in her head answered in a voice that sounded remarkably like her late mother's. A voice that was practical. Bossy. *You must try something. The pills and talk therapy don't seem to be working anymore. Do you want to live like this for the rest of your life?*

As if walking among daffodils and the first buds of spring was going to help her get over this. Mark was gone, and she was alone. She would always be alone.

Stop that. He's gone, and you need to move on. You need to find your old self... the Sylvia you were before this dark cloud settled over you. Before Mark.

Sylvia nodded in agreement with her mother's voice, squared her shoulders against the breeze, and continued to walk.

She had promised the doctor, and now that she was here in the gardens of the city park, she would try to enjoy the morning. It was a normal thing, to take a morning stroll. And it was safer to walk now than in the afternoon. She was less likely to run into people in the morning. She wasn't ready for people yet. Especially men. She hadn't been comfortable around people since Mark's illness and death two years earlier. Since the black...

What was that? Something caught her eye.
Small and...

Black.

Sylvia paused in the middle of the path to take in the sight before her, and a small sigh of contentment escaped her lips. How long had it been since she'd smiled? It felt like two long years. And yet here she was, smiling over a little black cat napping in the first rays of warm spring sunshine that had penetrated the clouds above.

Sylvia lowered herself to the bench nearby, happy to find this quiet spot away from people. People made her nervous. But animals, especially this cat…

The cat startled from its sleep and leaped to all four feet. Sylvia jerked in surprise.

"You scared me," Sylvia said. The cat faced her, eyes wary, as it backed toward the underbrush near the path.

"Oh, don't rush off so soon. Here, kitty, kitty." Sylvia rose and stretched out her hand, willing the cat to approach her. The cat turned and ran to the safety of the tangled underbrush, pausing to turn, frozen in place, watching Sylvia.

"You won't get that one to come out," a deep voice said from behind her. Sylvia whirled to see a tall man dressed in overalls, smiling at her from under the brim of a conductor's cap. "That cat's been here for years," he continued. "I see it in the mornings when I come to work. She doesn't like people much. I've tried to be friendly, but she runs away."

"Perhaps she's always been feral." Sylvia's heart pounded. The anxiety that had been her near-constant companion in recent months rose in her chest. She was surprised she could even get the words out.

"I don't think so," the man said. "I was told she belonged to an elderly couple who used to live across the street. They died in a fire a few years back, and she's been here ever since."

"How sad," Sylvia said. She glanced at the cat, feeling a sudden kinship with it. They'd both been yanked from their old world and forced to find their footing in a new one.

"She gets a lot of mice, though. We don't see many at the train station."

"Train station?" Sylvia asked, congratulating herself on her nearly normal-sounding voice as she fought to relax and breathe as if she talked to strange men every day.

"Yes, behind there." The man pointed to a wall of boards painted to appear like a stone fence. "There's a train that runs all summer for the children. I drive it and do some of the maintenance. The season starts in two weeks, so I'm here getting ready for our spring launch."

"The children must enjoy that," Sylvia said, mentally kicking herself for continuing to engage with this man. She wanted to be alone to commune with the cat she was watching. The cat was watching her in return.

"Oh, yes, the children seem to like it. I enjoy it too. Always wanted to drive a train, so I took it up after I retired." He smiled.

"Uh-huh." Sylvia nodded. He didn't look old enough to be retired. He looked about her age.

Was she noticing a man? What would Mark say?

"My name's Jack Robertson." The man extended his hand toward her, interrupting her thoughts.

Sylvia looked at it before slowly shaking. "Sylvia Tremblay." She looked into his hazel eyes that, for an instant, seemed to reveal pain. For a moment Sylvia got lost in that pain. Was Jack feeling as hopeless as she was? Wondering, like her, if that feeling would ever go away?

Maybe he was like her. *Alone*.

Or…

Lonely.

"I haven't seen you around before. Are you new to the area?" Jack asked, breaking into an easy smile in a face lined from a lifetime of laughter. Sylvia found herself returning his smile, hoping hers appeared genuine.

"No, I've lived here for years," Sylvia said. "I don't get to the park often, though." Could he hear her heart pounding? The loud bongo beats in her ears made her momentarily dizzy, and she felt heat rise under the collar of her coat; her face was surely flushed. She felt the heat in her cheeks deepen. Jack glanced at her, then at the cat, and raised his arm to read the time on his watch.

"Well, I should be getting along. Good day to you, Sylvia."

"Yes. H-have a good day." The cold sweat that had begun to climb up her back receded as she watched Jack walk toward the back of the garden and disappear through a door in the fence.

"Well, that was embarrassing." Sylvia seated herself shakily on the bench again and turned her attention back to the cat. "I haven't talked to a man in a while. Except doctors, of course, but they're not the same. Not in their professional capacity anyway." And she would know. She'd encountered an assembly line of medical professionals after the accident and during Mark's extended illness. Sylvia shook her head, pulling herself back to the present. Going down the rabbit hole to the past always led to pain.

Remember the objective, Sylvia. She needed to find her way back to the world, not drift rudderless in a sea of old memories. The cat looked at her, an unblinking statue.

"But enough about me. Tell me, how do I get you to come out of your shell, little one? You look a bit lean. Haven't you been eating well?" The cat blinked, turned, and walked deeper into the underbrush.

Sylvia sat, staring at the spot where the cat had disappeared, until she became aware that the cold spring air had seeped through her too-thin jacket.

"Well, I guess that's that," Sylvia mumbled. "Time to get moving." She stood and began to walk the path that wound its way through the gardens, glancing into the underbrush intermittently to see if she could find the cat.

When she got to the little bridge that crossed the creek at the centre of the grounds, she paused a moment to watch a mallard duck and his mate drifting in the slow-moving water. Her heart lurched. It was hard to be single when she had so long been part of a pair. She would need to get used to it; there weren't many men interested in a plump sixty-year-old, particularly one with dark clouds invading her every thought. She thought of Jack then quickly dismissed the memory. Just because he was the first man she'd spoken to in months didn't mean he was interested. Maybe he wasn't even suitable. Though he did have a kind face.

At least she wasn't alone in her misery. The online support group she'd found had women from all corners of the Western world bemoaning their new fate. They logged into the chat room or discussion threads, each sharing her story, each one worse than the last. But in some ways, it was a comfort to know other women shared her fate. She was a member of an exclusive club with the ultimate hazing ritual: all you had to do was be the surviving spouse.

Sylvia strolled past an oval track where several men and women walked in a random yet organized pattern, some alone, some in groups, some clockwise and others counter-clockwise, all coexisting despite their different rhythms. People smiled as they passed, and she forced herself to turn toward them and smile in return.

Her doctor would be proud. She'd done what she promised she'd do.

But what now?

Sylvia pulled the bus schedule out of her pocket. If she hurried, she could be home by ten thirty. Where she'd…

Spend time locked in a chat room with other women who were dealing with grief through pills and pity?

No. Today she'd made the effort to come out, and now that she had succeeded, she wouldn't go home right away. Today she would go to the store and buy some necessities: milk, eggs, fresh vegetables, perhaps some cat food.

Resolved, Sylvia walked out of the park toward the small supermarket she normally called to deliver her groceries. It was early on a Monday morning, and there were few cars parked outside.

"You can do this," Sylvia told herself under her breath. "You've shopped here for years." But she knew it was more than that. This was the first time since Mark's death that she had ventured out to do her own shopping. The bongo beats were back in her ears. *Breathe, Sylvia.* She walked toward the long line of shopping carts, pulled one from its nest, and manoeuvred it toward the automatic doors at the front of the store.

The aisles were almost empty, and she soon located the milk and eggs. As she walked past the dairy section, she paused a moment to read the yogourt containers. She had seen ads on television for Greek yoghurt, and before she could talk herself out of it, she picked up a small container. Time for the vegetable aisle.

Sylvia stopped for a few minutes, taking in the colours of the vegetables: red peppers and orange carrots bright against the green beans beside them. Rows of root vegetables and mushrooms—shitake, white, and portobello. Her stomach gurgled, but she stopped herself from loading her cart. She couldn't be bothered to try new recipes for one. When Mark was alive she had enjoyed cooking for their many visitors, but now…

She took a long, steadying breath and willed the wild bongos to silence. She would stick to the easy food, though she did sneak a bunch of spinach and some lettuce into the basket, along with carrots and red beets to make a fresh salad. Her doctor would be happy to hear that she was attempting to eat healthier. Satisfied, she made her way to the pet food aisle.

There, the bongos returned, and she felt dizzy as she scanned the array of cat food. How would she ever choose? What did a cat like to eat? Pausing a moment to breathe deeply and count to ten, she waited for the anxiety to recede and then examined the options again. Why did she come here? She wasn't ready to be out shopping.

"But what about the cat?" she mumbled. "It's all alone, and skinny from so few meals. You can do this."

There were four different varieties, and she took one of each, placing them quickly into the cart before steering it toward the checkout. Soon she was back outside, holding two newly purchased cloth bags full of groceries.

"You did it," she said, turning toward the street and walking to the nearest bus stop.

JACK WALKED into the shed where the trains were kept. After his winter break, it was good to be back amidst the smell of engine oil and the tools he loved. The train hadn't run since the Christmas season, when he'd driven it through the winter garden brought to life by the lights decorating every branch. He smiled as he thought of the children enjoying the holiday rides. It was one of the joys of his job, listening to them *ooh* and *ahh* over the scene and then cheer when they were herded off at the end to enjoy hot cocoa.

He walked over to the chest and laid out the tools he needed to tune up the engine. Jack loved this part of his job. He used to enjoy tinkering on the weekends before he'd retired from his job as a bank manager two years earlier.

"Hey, Jack." His co-worker, Tyler, greeted him as he stepped through the door. "You're here early."

"Well, I like to get an early start."

"Really? Or is Cassie still smothering you?" Tyler smirked.

"She means well. And it's not as bad as when she first moved back to town." Jack's grown daughter, Cassie, had arrived about two summers earlier, a few weeks after Emma, his now ex-wife, left him.

"Well, it's good to see you and great to be back on the train," Tyler said. "Plus, it beats the landscaping they had me doing the past few months."

"Still planning to take the mechanics course?" Jack asked.

"I've been saving for it since we talked at Christmas. Should have enough by September."

"Good for you, Tyler." Jack slapped the younger man on the back. "A man's got to go after what he wants in life." Or who he wants.

Jack thought back to his encounter with Sylvia. Her hair was a mass of long blonde curls, so unlike

Emma's dark red bob, and she wore ordinary clothes, not the high-fashion outfits that Emma had worn the two years before she left him.

Jack tried to focus on what Tyler was saying. Why was he even comparing the two women?

Emma had left. Just like that.

And Sylvia? Pain was there, in her words and expressions. Maybe she was like him, searching for the missing piece that had been missing for far too long.

"I forgot the best part," Tyler said, bringing Jack out of his reverie. "I talked to the boss, and he says there may be a job with the city once I'm done."

"That's great news." Jack was pleased for his young friend. "Now let's get this engine oiled and ready for the summer."

"All right!" Tyler rubbed his hands together and walked over to where Jack had already laid out the tools. They began to plan the work that needed to be done.

*J*ack walked home, glad to have put in a good day's work. As he passed through the gardens, he saw the little black cat crouched low to the ground, watching a robin. The bird strutted around the lawn, pausing every few steps to peck at the ground. Jack stopped to watch the cat creep toward the bird, her belly close to the ground, ears forward, focused. Jack held his breath as the cat increased her pace and pounced, then shook his head when she landed at the spot where the bird had just been.

"Too bad," he said as she picked herself up and looked at the tree where the robin now perched. The cat turned and walked in the direction of the train station. Hopefully she would find a mouse tonight. She looked skinny after the long winter.

Jack looked around the clearing, half hoping there was someone else who had witnessed the failed attack —a woman with blonde curly hair, someone he could share his thoughts with. The clearing was empty except for the robin that had flitted back to the ground to resume its hunt for worms. Jack brushed away the thought. He might never see Sylvia again, and continuing to think about her was fruitless.

He resumed his walk home, and as he approached the small rancher where he had lived for nearly thirty years, he could already smell the roast beef that Cassie had promised she would make to celebrate his first day back at work.

"Hi, Dad," Cassie said as he entered through the kitchen door. "Dinner's almost ready."

"Thanks, honey." He smiled as he moved past her to the bathroom to wash his hands and change out of his work clothes. He listened as she moved around the kitchen. She was in a good mood. Maybe today they could have a nice meal without all the drama.

Jack joined her at the table as she placed plates heaped with food onto flowered placemats he hadn't seen in ages. Emma had bought them in

Hawaii four years earlier, when they had celebrated their thirtieth wedding anniversary. He hated those placemats and made a silent vow to dispose of the things.

"How was your day?"

"We got quite a bit of work done. Tyler's back helping again." Should he ask her the same? What the hell. "How was your job interview?"

"Fine, I think." Cassie didn't look him in the eye. "Not sure I want that job, though."

"What kind of job do you want?" As if he didn't already know. Why couldn't he just shut up? He knew this line of conversation wouldn't end well, and he had just wished for no drama.

"They posted the jobs for kids' summer day camps. If I do that along with the fitness classes I'm teaching, it will give me more experience before..." Cassie took a deep breath, and Jack braced himself. "Dad, I contacted the university and told them I'm coming back in September."

"I see." Jack's heart sank. "So you still have your mind set on this."

"What did you expect?" Cassie looked at him as though he had two heads. "I have to get a career going sometime. I can't just look after you. I'm twenty-two years old."

Jack took a deep breath and counted silently to ten before speaking again. "You don't have to look after me. I'm not a child."

"No, but you did have a heart attack." Her voice softened. "And I know it's in the back of your mind all the time." Jack couldn't deny that. Though he put up a brave front with Tyler and pretended that Cassie was overprotective, he was afraid of what would happen if she left.

"Isn't there any way you can finish here?"

"Dad, we've been over this a thousand times. I need to move back to Kelowna to finish my courses, or it will take forever. I only have one more year, and if I don't go in September, I'll have to repeat a bunch of classes."

"You say that, but we both know you'll leave and never come back." Jack's voice rose, and he was already ashamed of where this was going.

"Could we just have dinner?" Cassie waved her hand back and forth between them. "Let's just eat."

"You'd probably be happy to move me into a home," Jack muttered.

"Now you're being ridiculous." She sawed off a piece of roast beef, put it into her mouth, and chewed.

But for the sounds of cutlery scraping against china, they ate the rest of their meal in silence. When they were done, Cassie collected the plates and cleared up.

"I'll be back later. I'm going for a run."

Jack nodded as he went to the living room and settled into his recliner. Taking up the TV remote, he flipped to the news and saw pictures of the familiar face of the TV anchor he had watched for decades, while the young woman now sitting in his chair talked about the anchor's long career.

"He'll be missed as he moves on to another chapter in his life."

"Like hell he'll be missed," Jack grumbled. "He'll be forgotten inside a week."

He looked around the familiar room, the walls feeling too close, too confining.

Nothing in this house was comfortable since Emma had left. What used to be a sanctuary now felt like a prison.

The shelves nearby held photograph albums full of memories he no longer wanted—memories of a life shared with the woman who'd broken his heart.

"I'm going for a walk," he said to the empty room.

Outside in the fresh air, Jack puzzled over what to do about Cassie. He wasn't ready for her to leave, but he felt like a heel trying to get her to stay. He hadn't raised her to be his nursemaid, but he wasn't sure what he would do on his own. The house was too much work for him. Bloody Emma. How could she leave them the way she had? He still felt the punch in the gut as though it were yesterday.

Only six months after the heart attack that had forced him into early retirement, he had come home, excited to land a new part-time job working on the trains at the park.

Emma was there, dressed to go out, sporting a new coat and a new haircut and colour. She had been going to the gym and wearing clothes that took years off her appearance. He was proud of this new, radiant Emma, and his heart swelled, knowing this beautiful creature was his. Then he saw the two suitcases he'd purchased for a trip to Europe. They had been planning the trip for months, but now the suitcases were sitting beside the door.

"Jack. You're home early." She looked past him at the closed door, a frown on her face.

"What's going on?" His heart began to pound.

"We've talked about this." She walked past him to look out the window and checked her watch.

"What are you talking about?" But he knew, had known for some time, that things weren't good between them.

"I left you a letter." She waved at the envelope sitting on the mantel. "But since you're here, I'll tell you in person." She took a deep breath and looked him straight in the eye. "I'm leaving you. I realized a few months ago, before you got sick, that I wouldn't be happy retired with you."

Jack felt dizzy. "What are you saying? We've been planning our retirement for years. You wanted to volunteer at the museum, play golf, maybe take a trip or two. We had our life laid out. Together."

"No, Jack. We've been over this many times. You know I want more than golf and a local volunteer job. I need to spread my wings, see how far I can fly. We've grown apart, and I'm sorry, but I must do this." She was shaking her head at him in… was that *pity*?

"You haven't even noticed, have you?"

"Noticed what?" He was about to say more when the sound of a car horn interrupted him.

"I have to go. Lorenzo is here."

"Lorenzo Baldonado? Your boss?"

"Yes. Don't look so surprised. You must have known that I haven't been invested in this marriage for a long time. And now that Cassie's in college… I can't go on like this, pretending there's something between us. Lorenzo asked me to go with him to Spain for a few months, and I said yes."

"You're having an affair with Lorenzo?" He grabbed the back of a nearby chair and steadied himself. Damned if he would crumble in front of her, but it was tough to stay upright with the floor swaying.

Emma looked at him for a few moments and then spoke slowly and deliberately, as if she was speaking to a child—or even worse, a frail old man. "Don't be difficult. If you think it through, you'll realize this is for the best. We don't have anything in common now that Cassie is grown and gone."

"How long?" How could he not have known? And why wasn't he able to do anything but ask questions?

She moved toward the door now, opening it and putting the suitcases outside on the porch. "I'll be there in a moment," she called and turned to face him. "A couple of years."

"A couple of years?" There he went with another question.

"I have to go. Everything else is in the letter."

"What did you tell Cassie?"

"I phoned and told her that you and I had grown apart —that we both love her, but that we don't love each other any longer."

"How did she take it?" His little girl had finally returned to school after missing a semester after his heart attack. Now she would be thrown into the emotional soup again, and nothing he could do would stop it.

"She sounded surprised, but she'll be fine. It's not like she needs her mother anymore. I told her I'd send her a ticket once we get settled, so she can come and visit. Lorenzo is looking forward to showing her around Spain."

"You know how much she relies on you—on us. She'll be crushed."

"Don't try to make me feel guilty. Cassie isn't a child anymore. She'll get over it." She turned toward the door, pausing for a few moments to look around the room. "I don't know if this will help you make sense of it all or not, but I think of this as a completed marriage, not a failed one."

He stood and stared at her, his mouth open. No more questions. No more words. No more sound.

"Goodbye, Jack. I wish you a good life." And then she was gone. He collapsed onto the sofa, staring at the closed door, and without conscious thought, the sounds trapped in his throat erupted in a howl of anguish that reverberated around the room, continuing until he collapsed from exhaustion.

Over the following months, he discovered that Emma had been planning her escape for a while. She'd cleared out their savings accounts and sold off some of their assets, leaving him with the house, his pension, Cassie's education account, and a small account that he had been using to secretly save for a gift for Emma: ironically, a three-month vacation to Spain. The note had spelled out her plans in detail, including her assumption that he would sell the house, which amounted to half of their assets.

Jack shook his head to chase away the memories, bringing himself back to the present, where he found his steps had taken him to the park.

As he walked around the gardens, he breathed in the spring air and began to relax. He'd always loved this place and wished he had someone to share it with. Emma had been right about one thing. They didn't have a lot in common anymore.

He couldn't remember the last time Emma had walked in the gardens. She much preferred to walk in the mall, on the city streets, or on the treadmill at the gym. Even when they visited Hawaii, she refused the option of walking in a fern grotto to see the Akaka Falls, missing the scents of fresh hibiscus flowers in favour of sunning herself poolside at the hotel.

As he passed the bench where he'd last seen the cat, he was mildly disappointed not to see Sylvia, who had taken the time to try to coax the wild cat out from the shadows. Something about her stuck with him. Perhaps he'd see her tomorrow. For now, he needed to get home and see that Cassie was all right. She would be home from her run soon.

CHAPTER 3

The following morning, Sylvia lay in bed. Her right leg ached, and she felt miserable. The sun peeked at her through the slats in the window blinds, urging her to come out and play.

Time to get up, her mother's taskmaster voice said. Her mother had kept moving through life despite losing her first child, her home, five siblings, and two husbands. She had never understood her eldest daughter's infrequent but severe bouts of depression.

"Snap out of it," her mother would say.

Sylvia didn't want to.

That's the depression talking. You need to get up, or that cat will go hungry again.

Sylvia got up. She moved her legs toward the edge of the bed, reluctant to leave the warmth of the covers.

Move it!

"Okay, okay," she muttered, forcing herself to rise, dress, and eat a healthy breakfast. She chose a warmer coat than the one she'd worn the day before and searched her closet until she found a good pair of walking shoes.

She hadn't worn those shoes for three years—not since she was wrenched from her former life by someone who sped through a red light and slammed into her car. She and Mark, who had been driving, were rushed to the emergency room.

Sylvia had awoken in the strict, sterile surroundings of the critical care unit, trying to identify her location, feeling nothing but the fog and extreme thirst that came after a general anesthetic. She felt pain in her right leg. It had been broken in three places, requiring surgery and a full leg cast. Mark was there, waiting for her to wake up. He had walked away with only a few scratches and a dull, persistent pain in his back, something he had felt occasionally before the accident.

She healed quickly and hadn't experienced any ill side effects other than a ghastly scar. *Better a scarred leg than no leg at all*, her no-nonsense mother would have said. *Snap out of it.*

"If only I could," Sylvia said aloud.

The simple song of a thrush pulled Sylvia from her musings, and she focused on the path she had followed the previous day. She breathed in the gentle scent of cherry blossoms and smiled. When she arrived at the bench where she'd noticed the cat, she sank down and leaned forward to scan the bushes, straining to see or hear any sign of movement. Sylvia sat, watching and waiting, and then pulled a can of cat food and a little tin dish from a bag. She opened the can and dumped the contents into the dish, placing the food just under the low-hanging branches of the bushes.

She returned to the bench, her mind wandering. She and Mark had been grateful for their close call.

"I could have lost you," he'd whispered to her as he sat beside the hospital bed, holding her hand.

"I'm not so easy to get rid of," she answered, you aren't going to get out of taking me to France."

He grinned. "Do you want to hear about the catacombs? I found a tour that will take us there for only a few euros."

"As long as you find something cheerful to end the day with," she said. "They buried millions of people down there."

His eyes sparkled with mischief, and he pressed her hand between both of his. "We could go out to Normandy afterward. To see the battlefields."

She shook her head.

"Seriously, I've been looking at the shows as an option. The Moulin Rouge?"

"That sounds lovely," she'd said, before drifting back asleep.

When she returned home from the hospital, they continued to plan. They were to work only thirty-six short months before retiring and embarking on a year-long trip to Europe, Asia, and South America. They'd begun to downsize their house, selling off their bigger belongings, giving away old clothes, books, and gadgets with a forgotten purpose, making room for their new life.

Sylvia shivered as she remembered what came next.

It was August 18 when the doctor's office called to say it was urgent that Mark come in for his test results. Mark came home from work after lunch, and she accompanied him to the doctor. "You're better with details," he'd said, but she knew he was concerned. The pain had been getting worse.

Neither of them returned to work. Their days became a whirl of visits to labs for more tests, to doctors for second opinions, and finally to the oncologist, who confirmed the grim prognosis of cancer.

Come on, snap out of it, the taskmaster urged.

"Yes, I know, life is for the living," Sylvia said. She sat a few minutes longer, watching the leaves and waiting for a sign of movement. Disappointed, she walked around the gardens and down the path toward the oval track. There she leaned against a chain-link fence and watched people stroll around the track. Some of them she'd seen the day before. Gathering courage, she walked through the gate, stepped onto the outside ring of the track, and began to walk, smiling at those passing in the other direction. When she'd walked the whole oval, she went back to where she had left the little dish. The food was gone. She sighed happily.

"HELLO AGAIN." Jack stepped onto the path behind Sylvia, startling her. He nodded toward the empty dish. "It looks like you're making progress with the cat."

"It'll take a while yet," she replied, turning briefly to look at him before shifting her attention back to the bush. "But I have patience."

He glanced at the hands clasped together behind her back. No rings. Funny, he hadn't tried to determine a woman's marital status in years, not since before he met Emma. After Emma left, he avoided reaching out to women. The young ones scared the devil out of him with their energy and ideas. The older ones scared him too. They were even more complicated with their past lives and relationships.

He watched Sylvia now as she peered under the leaves. "The cat's lucky you're feeding it."

"I'm lucky she needs my help," Sylvia said. "I haven't had a reason to venture out much in the past few years."

"Have you been ill?" he asked, then mentally kicked himself. Was he prying too much?

"My husband died." She was still looking at the bushes but turned her head to look at him. "I've been finding it hard to begin again. I don't really know where to start." Her sky-blue eyes welled up with tears.

"I'm sorry for your loss," he said gruffly.

"Thank you," she answered, looking away toward the bush again. "I know people think I should be long past it. In some ways, it seems he's been gone forever. In other ways, well, it seems like yesterday."

"Everyone has to grieve at their own pace." Jack found himself quoting the many people who had told him that when he had lost his parents.

"I suppose they do." She turned again to look at him. Was that gratitude on her flushed face? "I… I had best be going home," she stammered.

He didn't want her to go and searched for a reason to make her linger a little longer.

"Listen, the train will be ready for the spring season in a couple of weeks. Would you like to be the first passenger?"

She nodded tentatively. "I would like that."

"If you meet me here on Monday the week after next around ten in the morning, I'll come and get you."

"Okay," she said. "I'll be here." She turned and began to walk away, then paused and turned back. "Th-th-thank you."

He watched her go, pondering what he had just done. Did a train ride count as a date? Maybe. She looked like she needed a friend, and he was being friendly. He wasn't really interested in a woman who seemed afraid of her own shadow. He stood a little longer, watching her walk away, noticing the way her hips swayed.

"What is it about her?" he asked no one in particular.

"Meow," came a reply, and he turned to see the little cat sitting under the leaves not far from the empty dish. She was licking her paw and washing her face, content after her meal.

"Well, it appears someone agrees with me," Jack said to the cat.

SYLVIA WALKED QUICKLY AWAY from Jack. Had she just accepted a date? No, he was just being friendly. Like those times when people say, "Let's do lunch." He would probably forget all about it by next Monday. But what if he didn't forget?

Well, she would just have to go on a train ride. Where would the harm be in that? So what if she was a grown woman? She told herself to relax and take it one day at a time. If he was there at ten that Monday, he was there. If not, no hard feelings. Meanwhile, she'd continue to feed the cat.

She hoped he would be there. He had kind eyes.

* * *

"It's definitely a date," Sylvia's sister Alice proclaimed when Sylvia phoned to tell her about her day. "What are you going to wear?"

"I hadn't thought that far ahead. Who knows if he'll even remember?"

"I think you should wear that blue T-shirt. The one we got last fall. The one that makes your eyes pop."

"It's only a train ride."

"And go out and buy a good bra. One that shows off the girls."

"Alice!"

"Don't *Alice* me. You know I'm right. It isn't as though eligible men are falling from the sky. Oh, and make sure you get some condoms. It's not like when we were young. Lots more diseases out there now."

"What would you know? You've been married forever."

"I have friends. I hear stories. Anyway, think about making a bit of an effort. Maybe get your hair done. When was the last time you took the time to pamper yourself?"

"I'll think about it. And… Alice? Thanks."

"Anytime, Syl. I'll talk to you in a few days. I'm glad to hear you're getting out again. I've been worried about you."

When she hung up, Sylvia grimaced. Trust her sister to make a big deal about a little thing. She picked up the phone again and dialled Elaine. She hadn't heard from her stepdaughter in weeks. In fact, Elaine rarely called anymore. She had called more often when she first began to get gigs and sing professionally, to share her successes and her failures. She had a steady job now, singing in a band that travelled a circuit, performing in venues in Vancouver and sometimes Toronto or Montreal.

Elaine was living and loving her life, and Sylvia was proud of her, though she did miss hearing from her. She was playing in Toronto these days, and with the time difference, it was more difficult to connect.

Maybe, she thought, Elaine didn't really want to hear from Sylvia anymore. Elaine had once been very close to her, before Mark died. Before her mother came back into her life. *Oh, go away*, the taskmaster answered. And she was right. There was no need to jump to conclusions. Elaine was probably just busy…

The call went to voicemail, and Sylvia left a brief message. "Just thinking about you and thought I would see how you're doing."

Forcing thoughts of Elaine out of her mind, she wandered to her office to log in to the depression chat room, but she soon found herself surfing the Internet, reading customer reviews of nearby hair salons. An hour later she made an appointment for a cut and colour the following week. Alice was right. Although she hadn't said it directly, Sylvia knew she had let herself go over the past few years. It was time to put some effort into her appearance, to look after herself again.

Sylvia travelled to the park over the next few days, bringing cat food and emptying it onto the little tin dish. Every day she moved the dish closer and closer to the bench, and every day the dish was empty when she returned from walking the oval track. Her stamina was increasing, and she was now walking five times around the oval and looking forward to her new routine.

On Sunday, she noticed a folded piece of paper under the tin dish. It was probably from Jack. Cancelling their train ride, she assumed. She had been looking forward to it. Glancing around to see if anyone was watching, she opened the paper and read the words that had been written in perfect cursive.

Hello, I notice that you feed the cat every day. I just lost my cat after many years and have cat food that I'd like to donate. Could I arrange to meet you and give you the food?

Sylvia glanced to her left and right but saw no one watching. Carefully she refolded the paper and pushed it into her pocket.

She opened a can of cat food and emptied it onto the dish, placing the dish slightly behind the bench. She sat again, considering how to respond to this unexpected correspondence. She pulled a pen and small notepad out of her pocket—she had been carrying them with her since Mark first became ill, to write down instructions, medical terminology, and to-do lists.

She began to write.

I am sorry you lost your cat. I know how difficult it is to lose those you care for. I think that this cat would welcome the food you have. Would you like to share the feeding?

She paused a moment and, taking a deep breath, added her cell phone number to the bottom of the note. She folded it quickly, went to the dish, shoved it underneath, and walked away. She glanced back only long enough to notice that the cat had crept out of its hiding place and was devouring the contents of the plate.

Sylvia climbed onto the bus shortly afterward, reminding herself to breathe so the anxiety didn't creep into her brain and start her heart palpitations again. What had she been thinking, leaving her phone number on a note in the middle of the park? What if the writer was an axe murderer? Or… Or what?

The psychologist she had seen after Mark died had told her about ANTs: Automatic Negative Thoughts. She needed to kill them by questioning their validity. Perhaps she had not been particularly smart to leave contact information for a stranger, but really, what was the risk? She had given her cell phone number. Her land line, not her cell, was the one connected to her address. She could change the number if anything happened. Besides, how many axe murderers had perfect penmanship?

She took a few moments to breathe deeply, thinking through the situation. Most likely the person was just trying to help and get rid of old cat food. She might as well take the note's author at their word. She began to relax, and the anxiety that had been spreading up to her chest subsided. *Think positive thoughts. Don't let the negative thoughts in. It's just the depression talking again.* As she listened to the warring voices in her head, she was glad no one could hear them, or they would know she was going crazy.

Sylvia looked out the window and watched the buildings go by. The distance to her neighbourhood was relatively short, only two or three miles. Perhaps she should try walking to the park tomorrow. Or riding a bike. Could she ride a bike? She had sold her bike after she married Mark. He preferred to jog or swim instead. Ten years was a long time, but taking it up again was supposed to be, well, like riding a bike.

A few hours later her cell phone rang, and she reached for it, expecting it to be Alice or Elaine. Instead a reedy voice at the end of the phone said, "I'm phoning about the cat."

"Oh, you're the person who left the note."

"My name is Isabella. I'd be happy to share the feeding of the cat, but I only go out early these days."

Sylvia talked to Isabella long enough to set a time to meet the following day. "I'll show you the routine, so we can keep building the cat's trust," she said. "And I would love your ideas. I've never tamed a wild cat before."

She took care getting ready the next morning. She defrizzed her curls and put on some makeup, rubbing it off twice before getting it right. It had been so long since she had put on blush or mascara, she was all thumbs.

She considered her reflection. She looked good, and she hoped the trip to the salon would further improve her confidence. Her anxiety had been at bay all morning. She was going to meet a woman about the cat, and then she was going to the salon. Normal things for a normal day. Nothing to be anxious or worried about.

A tiny elderly woman was sitting on the bench when Sylvia arrived.

"Isabella?"

The woman turned toward her, and Sylvia realized she had been mistaken. This woman was about Sylvia's age. She beamed and rose to shake Sylvia's hand.

"I'm pleased you responded to my note. I felt rather silly, but my daughter told me I had nothing to lose, that I had to reach out or stay stuck indoors forever. My husband died recently." Her face reddened. "But you don't need to know that. Why don't you tell me about the cat instead? Does it have a name?"

"Angel. I named the cat Angel. And I know how hard it is to start over when you lose someone you care about. I lost my husband two years ago, and ever since, life has felt empty. But then I happened upon Angel."

Isabella smiled. "You do understand. Thank you for saying so." She reached into her bag and pulled out a can of cat food.

"Oh, she seems to really like that brand. How wonderful," Sylvia said when she saw the tin. She showed Isabella the routine that had begun to build the cat's trust. "I'm hoping that by summer she'll trust me enough to let me take her to the vet and make sure she has her shots and is spayed. I'd like to be able to get her indoors before winter comes."

"Admirable goals," Isabella said. "I'm happy to help." And with that she picked up the small dish and loaded it up with cat food, placing it behind the bench, a little closer than where it had been the day before. "Do you come every day to the park just to feed the cat?"

"When I first started to come a few weeks ago, it was to get some fresh air. And, yes, I suppose I did come to feed Angel. But now I stop over at the track past the trees and walk before I go home again."

"I didn't know there was a track." Isabella was grinning. "I used to be a runner. Before. Well, before my husband got killed. Would you mind showing me where it is?"

Sylvia led the way across the park, and the two women walked together for several laps.

"I've always wanted to run the Boston Marathon," Isabella said. "I haven't run for years."

"It's been a long time since I've even considered what I want to do," Sylvia said. "I always wanted to travel more. My dream was to go to Italy on a culinary tour, and once, when I was much younger, I thought it might be fun to ride a bike around one of the Gulf Islands."

"What's stopping you? There must be groups of people who take bike trips together."

"I have to learn to ride a bike again first." Sylvia laughed. "It's been forever since I rode even a stationary bike. Besides, I have to befriend Angel."

"Thank you for letting me share her," Isabella said. "It's been a long time since I had anyone, or anything, depend on me. It's good to have a reason to get up in the morning."

They said their goodbyes, and Sylvia felt lighter than she had in months. *I may have just made a friend.*

She fought off the usual negative thoughts and looked at her watch. She'd have to run to catch the bus. She didn't want to be late for her appointment at the salon.

When Sylvia rose from the salon chair a few hours later, she ran her fingers through the curls of her new bob. The grey was gone, and her head felt light, as though a weight was lifted with her long tresses gone. She stared at the mirror for a long moment, having trouble believing it was her own reflection staring back.

"You've changed my appearance completely," she said to the young woman who had cut her hair. "I look like the old me." *The me before Mark got sick. The me before…*

In the back of her mind, she wondered if it really mattered what she looked like, since no one was likely to notice anyway. But she closed her eyes and shook off the memories.

Don't listen to the depression, her strong voice said. *Don't let it win today.*

She ran her hand through her hair again. She looked great, and she'd begun to make a new friend. Today was a good day. She pasted a smile on her face and walked toward home. She was going to stop off at the grocery store to get some fresh vegetables, pull out her favourite cookbook, and make a nice dinner. Even if she was alone, she deserved a good meal.

* * *

JACK GRUMBLED as he walked home, his stomach growling. Cassie had announced three evenings before that she would be working with the kids' day camps that summer. She was going to a planning retreat for the week.

"I'll have to be away for five nights, Dad. If you need me, you can call the office. They'll get me the message."

He didn't have a lot of say in the matter and told her he'd be fine. But he'd woken up late and had forgotten to make his lunch the night before. Then he'd left his wallet on the bedside table, and Tyler had called in sick. He'd planned to borrow a few bucks from his young friend. His stomach growled, reminding him that he had miscalculated the day entirely.

Arriving home, he went straight to the fridge to root around for something to eat. He didn't mind cooking, but he rarely had the chance. Emma had hated his cooking, and since Cassie had returned, she'd taken over that task. *Damn.* The fridge was nearly empty. Emma would never have left it this way, but Emma was gone, and Cassie was away too.

"Argh!" He went into his bedroom, changed out of his overalls, grabbed his wallet, and headed out. He'd have to go grocery shopping.

Jack steered the cart toward the edge of the supermarket, remembering what the nutritionist had told him. He was to stick to the edges of the store, where the fresh food and dairy were found, and avoid the middle aisles with the processed food. He placed a selection of colourful vegetables into the cart and walked toward the meat section.

As he rounded the corner, his cart grazed another.

"Pardon me," he said, and looked up to see bright blue eyes peering back at him. His heart skipped. "I wasn't watching where I was going."

Sylvia stopped and stared at him before she seemed to find her voice. "Jack! How are you?"

"Hungry, if you want to know the truth." He answered without thinking. "My daughter—I mean *I*—forgot to go shopping this week."

She peered into his cart and smiled up at him. "It looks like you have a good selection. What are you making?"

"I haven't the foggiest idea. I'm not much of a cook."

"Well, there are all kinds of possibilities in that basket," she said. "You just need to search for recipes on the Internet that go with the ingredients you have."

"I can't say I've ever done that. I'll have to get someone to show me one day."

"I can show you. I-I-I mean… if you have a few minutes, perhaps we can go to a coffee shop and I can show you on my phone. Most coffee shops have wi-fi."

"How about we go one better? How about I take you to dinner? There's a little Greek restaurant near here that I heard is very good."

"Oh… I'm not really dressed to go to a restaurant."

She looked down at her jeans and T-shirt, and his eyes followed hers. She looked just fine to him, and he said so.

"I was going to go home and cook dinner."

"Of course, I didn't think. You must have someone at home to cook for."

"No, no. It's not that. I mean, no, I don't have anyone waiting. I was just going to cook for myself."

"Would you join me for dinner?" he asked. "Then you can show me how to find the recipes, and I'll be prepared for tomorrow night." Emotions flitted across her face. He loved watching her make up her mind.

"Well… Yes, I would love to have dinner with you." She looked relieved to have made the decision. "But first, I need to pay for my groceries."

"Great!" Jack said, a little more loudly than he wanted to. "I'll meet you out in front of the store in, say, fifteen minutes?"

He pushed the cart over to the meat section, selected some lean meat, and took a detour to pick up a small bouquet of tulips. Sylvia seemed like the kind of woman who would appreciate flowers.

When he pushed his cart out front, he found her on the corner, looking up at a tree.

"He's a saucy thing," she said, pointing to a grey squirrel high in the branches above her head. "He's been teasing the birds." She was smiling widely, and

Jack found himself chuckling and sharing her delight. Emma would never have noticed the squirrel. She moved through life at breakneck speed.

He paused a moment longer, watching Sylvia. She was beautiful. How had he not noticed that the first time they'd met?

"You've cut your hair."

She lifted her hand toward her head. "Yes, I decided I needed a change."

"I like it."

"Thanks." She blushed, and he was pleased. It had been a long time since a woman had blushed in his presence.

"Shall we go to the restaurant?"

He led her to his car and opened the passenger door for her before loading their groceries into the cooler bags Cassie insisted they keep in the trunk. As he slid into the driver's seat, he reached over to hand her the tulips he'd purchased.

"I thought you might like them," he said, feeling a little shy.

Sylvia brought the bouquet close to breathe in the scent. "Tulips are one of my favourite flowers," she told him. "They come in so many colours and brighten up the world after the winter is done."

"Have you ever been to the tulip festival in Washington state?"

"No, but once, a long time ago, I went to the one in Agassiz. There were acres of flowers. It was breathtaking. And you?"

"Unfortunately, I haven't travelled as much as I would like, except for the occasional trip for work."

"Where would you most like to go?" she asked

"France, I think. I always wanted to see Paris."

"Mark and I had planned to go there this year but, well…"

"You could still go," he said. Mind you, he didn't think he'd ever go to Spain. Not now that Emma had ruined it.

"I suppose I could. But where I really want to go is Italy. With all the movies about Tuscany, and the shots of the vineyards, I think it must be a wonderful place to visit. All that amazing food. I'd love to take a culinary tour."

"For tonight, we'll have to settle for Greek fare." He pulled the car into the restaurant lot.

"Perfect," she said. "I'm starved."

And he realized he had been enjoying her company so much he had forgotten his hunger.

They lingered over dinner, sharing stories. He told her about his job at the bank, his new work with the trains, how he mentored Tyler. She told him about her life as a teacher before she had left work for good. They talked about their families, their childhoods. She told him about Elaine and Alice, and he told her about his daughter.

"Cassie sounds like a wonderful girl."

"She's my great joy."

"And what would she like to do for a living?"

"She wants to be a teacher," he answered. "In fact, she only has a year of classes left."

"You must be proud."

And he was in that moment. He was proud of his daughter and truly wanted her to get her teaching degree. In Sylvia's presence, he felt this was a real possibility. She made him feel less lonely. Less needy. He felt like his old self for the first time in a very long while.

The waiter began to hover as they drew out the evening with conversation. "Could I get you anything else?" he finally said. "We're about to close."

"Oh." Sylvia looked out the window at the darkened garden in front of the restaurant. "I don't think the night has passed this quickly in a long time." She reached for her purse.

"Please," Jack said, placing his hand on her arm. "Let me get dinner."

She looked up into his eyes and smiled. "All right, as long as you allow me to cook for you one day soon. I'm a really good cook."

He drove her to her house and paused a moment before getting out of the car to open her door. She was already standing on the sidewalk, holding the tulips and ready to get her groceries.

"Thanks again for dinner," she said. "I had a lovely time."

"Thank you for joining me—and for being such charming company."

She blushed again, and he found himself pleased. Pleased that he was the reason she was flustered. He grabbed her second bag of groceries and offered to carry them in.

"It's okay—I've got them," she said. "I'll see you next Monday?"

"Ten o'clock." He watched as she walked up to her little house, reached into her pocket for her key, and let herself in.

He couldn't wait until next week.

* * *

SYLVIA HEARD the beeping of the message machine as soon as she got inside. Alice had called more than once while she was out, and the third call had only been thirty minutes earlier. Her sister sounded decidedly worried, so Sylvia dialled her number.

"Hi, Alice. Sorry to call this late."

"Thank God! I was worried. Where have you been?"

"Well, I was out on a date with Jack."

"Jack? The train engineer Jack? I thought you were going on the train ride next week."

"I ran into him at the grocery store. It was an impromptu thing. Anyway, he took me out for dinner."

"Eeee!" Alice squealed, reminding Sylvia of their childhood. "Spill. Tell me everything."

There was a knock at the door. Sylvia frowned and sidled over to the window to peek through the blinds. Jack stood on the porch, her purse in his hand.

"Listen, it's getting late. I'll call you tomorrow, okay? I just wanted to let you know I got home safely."

"All right, but I want details!"

Sylvia hung up and went to the front door.

"Hi," he said. "You forgot your purse, and I remembered… Well, I forgot to get your phone number."

"Hi," she said in return, grinning at him as though she were a teenager with a crush. *Don't be such a twit, Sylvia. He's just being nice.*

She told her depressed brain to shut up and go away. She wasn't about to let it ruin the evening for her.

"Thanks for bringing it back," she said. "I don't know what I would have done when I realized it was missing."

He looked into her eyes, silently waiting. Her heart pounded.

"Would you like to come in for a coffee or tea?" she said, breaking the silence.

He stepped across the threshold before she could change her mind, dropped her purse on a chair near the door, and then took her face in his hands. He leaned in and whispered, "And I forgot to kiss you goodnight. May I?" She nodded slightly before his lips descended on hers, questioning at first and then gaining force as her hands crept up his chest and around his neck.

His hands left her face and slipped down her back, pulling her closer as he deepened his kiss. A long moment later, they broke apart. "That was even better than I imagined," he said, and she felt the heat of a blush rise to her neck and cheeks. "Now, before I leave, how about that phone number? I'd really like to be able to call you later."

She laughed at the earnest look on his face, and a little thrill went up her spine. She had forgotten what it was like to be desired by a man.

It's not you he desires. His wife left him. He's probably just lonely. Her depressed thoughts intruded on her glow.

"Let me get a pen and paper," she said leading him toward the kitchen. As she wrote her name and number on a pad of paper near the telephone, she watched him survey the room.

"You weren't kidding about liking to cook, were you?"

"Nope. I love trying new recipes. When I left my job, I think my co-workers missed my potluck dishes more than they missed me. Here you go. My number."

He took the paper from her hand and then pulled her close for a second kiss. "I'll skip the coffee, if that's okay. I have to go to work in the morning, and caffeine keeps me awake."

"A rain check, then." She made a mental note to get some decaf. She closed the door behind him, hugged herself, then danced into the kitchen to put away her groceries—and put her flowers into water.

The following day, Sylvia was on the bus on her way home from the park when she noticed a Canadian Tire store, and on impulse she got off at the next stop. She'd look and see if they had a sale on bikes. She had some insurance money, and she'd never replaced their car, because she hadn't the courage to get behind the wheel again after the accident.

With a bounce in her step, Sylvia walked into the store and scanned the signs above the aisles. Not seeing the bikes, she moved to the seasonal aisle, and there they were in bright red, pale blue, and metallic green. Which one? Any at all? How much should a bike cost? Should she comparison shop? Maybe she couldn't ride one anymore. Why did she get off the bus? Was it going to rain before she got home?

She quickly saw that the choices were fewer than she anticipated. Some were for children, others for men. She looked at the four models that were nearer her size and decided to try the powder blue one at the end. She pulled the bike forward, straddled it, and kicked up the kickstand. She used her feet to push the bike along the aisle then stopped to look at the price tag. Fifty percent off. She climbed off the bike, walked down the aisle, and found a helmet that matched. She hadn't indulged in colour-coordinated accessories for years. Then she found a basket for the bike. She liked the idea of having a bike like Angela Lansbury's in the old TV show *Murder, She Wrote*—one that she could ride through the lanes, carrying her shopping in the little basket in front.

"Can I help you?" a man asked from behind her. Startled, Sylvia jumped and, taking a calming breath, turned to see a young man in a store uniform smiling at her expectantly.

"Yes," she said. "Could you please tell me how this basket attaches to that bike?"

"May I?" he said, taking the basket from her. He turned it over in his hands and fastened it easily to the front of the bike.

"Pretty easy," he said, showing her the mechanism she would need to attach and detach the basket in moments.

"So it is," she said, smiling. "I'll take it."

He nodded and began to remove the basket.

"Oh, no," she said. "I'll take it all." She placed the helmet in the basket and pushed the bike toward the checkout area.

Looking in the plate-glass window outside the store, she took the time to put on the helmet and check it for fit. Her newfound courage almost escaped her as she stood looking at the woman in the mirror of glass. Discarding the helmet's packaging inside the store was a rash decision she was beginning to regret as she fumbled with the straps. What was she thinking? She would never be able to ride a bike as well as she had in her thirties.

No more ANTs, she reminded herself, and then, looking pointedly at her reflection, which seemed to agree with her, she gripped the handlebars, straddled the bike, and kicked up the stand. She would try here in the quiet parking lot, away from unexpected cars and prying eyes. She pushed off tentatively with her left foot. Wobbly at first, she began to pedal, smiling as the breeze brushed against her face and navigating around the lot without incident. She gripped the brakes on the handles slowly, bringing the bike to a stop in front of the store window.

Could she ride home? The side streets weren't very busy between the store and her house. What else was she going to do? She didn't want to figure out how to load the bike onto the front of the bus. Steeling herself, she gathered her courage and pedalled toward home.

Once there, she turned on her computer to check her email—the only messages were from the grief chat room. She replied to a few. One woman she often corresponded with had been anxious about Sylvia venturing outside. "What if something happens to you?"

Sylvia smiled as she answered. "Something did happen. I went on a date, and I bought a bike." Then she logged off the computer, made a cup of tea, and settled down to read a book.

Sylvia dressed carefully to go to the park the next day, wondering—hoping—that she might run into Jack. She'd bike there. She'd thought about biking quite a bit since her conversation with Isabella and hoped that having a goal might motivate her more. If, at sixty-plus, Isabella could train for the Boston Marathon, then there was no reason she couldn't train for an event too. She surfed the Internet and decided that her first bike trip would be to one of the Gulf Islands later that fall. She'd plan which one later, but meanwhile, she would bike an hour or so a day to build up her stamina.

She rode around one of the bike trails in the park for a half hour before riding up behind a man with a familiar gait wearing overalls and a conductor's cap.

Now that he was there in front of her she slowed a bit, waiting for the anxiety rising in her chest to subside.

"He's just a man," she whispered to herself. A nice man. And a great kisser. *He isn't interested in you. He's just lonely.*

Maybe at first he'd just taken the time to talk to a stranger about the fate of a little cat. But that kiss? It had desire behind it.

She pedalled a bit faster, planning to casually run into him. He was getting closer to the parking lot now and patting his pants pocket, probably looking for his keys. He would be gone soon, and she'd miss her chance.

As she put on speed—just enough to appear casual and not like she was chasing the man—he stopped abruptly and pivoted on his heel to face her.

"Jack!" she said, braking hard. "Ahhh!" She managed to dodge him and a young woman pushing a baby carriage before she lost control and crashed onto the paved bike path. She lay there a moment with the air knocked out of her.

"Sylvia?" he said as he ran up to her. "Are you okay?"

She tried to disentangle herself from the bicycle and winced at the pain shooting through her right leg. "I'm not sure. My leg. I think it's broken."

The woman with the baby carriage had stopped to see the commotion and offered to phone the ambulance. Sylvia lay back, feeling grateful that someone was there to help and at the same time stupid for riding too fast.

"Can you move?" Jack asked as he knelt beside her.

"No. I'm sorry, you must have other things to do."

"Don't worry about me," he said. "It's not every day a beautiful woman literally falls at my feet."

She looked up into his face and smiled through her pain. "I bet you say that to all the girls who crash their bikes in the park." Was she flirting? God, she was lying completely helpless on the ground, and she was flirting.

He chuckled. "So far it's only happened the one time." He sat beside her, talking and gently moving his hands over her arms and legs to see where the pain was coming from. When he got to her right leg, she squealed. "Yep, it looks like this leg is the culprit. I'm going to leave this to the professionals. Do you hear that siren? Hang in there. The ambulance should be here any minute now." As if on cue, the ambulance drove into the parking lot, and two uniformed attendants jumped out and rushed over to her.

"Thanks for waiting with me," she said to Jack.

"Not a problem," he answered. "Listen, if you need anything at all, give me a call." He rooted around in his pocket and pulled out a small pad of paper and a pen. "And if it's okay with you, I'd like to call and check up on you."

She nodded weakly. "I'd like that," she said, and he tucked the paper with his number into her jacket pocket.

"Meanwhile, call if you need anything. I mean *anything*." He waited until the paramedics separated her from her bike and transferred her to the stretcher. "I'll keep this at the station until you're able to ride again." He patted the bike.

She willed the paramedics to move faster and get her into the ambulance quickly. She didn't want to break down in front of Jack.

Finally, they opened the back door of the ambulance, pushed her stretcher inside, and closed the door on the several onlookers who had gathered to watch. The last face she saw was Jack's, worry etched on his brow as he gave her a little wave.

For the next twelve hours, Sylvia experienced a severe case of déjà vu as she entered the emergency room, was prepped for surgery, and woke up in recovery before being shipped to a bed on the acute care ward. The difference was that this time, she was alone. Mark wasn't there to greet her when she woke up.

"Good morning, Mrs. Tremblay," a nurse chirped. "How are we feeling today?"

Sylvia looked up at the woman who was no more than a girl and silently took stock of exactly how she did feel. "My leg hurts like the devil, but otherwise I seem to be in one piece."

"The doctor will be here in the next hour to review your chart with you. You can be discharged after breakfast, and the social worker will meet with you to make sure you have home care. Take this medication for the pain, and someone will bring a tray in to you in a few minutes."

"May I have my cell phone?" Sylvia asked, and the nurse obliged by retrieving a plastic bag attached to the end of the bed. She pulled the phone out of the bag and turned it on. Nothing happened. The battery was dead. How would she phone Isabella now? The poor cat would think they'd abandoned it again.

The nurse patted her on the hand and told her not to worry. There were spare cords at the nurse's station, and she would send one down with breakfast. "What we need to do now is to get you up and dressed. Get you to the bathroom. Do you think you can void?"

Sylvia told her she would try and marvelled, not for the first time, at how fixated those in the medical profession seemed to be on bowel movements. She struggled to shift her weight and swing her legs to the edge of the bed, took the proffered crutches from the nurse, and wielded them efficiently to the bathroom unassisted. "Unfortunately, I have a lot of experience with these," she told the nurse, who hovered nearby. "I'll be okay on my own." The nurse waited until Sylvia got into the bathroom and left, satisfied with Sylvia's assessment of her ability.

"I'll be okay on my own," Sylvia repeated to her reflection in the bathroom mirror as she pondered what she needed to order for food and how she would get work done around the house while on crutches. It would be challenging, especially for the first couple of weeks, but she was sure she could manage. She'd managed worse.

She settled back into bed just as the kitchen staff brought her breakfast and the promised cell phone charger. She plugged in the phone and waited for it to spring back to life. There were five messages: two from Alice and three from another number she didn't recognize. Before Alice, she dialled Isabella's number and told her what had happened.

"I'll be happy to feed Angel every day until you're better," Isabella assured her, and she admitted that yes, she had been training and was able to run ten kilometres now.

"That's wonderful!" Sylvia said, sitting up too fast and wincing as her leg protested. "I'll call again in a few days to let you know when I'll be back at the park."

Then, with a deep sigh, she dialled Alice's number.

"It's about time you called. Have you been out on another date?" Alice sounded annoyed, and Sylvia began to feel defensive. Why did Alice treat her like a child?

"Actually, I had an accident." She heard Alice gasp. "I'm okay. I fell off my bike and broke my leg again."

"What were you doing, riding a bike at your age?"

"What's that supposed to mean? I'm not ancient and decrepit."

"Oh, Sylvia, I know that. I've just been worried that you were out with that man again, and that he wasn't as nice as you thought he was."

"I appreciate that you worry about me, but I'm a grown woman."

"I do worry. You're my only sister."

"I'll be fine."

"How bad is the break?"

"It's pretty bad, but only in one place this time. They operated on me and put in a couple of plates. I'm in the hospital, waiting for the surgeon."

"You can come here while you recover. I'll come and get you."

"Don't bother. It would take you hours to get here, and it's not necessary. Wait until I talk to the doctor, okay?" Sylvia was surprised at the anger she felt. Alice was being overbearing, and for the first time in a long time, Sylvia realized she didn't want to answer her sister's questions or give in to her way of thinking. She certainly didn't want to go to Alice's house and be waited on like an invalid.

"If you need me, call me. I have some vacation that I can take."

"I will," Sylvia promised, ending the call with a groan. She knew why she was angry. Mark wasn't there, and she didn't want to be dependent on her sister. She closed her eyes at the memory of nursing him for several months before giving in to his request and surrendering him to the hospital for twenty-four-hour care.

One morning she'd found his ex-wife in the hospital room, talking to him as only someone with a shared history and child can do. She'd forced herself to interrupt their tête-à-tête, asking how long ago their reunion had been.

Mark looked at her apologetically. "We've been corresponding for a couple of years, since our accident and my diagnosis," he said, and Sylvia's knees buckled so she had to take the seat on the other side of his hospital bed.

"Why didn't you tell me? Was there something to hide?"

"No. No," Dierdre said. "It's just that we know how much you already have on your plate, and I've been trying to help Elaine with her singing career. We all know that I've failed as a parent." She looked at Mark. "And as a wife."

"Is it in her best interest to go into music?" Sylvia looked at Mark. "It's not a very stable career."

"That's why I called Deirdre. She's made it in the business." He turned toward Deirdre, excluding Sylvia from the circle again. "She can give our daughter guidance."

Ah. Elaine was *their* daughter. "And I'm just the substitute who has raised her for the past ten years." Sylvia glared at them, anxiety overtaking her and making her dizzy. Elaine had been an angry lost soul when Sylvia married Mark and taken the girl under her wing. Deirdre had abandoned her daughter to pursue her career on the road. Now Sylvia was the one who was to be abandoned. By Mark and by Elaine.

"It isn't like that," Mark said. "I love you. Elaine loves you. After I…" His voice cracked. "After I leave, Elaine is going to need you more than ever. You and Deirdre."

Sylvia looked from one parent to the other. She saw Elaine's features in their faces—her mother's pert nose, her father's slow smile—and she relented. The child she had taken to her heart didn't need to know how betrayed she felt. Elaine didn't need to believe that Sylvia didn't support her dreams. She only prayed that Deirdre was true to her word—that she would watch over her daughter as she ventured into this fickle business.

"Okay, I'll support this," she said, turning toward Deirdre, "but you'd better swear to help where you can. She's very vulnerable right now."

"Thank you." Mark and Deidre breathed a sigh of relief, and Sylvia left the room to consider how to live with this new revelation.

A month later, she stood at Mark's graveside, tears streaming down her face, and recommitted to helping Elaine in the months that followed. She stood by, strong, and helped Elaine move forward with her life, facilitating the renewal of her stepdaughter's relationship with Deirdre. Sylvia supported Elaine as she launched her band, found an agent, and started playing on the national circuit. She helped Elaine until she could fly without Sylvia to hold her up. Only then had Sylvia fallen into deep grief and become consumed by depression.

"Well, hello again, Mrs. Tremblay." The surgeon interrupted her reverie. "How are you feeling?"

"Stupid, if you must know. I fell off a bike."

He chuckled at her rejoinder. "The surgery went well. We put in plates to hold the bone together, and it should heal fairly soon. You should stay off the leg for about four weeks, and I want you to come in for a follow-up appointment next week." She listened to him go on about the aftercare, about changing the bandages and watching for infection. "You can go home this morning. Do you have someone you would like us to call?"

"No. I have my phone." Who could she call? Elaine wasn't around. Alice lived three hours away and, after their earlier conversation, Sylvia didn't relish the idea of being carted all the way to Kamloops so her sister could harangue her for riding a bike. Maybe Isabella would be able to pick her up. She didn't know Isabella well, but she seemed like someone who might help.

Her cell phone rang then, and she reached for it, looking at the same unfamiliar number before answering the call.

"Sylvia." Jack's voice on the other end was a balm to her mounting anxiety. She calmly answered his anxious questions about her condition. "Do you have anyone to stay with you?" he finally asked.

"I don't think I'll need that. I've had a broken leg before, and I'm pretty self-sufficient." She didn't know if she was trying to convince him or herself.

"Why don't you stay with me for the first week?" He paused. "I mean, I have a guest room on the ground floor where my mother used to stay when she visited. It would just be for a week, until you begin to heal."

"But we hardly know each other."

"That's true. I guess I thought… or didn't think. At least let me drive you home."

"All right. I'd really appreciate it. They say I should be ready to go in about two hours."

"I'll be there," he said, and she sighed in relief. One problem solved.

WHEN JACK ARRIVED, the nurse went over the aftercare instructions. "You'll need someone to drive you home and stay with you for at least twenty-four hours, preferably forty-eight, until you are able to get around for yourself."

"That's fine," Jack said. "I'll look after her."

"But Jack…"

"We'll discuss it later, Sylvia. Meanwhile, let's get you home." Jack pushed the wheelchair to the hospital entrance and helped Sylvia transfer from the chair to his car. He arranged her crutches in the back seat and climbed into the driver's seat.

"Listen," he said. "I know you want to go straight home, but I was thinking that I could have you stay in my guest room for a couple of days. I feel partially responsible, and the nurse did say that you should have someone around. My house is just a few blocks from here. Why not come for lunch and then decide?"

"I'm pretty tired," she said, and then looked at his crestfallen face. "But I'm also a little hungry. And you're right. It's probably best that I eat something."

Jack grinned and drove the few blocks to his home. "I've been watching the cooking channel the last couple of nights," he admitted. "I've made a great vegetable soup that you might enjoy."

"Lead on," she said, smiling. "I wouldn't miss it for the world."

JACK FORGOT Cassie was returning on Friday until she walked through the back door. "Hi, Dad. I've got great news," she said as she dropped her backpack on the floor and turned to the table he had set up for two. "Oh, you made us dinner."

"Well…" He tried to think of a way to explain that he hadn't remembered she was coming home. He didn't want to trigger a scene. Not with a witness…

A very special witness.

"What did you make?" Cassie crossed the floor to the stove and lifted the pot lids. "This looks great." She turned to look at him. "Where did you learn to cook?"

"I've had a tutor the past few days," he answered, nervous about how to tell her about Sylvia. He had to do it soon, so he might as well do it now… Or maybe in a few minutes. "What's your news?"

"I talked to Mom the other day. She's coming home."

Jack placed his hands on the counter and looked across at Cassie. "Your mother has been gone more than two years. She isn't coming back." Even if she did return, would he want her back?

"That's not true." Cassie thrust her chin out at him and glared at him. "She Skyped with me when I was away. She said she was coming here. To our house. To see us. She misses home."

"She hasn't been in touch with me," he said slowly. "She's probably coming to visit you, not me." He realized this was the truth. There was no way Emma was returning to their marriage.

"That's not what she told me," Cassie said, wandering around the kitchen. "Do you want me to dish up the food? It smells great. By the way, who is your tutor?"

He took a deep breath and said, "My friend Sylvia has been staying with me while she recovers from an accident, and…"

"There's another woman here?" Cassie turned toward him, her face stark with shock. "What about Mom?"

"I told you. Your mother hasn't been in contact with me since she left."

Cassie glared at him. "Who is this so-called friend of yours, anyway?"

"I am," a melodic voice said from the kitchen doorway. "Your father let me stay here for a few days until I get used to my crutches and can do for myself."

"And in return, Sylvia has been teaching me to cook," Jack added, waving his hand around the kitchen. "She's really good."

"Where did you two meet?" Cassie's face was red, and Jack braced himself for the angry outburst. He had seen the signs before.

"We met at the park," Sylvia said. "And your father has been gracious enough to let me stay for a few days after I had a mishap on my bicycle."

"She's been staying in the guest room downstairs," Jack added, "and today we're celebrating the fact that Sylvia had a great check-up. No infection. Everything is mending as it should."

"And when will you be going home?" Cassie asked. Jack winced at the tone of her voice.

"Actually, your father was going to take me home this evening. I've been anxious to get back to my life— not that your help hasn't been welcome, Jack," she said.

Jack smiled at her. "It was a pleasure. I couldn't leave you alone to fend for yourself after you fell to avoid me." He wished they were alone and able to talk as they had the past few days. He saw in her eyes that she felt the same way.

Cassie cleared her throat and went to the cupboard and drawer to get another place setting. Jack knew that determined look in his daughter's eyes. They would have no further private time today.

"What do you do?" Cassie asked Sylvia as she sat down at the table.

"I took early retirement a few years ago, but before that I taught school," Sylvia answered. "Grade One, mostly."

"That's what I want to do," Cassie said and, by the time Jack joined them with a plate of grilled vegetable sandwiches, they were in a deep conversation about teaching. He watched as he ate and saw that Sylvia's generous nature was winning Cassie over just as it had with him.

Cassie came with them when Jack dropped Sylvia off at her home, and together they helped Sylvia into the house. Sylvia thanked Jack again for his hospitality.

"I'll be over tomorrow after work to see how you're getting on," Jack said, ignoring her protests.

She relented. "I'll be here. And maybe I'll have figured out how to get around enough to put together a dinner for you."

"I'd love to come for dinner." He kissed her on the cheek and noticed Cassie turning away. He hadn't meant to embarrass her. "I'm glad you're getting better," he said to Sylvia. "You still have to come on a train ride, remember?"

"I remember," she said, and leaned against the door jamb. The effort of getting up her front stairs had weakened her. He should go.

"I'll check in on you tomorrow." At the bottom of the stairs, he turned to wave goodbye, and she was still there, watching him. *Damn*, but that felt good.

THE NEXT DAY, Sylvia lay in bed, staring at the ceiling and thinking about what she needed to do around the house. The bathrooms needed cleaning, the fridge needed stocking, and she had only a few hours until Jack arrived.

Smiling to herself, she got up and struggled to make the bed. Several minutes later she was successful and faced the task of washing and dressing. Her leg still ached, and as she struggled down the stairs, she decided to stay on the main floor for the next few weeks. She would sleep on the day bed in her office.

By five that evening, she had finished making dinner and was setting the table when Jack called.

"Sylvia, can I get a rain check on dinner tonight? Cassie called to say that she made dinner for me—my favourite—and asked what time I was coming home."

"I see." Sylvia's buoyant mood plummeted.

"I'll be over after dinner, though," he said. "Cassie's been away for a few days and seems to be feeling left out. "

What had she expected? He had a daughter, just like Mark had. Cassie, like Elaine, was her father's whole world. "Well, why not come over for dessert, then?" she asked hopefully. *Have you no shame?* The ANTs were back again. She hadn't even noticed their absence until now.

"Do you mind if I bring Cassie?" he asked tentatively. "I mean, if she decides that she wants to come?"

"Of course not. I made a lovely apple pie and ice cream. I can't eat the whole thing myself."

"We… I'll be there," Jack said. "I love apple pie."

"I'll see you around six thirty."

JACK BEGAN to walk toward home. Cassie had called only an hour earlier, out of the blue and out of breath, insisting that he come straight home.

"I have a surprise for you," she said.

"What kind of a surprise?" he had asked warily. Cassie's surprises were not always good, and lately her refrain was that she wanted to go back to school in Kelowna. He hoped she wouldn't go to much trouble to change his mind. The week without her hadn't been as bad as he had feared, and he knew he would manage when she returned to school. For the first time in two years, he was looking forward to his future—and he hoped it included Sylvia.

He walked into the kitchen, noticed three place settings on the table, and smiled. Sylvia had sounded surprised and sad that he wouldn't be there for dinner, and meanwhile, she was planning to be here the whole time. He would have to remember not to play poker with her. She was an excellent actor.

Deciding two could play at this game, he delayed going into the living room to greet her, choosing instead to go upstairs to shower and change. He didn't want to ruin their surprise.

A few minutes later, he bounded down the stairway to the living room, pausing two stairs from the bottom to stare at the woman sitting there.

"Hello, Jack," Emma said. She was in the chair facing the stairs. Her chair. Jack felt like a ton of bricks had slammed into his chest and nearly lost his footing on the last two steps.

He looked at her and wondered for a moment if the last three years had been a dream. Her face, the same one he had looked at every morning for thirty years, was there smiling at him, knowing him, as lovely as ever.

"Emma. What are you doing here? I thought you were in Spain."

"She's come home to visit, Dad." Cassie made air quotes with her fingers around the word *visit* and smiled happily at them.

"I see. So this was your surprise?" he asked Cassie, still looking at Emma.

"I came to talk to you, Jack." Emma said. "Cassie invited me to dinner, and we've spent the afternoon catching up."

"I see," Jack said, remembering that Sylvia had used these same words with him not two hours earlier.

"Shall we have dinner?" Cassie asked, clearly pleased that the two of them were in the same room. "It's been forever since we had a family dinner together."

Emma looked at Jack, and Jack looked at Emma.

"Yes, let's eat," Emma finally said, speaking for them both. She hadn't changed. She still felt entitled to speak on his behalf and make decisions that included him without his consent. He followed them to the table Cassie had set with the best china, and they sat in their familiar chairs. He felt awkward as they passed platters around the table.

"You've been looking after yourself, Jack," Emma said, looking him up and down. "You've lost some weight, and Cassie says you've been walking more."

"Dad's been learning to cook too." Cassie handed Jack the potatoes. "He made the most delicious sandwich for me yesterday."

Emma's eyebrows rose as she looked at him. "Well, that's a switch. You've been making some changes."

Jack cut into his chicken and took a bite, chewing slowly, while he thought of what else to say. Had they always carried on conversations as though he were nothing but a puppet they provided words for? He listened to their conversation as he choked down bite after bite of food. Finally, the meal was over. Hopefully that meant Emma would leave soon.

"I thought you would have sold this place by now," Emma said as Cassie bustled in the kitchen, getting the coffee. "Isn't it too much for one person to look after?"

"Well, there are two of us living here right now," Jack answered. "I thought Cassie had enough of changes.

When she lost her mother, she didn't need to lose the house she grew up in as well." Emma's lips pressed together tightly, and he knew his words had hit home.

"But she's going back to school in the fall. What will you do then?"

"I'll manage." He glared at her. "Where's Lorenzo?"

"Lorenzo's downtown. He had a conference in town, and I came with him."

"I see." He paused as Cassie backed through the door between the kitchen and the dining room and turned to place a tray with two coffee cups, cream and sugar, spoons, and some homemade cookies onto the table.

"Aren't you joining us?" he asked as she began to walk toward the front door.

"Oh, I thought I would go for a run while you two talk," Cassie said. "I'll be back by seven."

Jack and Emma watched as the door closed behind their daughter.

"Tell me, Emma. Exactly why are you here?"

It was six thirty when Sylvia's doorbell rang.

"Right on time." She did love that about Jack. He was dependable.

She swung herself on to her crutches and hurried to the front door to find Cassie standing there, iPod on, earbuds in.

"Hi, Sylvia," she said as she removed her earbuds. "I was out for a run and thought I would stop by to see how you were doing."

"Thanks," Sylvia said, looking past Cassie to the street. "Is your father with you?"

"Oh, he's home with Mom," Cassie said blithely. "She came home today. She's missed us and has decided to come back."

"I see." *I told you so. No one wants you.*

She screamed at her depressing thoughts to stop.

"I thought I would come to see how you're getting on now that you're back home."

Sylvia smiled at Cassie, seeing so much of Elaine in this girl. The last thing Sylvia wanted to be was a home wrecker.

"I've made a few adjustments, but I'm managing. I even got outside for some fresh air this afternoon. Such nice weather."

"And you've been cooking," Cassie said, sniffing the air.

"Yes, I've even made an apple pie. I thought that it would be a good way to use up some of the old apples I had in the fridge. Most everything else had to be thrown out. But I was able to get food delivered from the local market. It was something I did often when Mark, my husband, was sick, and I couldn't get out to shop."

"I didn't know you were married."

"He died over two years ago. Cancer."

"Oh, I'm sorry." The smile Cassie wore slipped a bit before she added, "I'm glad you're doing well, Sylvia. I should be going. I told them I would be home by seven, and I still have a few kilometres to run before I'm finished."

"Thank you for stopping by, and please tell your father I'm fine. No need to worry about me," Sylvia said, closing and bolting the door and swinging her way back to the kitchen.

She sliced into the pie, cutting herself a big piece, and poured herself a large cup of decaf coffee before perching on a stool near the counter, putting her head into her hands, and sobbing. She was alone again, looking from the outside at a family reunited at her expense.

No use crying over spilled milk. Her mother's voice cut through the tears. She was startled into silence. The voice was back. She had to stamp out the negative thoughts.

"I'm getting better. This is just a little setback. He was lonely, and so was I. I'm sure it wouldn't have worked out anyway."

She raised her head and looked at the big piece of pie in front of her. She'd been eating so well the past few weeks.

Sylvia placed the slice back into the slot where it came from and then cut the pie into several more slices before covering it with plastic wrap and putting it into a basket. She was going to take the pie next door to her neighbour, who had three teenaged boys: a thank-you for all the times they had shovelled snow off her driveway.

She left her cell phone on the counter while she was away, and missed three calls: the first from Alice, the second from Jack, and the last from Elaine. She returned only two of those calls when she came home.

JACK WAITED for Emma to answer him and felt long-forgotten anger rise in his chest. She had left him. She had stood right there and told him she was leaving, letting him figure out how to pick up the pieces when she walked out the door.

"I'm here to talk about Cassie. You can't keep her tied to you. She needs to go and get herself a life."

"What makes you think I'm tying her down, or that I even could?"

"She makes dinner for you every night. I know she said that you were learning to cook, but Jack, we both know that's not true. She's fooling herself, covering for you."

"Emma, if that's why you've come all this way, then you've wasted your time."

"Did you spend all of her college fund? Is that why you won't let her go back to school?"

"You still don't listen, do you? I am not keeping Cassie from going back to school. She's already registered to go back in September."

"But she's reluctant to leave you. Worried you won't be able to handle things on your own."

"I can handle things just fine," he roared. "Not that it's any of your business what I do."

"It's my business when it concerns our daughter and her future." Emma raised her voice and stood at the other end of the dining room table. "I don't want her life to be like mine was."

Jack felt as though she had sucker-punched him for the second time that day. "Was living with me so awful? I thought we were happy."

"I swore I would never end up like my mother. I'd never be home nursing someone instead of grabbing life by the tail. I built my career so I'd never have to do that. And then when you got sick, well…"

"When I got sick you realized that you had made a mistake marrying me, is that it?"

"No." She walked over to the window and peered outside. "No, I can't regret marrying you, or I wouldn't have Cassie. She's a wonderful girl. We raised her well, you and I."

"Great. So the only reason you're happy I came along is so I could give you a child?" The pain of her earlier rejection tore into him again.

"Not exactly." She stood and pondered a moment. "You were a better man than my father."

"Joseph Stalin was a better man than your father. He was a drunk, a sloth, downright nasty, and well… it doesn't really bear going into, does it?"

"You were stable. You were good to me and to our daughter. You never had an unkind word to say to either of us. You were too good for me."

"You left because I was too good? What was wrong with me? What did you need me to do, to be? I don't understand."

She stood for a few more minutes before saying softly, "It wasn't you who was wrong, and it wasn't me, either." She waved her hand back and forth between them. "It was us. We didn't work anymore. Together we were less than we were apart. You weren't inspiring me to be better, and I wasn't inspiring you. We were old hat. Stale. And no matter what I tried to do to breathe life back into our marriage, it didn't seem to work. I'm sorry I hurt you. I'm sorry that I left the way I did."

"Things aren't all roses and rainbows with Lorenzo?"

"No." She laughed. "Lorenzo is too mercurial for that. Too passionate. But he pushes me. He makes me try harder. I'm always a little off-balance with him, and I like that."

"I don't really want to hear about Lorenzo's passion."

"I keep him off-balance too," she said. "I think he likes a woman who stands up to him."

"I wish you well with him." And he was surprised to find that he really did.

"He'll be here to get me in a few minutes. I hope Cassie returns before that. I'd like her to meet him. She said she would be back by seven."

"Seven." He looked at his watch. Six fifty-five.

Sylvia. He'd told her he'd be there at six thirty. "Excuse me a moment, I have a quick call to make." He dialled the number, and it went to voicemail. Where would she be? Perhaps the bathroom, or maybe she left her phone in her pocket in another room. He walked into the kitchen long enough to leave a voicemail message.

"Sylvia, I'm sorry I wasn't able to make it for dessert this evening. A family… emergency came up. I'll call you later to see how you are."

He returned to the living room to find Cassie and her mother in conversation.

"What do you mean? Lorenzo is coming here? Why would I want to meet him?"

"I thought you might like to meet your new stepfather."

"Stepfather? But you left him. You've come home for good."

"Why would you think that? Lorenzo and I are very happy together."

"No. That can't be true. You said you wanted to talk to Dad." Cassie paced the floor, and Jack stood back, watching the interaction, unsure how, or if, to intercede. Too late, Cassie saw him hovering.

"Dad, tell her you want her back. Tell her to come home."

"I can't make her do what she doesn't want to do. And your mother is right. Our marriage is over—has been for a long time." Was that a look of gratitude he saw in Emma's eyes?

"You should try harder! Tell her how much you've learned in the last few months about cooking, about doing things around the house. Tell her how much you've changed."

He walked over to Cassie, who was now in tears, and took her into his arms. "Cassie, as much as you want your mother and me to be together, it just can't be any longer. She's with Lorenzo now. She has a new life in Spain. My life is here."

Cassie tore herself away from him and hissed, "Is this because of that woman, that Sylvia?"

"Who's Sylvia?" Emma asked.

"Sylvia is a friend of mine," Jack said quietly. "She's a woman I've been spending time with over the past few weeks."

"She's been living here for the past week!" Cassie said, her voice rising.

"No," Jack said firmly. "She stayed here with me for a few days while she healed from her surgery. She broke her leg, and her doctors advised that she not be alone for the first while. I felt responsible for her accident because she fell off her bike to avoid running into me. She stayed in the guest bedroom." He found himself on the defensive, even though he didn't need to explain this to anyone, least of all Emma. "She stayed until she was able to wield her crutches on her own, and meanwhile she taught me a few things about cooking."

"What is she like, this Sylvia?" Emma asked.

"She's a nice woman, a widow. She loves walking in the gardens at the park, loves wildlife, and she can cook. Boy, can she cook." He smiled as he remembered the last time he had seen her. She was a great kisser too, but damned if he would share that with these two.

"So you like her?" Emma said, watching him closely.

"What's not to like?"

"Sylvia doesn't need you anymore, Dad. She told me to tell you that she's just fine," Cassie interrupted.

"When did you talk to Sylvia?" Jack's heart pounded.

"I went over there after dinner. Told her Mom was back. She seemed happy to hear you were back together."

"Why would you say that?" her mother asked her. "Cassie, Lorenzo has asked me to marry him."

"You aren't back, then? You aren't coming home again?"

"No," Emma and Jack said together. It was probably the first time they had agreed on anything in a very long time.

"No, not in the way you would like me to be," Emma continued. "Though Lorenzo has agreed to spend more time in Canada. I miss you." Emma smiled at them both. "Lorenzo will be here any minute. I'd like you both to meet him. It would mean a lot to me."

Cassie sank into the nearby couch. She looked small and fragile, more so than Jack had ever seen her. A horn sounded from the driveway.

"Please come and meet him, Cassie," her mother urged. "For me?"

Cassie sighed deeply, rose, and went outside to meet Lorenzo. He, in turn, was charming, something Jack had never really been. Lorenzo even managed to squeeze a promise from Cassie to visit Spain during school break that November. Emma beamed at them.

Before they left, Emma crossed the driveway to speak to Jack.

"I'm pleased to hear you're dating again. And you look well. I'm sorry I accused you of holding Cassie back. Please accept my apology."

"Thank you," Jack said, then kissed her on both cheeks and said goodbye.

Jack stood with Cassie while she waved them off.

"Dad, why didn't you fight for her?" she asked.

"Your mother isn't a prize to be won, Cassie. She's an individual with a mind of her own. She chose him. We need to accept that."

"Oh, Dad," she wailed and ran into the house and up to her room, slamming the door behind her.

Well, there was no going out tonight. The last thing Cassie needed today was to think that her father was abandoning her too. He needed to talk to someone. And the only person he really wanted to see was Sylvia.

He dialled her number, but the phone went straight to voicemail. He left another message and put the phone down. He'd need to make it up to Sylvia, and despite what he had just told his daughter about not fighting for a woman, he realized he would fight dragons for Sylvia. What was that woman doing to him? She'd only been in his life a few weeks, but she'd already made a home in his heart.

CHAPTER 7

Sylvia was going to visit her sister Alice. It had been a long time since she had been to Kamloops, the town where they had grown up. She limped around the bedroom, packing her clothes, and carefully rolled the suitcase while leaning on one crutch.

"I can do this," she said to herself. She was soon in the cab on the way to the airport.

When she landed in Kamloops, Alice swept Sylvia into a hug and held her. "It is good to see you, Syl. You look fantastic!"

"I do, don't I?" Sylvia answered. She had lost fifteen pounds in the past month and, despite her leg, felt healthier than she had in years.

"How long can you stay?"

"I'm here for two weeks, but then I need to get back. Isabella is going to Oregon to run a half marathon in early August. I need to be home to feed Angel."

"Angel. A very good name for that cat. She's certainly been an angel for you."

The visit with Alice was just what Sylvia needed. She spent time with her nieces and nephew while Alice was at work, cooked dinner for the family every night, and felt generally useful. She thought often of Jack, but pushed him out of her mind during her active days and found herself dropping quickly off to sleep every night, tired from all the activity. She was almost sorry to leave.

"I wish you could live here always," her fourteen-year-old nephew, James, said to her when they were seeing her off at the airport.

"I'll come back soon to visit. I promise. But right now, I need to get home."

"To feed Angel," her little niece, Elizabeth, piped up. "Aunty has to feed the kitty."

"Yes, exactly," Sylvia answered, kissing the children and giving Alice a huge hug. "Thanks for letting me stay. It was good to see you."

"You can come anytime. I haven't cooked at all. You really should go on that Italian tour you've always talked about."

"Maybe I will," she said.

She visited her doctor when she returned and was deemed ready for a walking cast. Glad to be able to trade her crutches for a cane, Sylvia walked a few blocks every day, feeling the strength return to her leg. She was pleased to take over Angel's feeding when Isabella left on her trip.

The afternoon before Isabella's flight, they met for a few minutes in the park.

Isabella smiled her usual broad smile. "Thank you for letting me help Angel. I feel like a new woman."

"You look like a new woman too," Sylvia said. "I barely recognized you!"

Isabella chuckled. "That's what George said when I saw him last week. He's an old friend of my husband's. We've been dating." She blushed.

"Good for you." Sylvia was pleased for her friend. "Have fun at the race."

"I will," Isabella said as she hugged Sylvia to her. "Wish me luck beating my time."

"Luck!" Sylvia said. "Wishing you lots of luck."

Isabella jogged down the path, and Sylvia sat on the bench to fill the cat dish and set it on the bench beside her. Angel was much braver now, jumping up onto the bench to eat her fill.

"Well, well," a deep voice said from behind her left ear. "I never would have believed it if I hadn't seen it with my own eyes."

Jack was standing beside her. She smiled tentatively up at him.

"My mother used to say that a lot can be accomplished if you are patient."

He walked around the bench to face her. "How have you been? I tried to call you several times, but I seem to have missed you. I wanted to explain about—"

"No need to explain," Sylvia said. "Cassie told me that your wife came home. I wish you well."

"That's just it," Jack said. "Cassie misunderstood the situation. Wishful thinking, I suppose. Emma isn't back. She only came to lecture me about my treatment of our daughter and to introduce her fiancé to Cassie."

"Her fiancé?"

"She and Lorenzo are to be married. It's taken a couple of weeks, but I think Cassie is finally accepting that our marriage is over. Cassie's going to travel to Spain to see where her mother lives."

"Your wife hasn't returned, then?"

"Ex-wife. No, our marriage is over. Dead."

"I see," Sylvia said.

"Do you?" Jack asked. "Sylvia, I'm so sorry if you were hurt by this. I just wanted you to know that."

"You must be on your way to the train," Sylvia said.

"Yes, I am. I have another couple of runs to do before we close for the day. Can I call you later?" He looked so hopeful and her heart beat faster.

"No, I mean… Well, I was hoping… You still owe me a train ride," she said.

He reached over to squeeze her hand. "Yes, I do. Come on."

JACK LED the way to the train and listened as Sylvia told him of her visit with her sister. He could listen to her all day and not tire of it. After driving the train twice around the track, he brought it to a smooth halt outside the station to off-load the children. Tyler was waiting for him.

"Hi, Tyler. You about ready for dinner?" He turned to Sylvia. "Tyler and I are going to try out that new restaurant at the edge of the park tonight."

"No can do. I have a dentist appointment," Tyler answered.

Jack narrowed his eyes at his young friend. "I didn't know you had an appointment."

"Just made it." Tyler held up his cell phone. "They had a cancellation, and they were able to fit me in. Rain check?"

Jack swallowed an exasperated sigh and turned to Sylvia. "Would you care to join me for dinner?"

Sylvia blinked at Jack. She'd been watching the exchange. "I-I…" She paused and looked into his eyes.

"Say yes," he said. "This ungrateful cur is abandoning me to my own devices, and I hate to eat alone."

"All right, then. Yes."

He resisted the urge to hug her. "I'll see you tomorrow, Tyler."

But Tyler was already on his way to the parking lot, and Jack could swear he heard him whistling.

They entered the restaurant, and Sylvia clapped her hands together in excitement. "It's Italian," she said. "I'm going to Italy in two months. I booked my ticket yesterday."

"So, you'll be taking your culinary tour after all."

"Oh, yes. And then, perhaps, I'll look for a job cooking in a restaurant like this one."

They spent the next several minutes looking through the menu, and the next hour flew by as they caught up.

"I've missed you." He took her hand in both of his.

"I've missed you too."

"Do you think we could start over—try this all again?"

"I'd rather just pick up where we left off," she said. "First dates are so awkward."

"I'd like that."

THREE MONTHS LATER, Jack stood at the airport arrivals gate and grinned when he saw Sylvia walking toward him.

"How was your trip?" he asked.

"My trip was wonderful." She let him fold her into his arms. "But it's so much better to be home."

COME HOME TO LOVE

For my parents,

who have supported my dreams for decades

CHAPTER 1

Susan McNeill stopped by the bakery to pick up two pieces of Black Forest cake, Richard's favorite treat. He hadn't been himself since retiring two months earlier. Maybe this would cheer him up a bit. She placed the pastry box on the front seat of the car and groaned when her cellphone rang for the umpteenth time that day. She answered it, put it on speaker and pulled onto the road toward home.

"It's true," said the voice of Jennifer Singh, her co-chair for the conference planning committee. "Siddhartha Jones is no longer with Blueback Technical Solutions, so he can't speak on behalf of the work they're doing on mental health with their HR department."

"Damn," Susan muttered under her breath as she approached the solid two-story home she and Richard had built together thirty years earlier, and saw the empty garbage bin sitting on the curb. The same bin Richard had promised to take in yesterday.

"Did you hear what I said?" Jennifer's voice was higher than usual, a sign that the stress was getting to her.

Susan parked the car in the garage and stared a moment in the rear-view mirror at the garbage can. "Yes, I heard. We can't use Sid as the keynote speaker." She sighed, then added. "Stay calm. We don't have to send out the conference brochure for another couple of days and we can always put a note on the website explaining that the keynote is being confirmed. It gives us some time. We can still find a replacement."

"Where? This is a disaster."

Susan turned the engine off and spoke more calmly than she felt. Richard had promised he would take it in this time. What was wrong with him? "I've got a list of potential speakers in my office here. If none of them are suitable, I'll email the speakers' bureau tonight. I've been working with them for years and they have pulled me out of this type of trouble before."

"Right. Yes. That makes sense." Jennifer's voice was returning to normal now, so Susan continued to talk through the rest of her plan.

"We've both handled tight timelines before. We just need to focus on damage control. I'll pull the board together so we can brief them in the morning. Can you start on a press release? Keep it light. Something like, 'due to circumstances beyond our control, we have booked a new keynote.' I'll work on getting a replacement by the end of day tomorrow."

"Yes. I can do that." Jennifer sounded relieved, knowing what action to take. "I'll send it to you by seven."

"Great, I'll look at it after dinner."

"Thanks, Susan. I appreciate you talking me down from this."

"I'll talk to you later. Now go take a break and get something to eat. It'll be fine." She discontinued the call and leaned back in the driver's seat, closing her eyes for a moment. Why would Sid leave his job? She would have to ask Richard about it. He was no longer working for Blueback Tech, but he'd still be up on the scuttlebutt. Richard. She opened her eyes to see the nasty pimple of a garbage can fester on their otherwise clean street.

"He's got to be kidding," she mumbled as she climbed out of the car. In a moment she'd dragged the bin up the driveway and shoved it into place between the recycling and compost bins where it belonged. Then she walked back to the car to retrieve the pastry box, her purse, and her laptop bag. It would be another late night and she wished, not for the first time, she hadn't agreed to chair the mental health conference. She wished she could just retire like Richard had two months earlier. Which she could, if he had kept to his end of the bargain and worked for a few more years.

She set the box and handbag on the bench outside the front door, fished for her keys, unlocked the door and stepped into the smell of stale air. No chicken. No pine scents. He had done no cooking or cleaning, but the television was blaring from the living room and the weather reporter from the six o'clock news was confirming what she already knew. Temperatures were dropping and a storm was coming to Sunshine Bay, and a storm this far south on Vancouver Island was rare.

The television grew louder as she approached the living room to find Richard snoozing on the couch, wearing the same sweatpants and tee-shirt he had worn at least three days in a row. She paused a moment, considering whether to yell at him so he would wake up, and decided against it. It would just make a hard day worse.

Instead, she went to her office, set down her things and continued to the kitchen to start dinner and stopped, anger rising as she took in the sight in front of her. There on the counter was a cutting board that had been used to slice cheese and tomatoes. An oily frying pan sat on the stove, used to make a toasted cheese sandwich. On another counter, an unrinsed tomato soup can was sitting beside the sink instead of in the recycling bin in the cupboard underneath. The bowls and spoons from breakfast and lunch sat on the counter above the dishwasher. He'd even left an empty instant oatmeal package on the counter. Seriously? What had he been doing all day?

She opened the dishwasher to find dirty dishes and the soap she had poured into the dispenser, waiting for him to press the start button. Growling, she took the dishes from the counter, shoved them in, and started the machine.

All the books she'd read about men retiring — well, the one book and a few online articles — said men could have a tough time adjusting and she should be patient. One article even said that retirement wasn't for sissies, though whether that one was talking about the retiree or their unretired spouse, she couldn't recall. What was she supposed to do until he adjusted? Work all day to come home to a slug of a spouse who left the housework, cooking, everything, for her to do?

She pulled a pan from the cupboard and set it to heat on the stove. Why didn't he understand she was having a frustrating month? She'd told him about the conference and the pressure she was under to mentor Jennifer. He knew Annette Taylor, the new executive director, had pushed them to hold the conference in a different venue so it could be twice as large as the last one. He also knew that Annette had then flown off to Australia for a month to deal with a family emergency, leaving her new director, Boris, to run things. The same Boris, who got the job Susan should have got. Would have got, if she hadn't told the board president, she was planning to retire in a year which she never would have done if she'd known Richard would take an early retirement package without even consulting her.

It wasn't fair for her to bring work problems home though. They weren't entirely Richard's fault. She needed to keep a lid on the emotions struggling to the surface and have patience. The last thing she wanted was to be a nag. But seriously, how hard was it to put away a garbage can, turn on a dishwasher and fry up some chicken?

Or even do something during the day? Judging by his appearance, he had done nothing in the past three days. This wasn't healthy for him or for their marriage. She would have to talk to him again.

She opened the fridge and removed the chicken breasts she had thawed and marinated, and vegetables to make a salad. Potatoes? No. They would take too long and she had work to do tonight. Work. Despite her trying to calm down Jennifer, she wasn't looking forward to this evening. It had been a long day and she'd much prefer to pour a glass of wine, read a book and turn in early.

She was tossing the salad when Richard shuffled into the kitchen fifteen minutes later, rubbing sleep from his eyes.

"Smells great. What's for dinner?"

The calm she had been trying to maintain disintegrated.

"Chicken." She said through clenched teeth. "The same chicken I left marinating in the fridge."

"Oh right, I forgot, I've been busy," he said. "Can I help?"

Well, he could have helped earlier, but why state the obvious? "Maybe set the table?"

She dished out the food and brought the plates to the table, then returned to get two glasses of water. Settling into her chair, she willed herself to stay calm, civilized. He picked up the remote control to the kitchen television, turned it on and dug into the meal.

"This is good," he said, chewing on a bite of chicken.

"Thanks," she said, reaching for the remote control to turn the volume down several decibels. "What have you been up to today?"

"Been watching a bit of TV. Reading." He spoke hesitantly, and his eyes didn't meet hers as he spoke. He did that when he had something to hide. Sometimes that was a good thing, like the time he brought home a diamond ring for their ten-year wedding anniversary and had to hide it for three days, but by the look on his face she knew that wasn't likely this time.

"And? You sound like you want to say something." She watched his face turn red. She hated being right. She had an awful feeling about this.

"Planning a vacation."

"A vacation?" From what? Netflix? Her patience was running thin.

"Rupert's been after me to visit."

Of course this would be about Rupert. It was always about Rupert. Rupert Cowen, his stepbrother, was like a third person in their marriage. Sometimes she wondered if she was the third person in their marriage. If Richard ever had to choose between her and Rupert, she still wasn't sure she'd win.

"Has he?" She tried to keep her voice casual, neutral. They both knew Rupert wasn't her favorite person this year. Not since he'd left her friend Lucy, his wife of three decades, to live in Palm Springs with a woman half his age. Was this what Richard wanted too? She looked at him more closely. He hadn't been himself since he retired and though she had tried not to, she had often complained, despite the online advice not to. Nagging, according to Google, would just push him away. Her heart pounded harder. Had she pushed him away? Was this his way of telling her he was going to Palm Springs to live with a girl half his age? Rupert had an enormous influence on him. Wait, his lips were moving. What was he saying now? She had to pay attention.

"Yeah, he might have a project I could be part of. I thought I'd go tonight. Sounded urgent. And I would be out of your hair for a while. I know how much work you're doing."

"What kind of project?" Rupert always had something up his sleeve and half the time it all worked out. It was the other half of the time she worried about. The times when he had resorted to sleeping on their couch because another of his bright ideas went south.

"I don't know. Thought I'd visit and find out." He ran his hand through his hair, and she flinched. Running his hand through his hair was something he did when he was nervous or needed to think of something to say. He was avoiding her eyes. What was Rupert getting him into now?

"How long would you go?"

"Two weeks. There's a last-minute deal returning on the twenty-fifth."

"Wouldn't your ticket cost more, ordering it so close to the time you leave?"

"No. It's still pretty early in March, so it was cheap."

"You already purchased the ticket? You already planned to go no matter what I said?"

He drew back, caught in the lie. When had he started lying?

"Yeah. The plane leaves here at ten and then the connecting flight from Vancouver leaves at midnight. I knew you'd be fine with it," he said, brushing away her words and her feelings with his hand. "Think of it as one of my business trips."

"You figured I'd be okay with it." She noticed his eyes were wary. Good. After thirty-five years of marriage, he should know by her tone that she was close to losing it.

"Look Sue," he put up his hands to ward off the tsunami they both knew was building inside her. "I'm sorry. I didn't think it would be a big deal. You're working all day and night on this conference of yours. I barely see you."

"What about our plans for next weekend?"

"Next weekend?"

"You were going to show me what you're getting from your pension plan and review our financial plan at the bank." She had it in her calendar, but he was shaking his head no and she raised her voice a little in desperation. "You promised."

"I haven't got all the information yet." He looked down at the table when he talked. Why couldn't he meet her eye?

"Isn't it all online?"

"No. I had to apply. The information won't be here for a few weeks. Maybe by the time I get home?"

"Why would you retire if you weren't sure of what you were getting?" This didn't make sense. Her voice was wavering now. What wasn't he telling her?

"It was the best offer I was going to get," he said in a low voice. "They weren't going to offer another buyout, so if I wanted to try something else, I had to go now."

"You never said anything about wanting to do something else," she said. What did 'something else,' mean?

"Well, I do. I just need some time to think about the best options." He was looking at her in the eye now. A determined look on his face.

"Meanwhile, I'm working so we can afford to pay our bills." Her voice was rising. "I'm working because you left your job. Don't you think it would be better if you stayed and helped around here? Do things like take out the garbage, do the dishes, cook the chicken I left in the fridge?" She needed to shut up. She needed to leave what she was thinking unsaid.

"I think it might be better for both of us if we take a break from each other."

Silence filled the room and all she could hear was the clock ticking on the wall, the ugly fish wall clock he insisted they keep because it reminded him of his beloved fishing trips. Tick. Tick. Tick.

She swallowed hard to keep her dinner from coming back up. "A break? What do you mean by that? A break like Rupert took from Lucy?" Her voice was louder than she intended. Was he leaving her? It was happening more often these days. Marriages breaking up after twenty, thirty, even forty years. Like Rupert and Lucy's marriage.

"No. It's not like that."

"Why can't you stay here? Work on figuring out our next life together?"

"I just need some time alone."

"But you won't be alone. You'll be with Rupert and his girlfriend and whoever she brings along. Will she bring a friend? Is that what this is about?" Her voice was close to a shriek now, and he blanched.

"She…" he seemed to search for words. Another lie? "She's away for a couple weeks. She won't even be there."

"Well, it isn't fair. I shouldn't have to continue to work just because you took a buyout and then sit home while you take off to Palm bloody Springs!"

"Look." He stretched both hands in front of him. "I'm sorry you still have to work. I'm sorry things aren't like you planned." She glared at him and he quickly added, "like we planned."

"How would I know what you plan anymore? We barely speak."

"Well now, you know. I'm looking for different work. I need some time to wrap my head around what I'll do next. I can't do that here."

She glared at the soup stain on his shirt, not trusting herself to look into his eyes, and willed herself to stay silent. She could feel herself losing control. Why did it always end up being about him? When did she get to fly off to Palm Springs? Never. She was too busy working.

"It'll do us good if I leave for two weeks," he continued. "I won't be underfoot anymore."

"Go then. Go to Rupert." The next words were out before she could stop them, "I'm sure his floozy can find a friend for you."

"Come on. I told you, she won't even be there." He ran his hand through his hair again.

"I just need some time to figure out my next move," he said. "They don't tell you retirement will be so boring. So final."

"I wish I knew what that was like," she muttered, stabbing at a piece of cucumber. "Why do you have to go to the States to think? Why can't you do it here?"

"I told you, Rupert needs me to help him with a project, and I need a break."

"From me, you mean." She put the fork down. She couldn't trust herself not to stab him.

He didn't answer. Just looked down at his plate.

"I've got some work to do in the office," she said, getting up and taking her plate and utensils with her. "I'll see you when you get back."

"Sue. Don't be like this," he called as she walked away. "It's not like Rupert to ask me to drop everything to come."

"What do you mean?" she said, turning to look at him.

He ran his hand through his hair again. "Nothing. It's only two weeks."

Two weeks with Rupert. Two weeks away from her. Two weeks could feel like a blink of an eye.

Or a never-ending waiting game.

"Have a good trip," she choked out, then turned on her heel and walked toward the office.

"I'll come and say goodbye before I leave," he called after her.

But she didn't look back. She'd be damned if she'd let him see the tears streaming down her cheeks. He could go to hell.

She entered her office and set her plate on the desk. The pastry box with Richard's favorite cake was still sitting there. She opened it and looked in. The scent of cherries and chocolate beckoned to her, promising to make her feel better if only she would try one bite. She could hear Richard walking up the stairs to their bedroom. She looked at the cake again, then closed the lid and shoved the box into the wastepaper basket.

*R*ichard had a pang of guilt as he handed the flight attendant his boarding pass for the trip to Cancun. Leaving Sue in mid-winter was bad enough, but now Rupert had him lying about where he was. If Rupert hadn't seemed so desperate, he wouldn't be going.

He settled back in the middle seat, a by-product of getting a last-minute deal, and cursed Rupert again. This would be a long, uncomfortable ride. A child about four years old climbed up in the seat next to him and began kicking the chair in front of him.

"Settle down, sweetie," his mother crooned from across the aisle where she sat next to another child, maybe two years younger. Their father, if there was one, didn't seem to be anywhere nearby. The child settled and then chattered about the trip and wiggled. Richard tried closing his eyes to ignore the little guy, and his thoughts wandered back to Susan.

He supposed she had a right to be frustrated that he was taking a trip without her. It was the first time he'd ever done that, other than a trip or two to visit his family in Winnipeg. But it wasn't like he'd ever told her she couldn't vacation without him.

They still had some extra money for her to take a short trip this year if she wanted to. As long as he found work soon. The severance package from Blueback Tech would only last a few more months.

The severance package Susan didn't know about.

How could he tell her they had laid him off after thirty years with the firm? She had counted on him working another two years so she could retire, and now she needed to work longer, at least until his investments started to pay off.

Much longer, if what he had heard about Blueback Tech was true. Shaheed, his friend and former colleague, was having trouble getting pension information from the company too. Shaheed was sure the pension plan would pay out less than expected, if it existed at all. But Shaheed tended to worry about everything. Pension plans were insured. There wouldn't be a problem. There was probably just a delay getting the information because of the number of people who had been laid off from the company at the same time. A backlog. Nothing more. Still, he hoped to have more information before he went home, or Sue would be really furious. It was good he was going to see Rupert. Rupert would help him figure out his next move.

Someone tapped his shoulder and he opened his eyes to see the child, hands sticky with chocolate, looking at him. Across the aisle, the mother was attending to the younger child.

This would be a long flight.

THE PLANE LANDED in Cancun at noon and Richard stepped from the air-conditioned airport into a hot wall of humidity he hadn't felt in years. It took a moment to adjust to the sunshine, the warmth, the enhanced odors that the heat brought out in everything. He followed the line of people to where the busses to the resorts waited and stood in the queue.

He didn't expect Rupert until noon, so he had some time to settle in, take a nap, relax without someone else around. He should phone Susan to let her know he had arrived safely, but he couldn't trust himself not to let it slip that he wasn't in Palm Springs. Why did Rupert think Richard had to keep this secret?

He looked at his watch. Best to wait until he reached the resort and Wi-Fi. By then she would be at work, and more likely to have calmed down. One thing about Susan was that she didn't stay mad for long, something he had never taken the time to appreciate until this year. He still couldn't quite believe he had mustered the courage to leave the way he had. But it was only for two weeks.

The bus pulled up and he soon settled into a worn seat, one that had taken thousands of passengers before him from the airport to the resorts, not stopping to experience the real countryside, the people and the culture.

The passenger who came to sit with him was a stocky older man with fading ginger hair, who looked around seventy. A man closer to Richard's age than he felt comfortable admitting.

The man didn't speak, closed his eyes and leaned his head back on the seat, exhausted from the journey.

Checking into the hotel, Richard went up the elevator to the fourth floor. The suite had a view, something he had been pleased to get given the last-minute deal. He dropped his bag on the bed in one of the two rooms and walked to the balcony to step out and look at the turquoise blue ocean, so different from the navy and green ocean back home. Everything seemed brighter here, full of possibility rather than the weight of the gray he had been dealing with for weeks.

He walked into the room to get the Wi-Fi password, signed into the internet and checked for messages. There was nothing from Rupert beyond a note to say that he had caught his flight from Palm Springs, and nothing from Susan. Had he underestimated her anger?

He knew she was angry he had 'retired' and she seemed to work harder than before. Taking on extra assignments. Training staff in their new positions. Trouble was, she was still working as though everything had landed on her shoulders and she had to fix it all. She never trusted that he could hold up his half of the relationship. Nor that he would be there for her, even after thirty-five years of marriage.

Even now she probably thought he had gone off to have an affair like Rupert had. When had he given her a reason not to trust him? Unless she had heard about the layoffs and the pension rumor. She had been speaking to Siddhartha Jones, who would be her keynote speaker. Sid who would do anything for Susan, but would he do anything to have Susan? Richard saw the way Sid looked at her during office parties or events, and he often wanted to strangle the man.

But no, Susan was steady. She'd never cheat. And she wasn't interested in Sid that way. She had told him so herself when they were driving home from his last office party. She had laughed at the idea, and he believed her. Besides, he would only be away two weeks, and by then he would have figured out what he had to do to get them back on track. He could talk to her then. She'd understand.

He sent a quick email to Susan to let her know he had landed and that she could contact him using WhatsApp. He wrote he was fine and would be in touch later once he and Rupert had visited a bit. That wasn't a complete lie. She didn't need to know that Rupert wasn't here.

He tried reaching Rupert one more time by email and also sent him a quick WhatsApp message. He wasn't online, but it was mid-morning and he was likely still in the air.

After unpacking the few clothes he'd brought, Richard decided against the nap and instead went to the pool, slipped into the water, swam up to the bar and sat under the little overhang, keeping himself out of the direct sunshine that was already hotter than he had felt in months. His skin was enjoying the heat and he would enjoy it even more once he got a mojito into him.

Several others at the bar were from the bus he had come in on. They, too, had shed their winter skins, forgetting the cold they had just left behind.

"Hey, you were on the bus." The stout man who had been sleeping beside him waded toward Richard. He looked younger. Relaxed. Warm. "Where are you from?"

"A town on Vancouver Island called Sunshine Bay."

"Yeah, I've been there before. You have some great fishing in those parts."

"What do you fish for?"

"Depends on the month. Steelhead trout, sometimes some Spring."

"Have you been up to Campbell River? They have some great fishing there."

He spoke to the man who introduced himself as Lorne McQuarrie, about fishing, camping and all the outdoors things he enjoyed but had done little of since their son Brian left home. Why hadn't he been doing these things? Maybe when he got back home, he could. After he found work.

Meanwhile, he wondered why Rupert had insisted on meeting here in Mexico and not Palm Springs, and why he had told him not to tell Sue. She would be furious when she discovered he had lied. And she would find out. She was like a bloodhound who could sense things. Every time. He glanced at his watch, and knowing Rupert wouldn't arrive for at least another hour, ordered himself another drink.

CHAPTER 3

Susan awoke to the alarm the next day and groped around for her phone to turn it off. Rolling onto her back, she held the phone close to her face and peered at the screen in the early morning light seeping through the curtains.

Five o'clock, only four hours since she had closed her eyes. At least she had managed to finish the communication plan and pitch for the board before going to bed and lying awake ruminating over how she and Richard had left things between them. He had come into her office when the cab arrived just before eight and given her a peck on the cheek, like a dutiful child would kiss his great aunt. There had been a definite pep in his step as he carried his bag down the driveway and climbed into the taxi, a swirl of freshly falling snowflakes in his wake.

At least he seemed happy for a change, though she worried about him visiting Rupert. Rupert had a talent for leading others down the garden path. Though not always. Maybe she should take him at his word. He just needed to figure things out for himself away from her. Maybe she would want the same thing in his shoes.

Groaning, she stretched up to find the lamp switch and turn it on. Nothing. Maybe the bulb was dead. She climbed out of bed and went to the window to peer out. The dim light of the rising sun revealed thick snow and heavy flakes falling. The trees had at least six inches on them, and the roof of the shed a good foot or more. The doorknob on the shed seemed closer to the ground, as though the entire structure had sunk into a silent cloud. Silence. The house was too quiet.

Shivering, she walked to where the main light switch was and confirmed her fears. The power was out and worse, as she walked down the darkened hallway toward the den at the front of the house, she could tell before she looked that the city hadn't plowed her cul-de-sac and knew from experience that it wouldn't be plowed for several hours. Or days.

There was no way for her to get to work to brief the board. She would need to do the next best thing and phone Boris, her director. Okay, not the next best thing, but the only thing she could right now. Knowing him, he would want to wait and ponder any options she could come up with. Why they promoted him so soon she would never know. He took forever to decide anything.

She walked back to the bedroom to get her cell phone. Almost out of power. She would need to find the power pack she always kept charged downstairs by the front door. As she walked, she dialed Jennifer's number. Jennifer answered on the first ring.

"I can't get out." Jennifer was in panic mode again. "I can't get out and it will take hours to shovel this stuff. Can you get to work?"

"No, and I'm almost out of power on my cell. I'll call Boris and let him know that I can't get to the meeting and I'll send out an email to the rest of the board." Susan said goodbye, then looked at the power on her phone again. Fifteen percent. Only a few more minutes. The phone battery was old. Tired. Like she felt this morning as she went to the kitchen to get a glass of water from the tap. No coffee today. No tea. No shower. Crap.

She used her phone to send out an email blast to postpone the meeting and was thankful she had thought to send emails to potential speakers and an email briefing to the board the night before while she was stewing in the office. Now on to Boris.

Boris didn't answer the phone right away, and when he did, he seemed distracted. He agreed canceling the meeting had been a good idea.

"That means I don't need to figure out how to dig out now," he mumbled. "I'll have a cup of coffee in that case."

"You still have power?"

"Yes. Though I heard most of town is out. There was a big slide outside of town that took down a power pole. It will be several hours, if not a day or two, before power is restored."

Great. That was all she needed. "Thanks, I have to go now. I don't have power here and my phone is almost out of juice." She hung up before he could talk longer. Boris could natter on if she let him. Now ten percent. Where was that power pack?

She rummaged around in the top drawer where it normally was before realization settled over her. Richard. Damn him. He always took it when he traveled. She checked the power company site to find out how long the power would be out. Boris was right. It looked like the power would be out for several hours. The last time this happened it had taken a week to restore the power. She hoped it wouldn't be a week in the dark, cold and alone. What was she going to do now?

Well, she could at least get dressed and try to dig out enough snow so she could walk to the garage. She could use the car to charge her phone and maybe get out and drive to a coffee shop if she could get the car to the main road. The power grid on the other side of town was still working and she was bound to find a warm coffee shop and breakfast.

She was soon outside, pushing the shovel that Richard hadn't bothered to put back into the garage, though she had asked him to do so. Good thing he hadn't listened. Though even he had to admit that a snow dump like this after March first hadn't happened on the island for so long, she couldn't even remember when the last time was. Crocuses had been blooming just the week before and the daffodils had already grown six inches. This was crazy.

Tightening the scarf around her neck, she continued to push the big scooped shovel from one side of the drive to the other, creating piles at least three feet high. This would take a while. The sun was rising in the sky as she leaned back on the shovel for a moment to appreciate the view. Any other year she would enjoy staying out here, shoveling snow in the quiet and then, in a perfect world, going inside to curl up with some hot cocoa and a good book. Unfortunately, she needed to get to a power source. Needed a cup of coffee. Needed to confirm a new keynote speaker and needed to keep thoughts of Richard from sneaking in. He would be in Palm Springs by now, sitting in the sun with a cold beer. Damn him.

The sound of an engine cut into the silence and she turned to see her neighbor, Jack Robertson, running a bobcat and scooping up snow. She waved at him and after a few moments he saw her and cut the engine.

"Good morning. I didn't see you there," he said, hopping down from the seat and walking to the side of the drive where he had just plowed. His gray hair was covered in a homemade toque and he wore a ski jacket over his burly frame. "If you wait about twenty minutes, I can come and do your driveway, too."

"Oh, you don't need to do that," she said, half hoping he would ignore her and half hoping he wouldn't so she would have something physical to do. Physical enough to tire her muscles so she didn't use them for something else, like punching a wall with Richard's imaginary face on it. How could she be so angry and so afraid at the same time? Was this how it felt to go crazy? Not crazy. She had told herself not to use that word anymore. Planning the mental health conference made her more aware of the stigma, but seriously, she couldn't think of another way to describe it. Confused? Angry? Relieved that he was gone a few days? Worried he wouldn't come back?

"Are you kidding?" Jack said, bringing her back to the conversation. "Sylvia has been giving me grief for buying this machine for months. If I can show her how much it benefits my neighbors and my landscape business... Well, you'd be doing me a huge favor."

She laughed. "Well, never let it be said that I didn't want to help a neighbor."

"Where's Richard? Traveling again?"

"Yes. Palm Springs this time."

"Well, he sure picked a great time to go. Though not as far as you're concerned, I suppose." He laughed, his hazel eyes alight, "When's he going to retire and give it all up? He talks about it all the time, but I haven't seen him in months. Must be busy."

"I'll let him know you were asking about him." She avoided the question. If their neighbors hadn't seen him, and they didn't know he retired, what had he been doing? Where was the Richard she knew? The man who led project teams in the IT world. Worked on projects worth millions. What had happened to him?

"Thank you, Jack," she said. "I appreciate this."

"Not a problem," he answered. "Hey, do you have any heat? I ask because I still have an old wood-burning stove that we've started up in the living room. Why not come over for some coffee and a bit of breakfast in about half an hour? I'll let Sylvia know."

She hesitated a moment, looking at Jack and remembering how many questions he asked, and then she looked at the road still covered in mountains of snow. Her stomach growled and won the argument in her mind. "I'd like that," she said. "Is there anything I can bring?"

"No, just yourself. Sylvia will be pleased to have someone else to cook for. You know her."

She smiled. Yes, she knew Sylvia. A lovely woman, ex-teacher, who had come into Jack's life only a couple years earlier after his wife left. After they'd been married for years. Like she and Richard.

After he retired. Like Richard.

She said a quick thank you before turning to go inside. She had to focus on something other than Richard. He was just on a holiday, figuring out his life. Figuring out what to do next.

But why couldn't he do it here? With her? Together?

She took the shovel up onto the porch and removed the snow from the stairs before going into the house. Closing the door, she quickly peeled off her wet boots and pants, placing the boots on the mat beside the door and then took the pants into the laundry room to hang them on a rack to dry before she got puddles of water all over the house.

Naked from the waist down but for her underwear, she bounded upstairs and into her bed to warm up. The air was frigid, and she was having difficulty feeling her toes.

The duvet settled over her and her feet thawed. She wiggled them a bit and then brought one foot onto her lap in a half lotus position and rubbed the feeling into it before switching to the other.

Finally, feeling her toes again, she leaned back on the pillows, waiting for the warmth to travel up to her legs. She turned over toward the center of the bed and looked at the empty pillow a moment before grabbing it and wrapping her arms around it. It smelled of his aftershave, his scent. She closed her eyes and breathed it in, pretending for a moment that he was just downstairs brewing coffee as he often did on weekends before he retired. If she could just stay here, she wouldn't have to go downstairs to confirm he wasn't there. She could just believe for a little while that everything was like it had been until three months ago.

Her stomach growled and broke the spell. She patted the pillow back in place, before she got up, and flipped the sheet and duvet into place, and pulled on dry pants. Sylvia's breakfast would hit the spot right now and she didn't want to be alone in a house with no power, no heat, no internet, and no Richard.

"Hey buddy," Rupert said when Richard met him in the hotel's lobby. He grabbed Richard in an enormous bear hug that normally made Richard uncomfortable, but today felt like a flood on parched skin. He had missed the big guy.

Richard reached up and slapped Rupert's broad back before stepping back and looking at his friend. "Good to see you." Richard took in Rupert's altered appearance. His normally solid frame was gaunt, his tee shirt hung off him and the creases on his face had deepened, as if the six months he had been away were six years. "Come. I'll show you to the suite." Rupert picked up his laptop bag and carry-on while Richard dragged the enormous bag that would have kept Richard in clothes for a month. "Pack light, do you?"

he said when they got to the elevator and waited for the car to come.

"I thought I might stay down here a bit after you head home." Rupert said, not meeting his eyes.

Richard took the hint not to ask anything further and when the door opened, hit the button to take them to the fourth floor. "You'll like the room, I think." This was awkward. No girlfriend, and now he was thinking of not going back. Must have broken up with Mindy or Missy or whatever the girl's name had been.

"I'm sure it'll be fine," Rupert said. "You may as well know. Mandy's left me."

Mandy. He had been close anyway. "Sorry to hear that." He would need to stick to texting with Susan. She would get this out of him in no time if he spoke to her, and he was sure Rupert wouldn't want Lucy to know about it.

"It was bound to happen. She was too... you know."

"Young?"

"Bouncy. Never wanted to stay in one place. Always moving. Exhausting."

Richard laughed as he opened the door to the room with his key and handed Rupert the other one. "Well, there are more fish in the sea."

Rupert looked at him for a few moments. "Right. Got anything to drink?"

"You're in luck. They supply drinks here." He pointed to a small bar fridge. "And that's your room there."

"This is what I call an all-inclusive." Rupert parked his bag in the middle of the room and headed for the liquor. Pouring himself a scotch, he said, "Listen, I'm bagged. I'm gonna take a nap, but I'll join you later. Where will you be?"

Richard motioned him to step out onto the balcony and pointed toward the area he had been swimming. "I'll either be there by the pool or at that café there."

"Got it. See you in an hour." He picked up the drink and dragged his bag into the bedroom and kicked the door shut.

Richard stared at the closed door. It wasn't like Rupert to drink; he had quit years ago and rarely touched it. Something about Rupert wasn't right, but he couldn't quite put his finger on it. He was thinner. Tired. Must take a lot of energy to keep up with someone who bounced all the time. He went into his adjoining room to grab the book he had started on the plane and looked at his cell. Susan hadn't responded. She must still be mad. He hated it when she behaved that way. It was immature.

He walked downstairs and saw Lorne lying on a lounge chair alone. There weren't many at the poolside, come to think of it. Nor at the hotel. The following two weeks would pick up when Spring Break started, though. He had been here one year with Sue, their son Brian and Rupert and his family, and it had been a madhouse then.

"Hey," Lorne said as Richard sat in the lounge chair next to him. "We got here just in time."

"For what?"

"They grounded the planes after we left Vancouver. My wife is mad. She was booked on a plane for tomorrow morning, but now she's delayed at least two days. They're digging out of a storm like they haven't seen since 1996."

"You're kidding." The storm of '96 had paralyzed Sunshine Bay and all of Vancouver Island for weeks. Digging out had been near impossible in their cul-de-sac. They had waited for three days to get the car out. Luckily, they could walk once they got out their snowshoes. Where would they be? He tried to picture them in the garage. Did they keep them or give them away since then? Susan would know.

Susan. No wonder she hadn't texted back. She was outside digging out the car. That would take hours.

She would really be mad at him now. A server came by then and asked if he wanted a drink. After ordering a mojito, he turned back to listen to Lorne.

"The Island got it the worst."

"Thanks for the heads up. I'll check in and see how my wife is doing when I go back to the room." He hoped it wasn't as bad as Lorne was making it out to be, but he was sure that it was, and here he was, lounging by the pool thousands of miles away.

Feeling guilty wouldn't help, so he may as well make the best of it. He'd come to see Rupert who seemed to need someone and there was no way of getting home now, anyway. Besides, Susan was resourceful. She could handle things while he was away. She didn't need him.

The server returned and he signed for the drink, took a long sip and looked out at the sun glinting off the blue pool water. That was the trouble with Susan. She never needed him anymore.

CHAPTER 5

Susan trudged through the snow to the neighboring house. Jack had finished digging out her driveway and she could get into her garage to start the car. Damn. She knocked her forehead with her hand. The power was out so the garage door wouldn't open. She couldn't start the car without risking carbon monoxide poisoning.

Without being able to start the car, she needed to find another way to charge her phone. Had Richard tried calling? She wouldn't know until the power came on again. Meanwhile, her stomach was growling again, and Sylvia's cooking was always a treat.

"Welcome," Sylvia said when she opened the door. "Jack's just inside by the fire. Go on in and get warmed up, I'll be there in a minute."

Susan walked toward the smell of coffee and as she entered Jack was pouring her a cup from a pot on the wood stove. "We picked up this percolator for camping last summer. It's one of the best investments we made last year." He handed her a cup. "There's milk and sugar there on the coffee table. Help yourself."

"Thank you, this is fantastic." She sat on the couch, wrapping both hands around the mug to get them warm again before adding some cream and taking a sip. The warm liquid slipped down her throat and warmed her. "And thank you again for digging out my driveway. It would have taken me hours."

"It gives me something to do in winter. My job at the park doesn't start for a few months. I used to run a bobcat for a landscaping company before I went into finance. After working in the bank for years, I find I enjoy having projects where I can see what I've achieved by the end of the day."

"So, you've adjusted well to retirement," Susan said. "I should get you to talk to Richard when he gets back. Maybe you can give him some ideas about what to do in his retirement."

"He doesn't seem like the kind who would want to stop working for a while yet." Jack said. "He's always talking about his job when I see him. Seems to like the challenge of running an IT team."

"Yes, I suppose he does." She thought about this as she took another sip of coffee. If Richard liked his job so much, and Jack was right, he talked about it all the time, why would he have retired early? It made little sense. Unless. Was he sick? Was that why he had been sitting around the house so much and always seemed so tired?

"Well, are we ready for breakfast?" Sylvia walked into the room with plates, cutlery and maple syrup and Susan returned her attention to the present. Sylvia set the items on a table near the wood stove and lifted the lid of a pan at the back to reveal a stack of pancakes and sausages.

"That looks wonderful," Susan said. "I am so glad you're my neighbors. I was destined for cold cereal today."

Sylvia piled pancakes and sausage onto the plate and handed it to Susan and then another to Jack. "Well, eat up you two. It's cold out and you'll need your fuel."

Susan took a bite and groaned in appreciation. "Blueberry pancakes. I love them."

"We picked them over the summer from the farm down near Parksville." Sylvia said. "One of my favorite things about summer."

"I used to do that when Brian was young. I would take him out picking, and we had a small garden in the backyard. But I have had little time since I started at my current job. Always too many things to do and not enough time to do them."

"That's one reason I was glad to get out of banking," Jack said. "The stress was too much and probably contributed to my heart attack. At least that's what the doctor said."

Susan knew what it was like to work in a job she didn't enjoy.

"Now he just plays with his new toy," Sylvia teased.

"Speaking of which, I thought I'd dig out Yasmine and Farouk's place next."

"That's a wonderful idea," Sylvia said. "They have that new baby and a three-year-old to entertain without electricity. I'm sure they'll appreciate it."

"Then I'll get over to the others for as long as I have gas for the machine," he said. "Glad I filled the tank earlier this week. I still have quite a few hours left."

"Well, I'll keep the home fires burning and if they want to come over and get warm send them along."

He stooped to kiss Sylvia on the cheek and moments later they heard the machine's engine. Sylvia chuckled. "He loves running that thing. And it gives me time alone to do what I enjoy."

"Your cooking. Thanks so much again for breakfast. You make a wonderful pancake."

"Yes, cooking, and in the spring, if it ever comes back," she scowled at the snow outside, "I have started an organic garden. That way my food is as fresh as possible."

"And during the winter?"

"I started taking yoga two years ago to help strengthen my leg after I was in an accident. My practice is regular and so next month I am signed up for a certification course. I thought I could teach it."

"That's wonderful. Turning something, you love into a job. I wish I could figure out what I love," Susan added.

"Well, it took me a while to come to this. Believe me," Sylvia said. "When I had to leave work to look after my first husband when he got sick, I wasn't ready to retire. I even went into a deep depression after he died. Thankfully, I had Angel here," she picked up the black cat that was rubbing against her legs and patted her, "and Jack to bring me back. And I traveled."

"I've always been a little afraid to travel. When I do, it's with Richard. He's been everywhere."

"Isn't there somewhere you have always wanted to go? Or something you have always wanted to try?" Sylvia asked, stroking Angel's fur. Angel purred.

"It's been such a long time since anyone's asked me that. I will need to give it some thought."

"I wish I had given it more thought when I was younger. I learned too late that you never know how long a man will be in your life. You need to have a life of your own."

They were silent for a few moments, and the cat got quiet.

"Maybe I should make one of those bucket lists people talk about."

"Yes, a list of things you always wanted to try. What is life for but to experiment with what you love?" She laughed and the cat startled awake, hopping down on all fours. Alert. Ready. Sylvia laughed again. "I'm sorry, Angel. Did I disturb your sleep?"

The cat glanced up at Sylvia in what Susan thought looked like a scowl, then tail high, turned and walked to the corner of the room to curl in a tight ball on her cat bed only to stand alert moments later when they heard voices outside and the high-pitched squeal of a child.

"Sounds like Farouk and Yasmine are here." Susan said. "Let me help you with these dishes while you get the door." She picked them up and wandered into the kitchen, scraped the remaining food into the compost bin she found beneath the sink, and placed the dishes into a sink of lukewarm soapy water. Sylvia had thought of everything. What a lovely way to start this day.

She washed the dishes and then rinsed them in cold water from the tap, then found a tea towel hanging nearby. As she dried the plates and opened a few cupboards to find the place to put them, she thought about her earlier conversation. What would she love to do? How long had it been since she had asked herself that question?

After putting away the cutlery, she went into the living room to greet her neighbors, who were thanking Sylvia for offering them her warm house. Sylvia had brought out a box of Lego for the child to play with and he was now sitting quietly on the rug pushing the pieces together, building a tower of sorts. Angel had abandoned her corner to perch on the windowsill, her eyes tracking the child's movements, tail swishing slowly back and forth. Poor cat. Susan knew how she felt. It was unsettling to have a change in a routine like when Richard retired so suddenly. Though in some ways, maybe it was more unsettling to have routines remain the same. Or boring. Was that why Richard had left so suddenly? Was he bored with her? If he was, she couldn't blame him. She bored herself. What had she been putting off until she retired or had more time? And what would she do about it?

There was a knock on the door and Sylvia went down the hall, and soon ushered the Turners into the room, a couple with two toddlers from down the street. "Make yourselves at home. Would you like some coffee or breakfast?"

Susan gave Sylvia a hand welcoming other neighbors Jack was sending their way and fetched and carried cups, water and plates from the kitchen until nearly two hours later when the lights flickered on and the radio sprang to life. The little group cheered the return of the electricity and visited a few minutes longer before saying their goodbyes and trudging back to their own homes.

Susan departed reluctantly to go home and was a little disappointed when her computer sprang to life as soon as she turned it on. She could get at least a half day's work in now. Ah, well. Back to reality. Her phone rang a few moments after she plugged it in to charge. Boris. Of course, it was Boris.

"Did you confirm the new keynote speaker?" he asked her, frantic. "I've been trying to reach you for hours."

"I told you we didn't have power at this end of town," she said, miffed.

"Right. Well." He paused and then plowed on as though he hadn't heard her. "What about the keynote?"

"I'll get back to you after I read my emails. The power only came on twenty minutes ago. Give me a few minutes."

Several hours later, she finally found another speaker, reviewed the press release and discussed it with a much calmer Boris and the executive. At nine o'clock she switched off the computer and climbed the stairs to her room to take a shower. She glanced at the messages on her phone to see a missed text from Richard.

Richard: Got here safe. Hope you're okay. Heard about the snowstorm.

She stared at the message and exhaled the breath she didn't realize she was holding. At least he was taking time to check on her. She texted back.

Susan: Yes. All is well here. Jack helped me out with his new Bobcat. How's Rupert?

No answer. He was probably out or asleep. She would check again later, but first she would stand under a stream of warm water and then climb into bed with a good book.

A few minutes later she was towel drying her hair and feeling more refreshed than she'd expected. A lot had happened that day, but she still had some energy left. She wandered to the bookshelf where she had several empty journals. Journals she always thought she would find time to use, but somehow never did. She selected one with a dancer on the cover and settled down in the comfy armchair in the corner of her bedroom. Taking up a pen from the table nearby, she wrote a list of things she wanted in the next five years. After half-an-hour she sat back and read the list through and wrote the numbers one through three beside those that popped out at her. First was to take tango lessons. Second was to buy a red dress, something she had never had the courage to wear before and get a new job. Third: If she had to work at least another five years, she wanted to earn what she was worth and not work for someone who was doing the job she should have had.

She was sorry she had told the executive director she was planning to retire in a year, but there was no use crying over something she couldn't change. She could only move forward from here. Maybe it was time to shake up her work life and grow new skills. Much as she enjoyed working in family services, there were other organizations out there. She just needed to look.

She reviewed the list one more time and, satisfied she had thought of everything for now, she picked one thing to do to maintain momentum, a technique she had used many times at work to get through her 'to do' lists. She surfed the internet on her smartphone and found the schedule for Armand's School of Dance. Tango lessons were being offered on a rotating schedule and it looked like the next ones started in a week. Perfect. She could register for the beginner's class. Richard would be back around then. Maybe he would join her. She would ask him the next time they talked or texted and then register them both.

She walked toward the bed and paused again at the bookcase to pull out a romance novel she hadn't read yet. She hadn't indulged in a love story in months and according to her friend Lucy, this one was excellent. Thinking of Lucy brought Rupert to mind. What on earth was going on with him that would require Richard to drop everything to join him in Palm Springs? She hoped Lucy didn't find out where Richard had gone. She would never hear the end of it.

Richard woke to find himself still under the festive umbrella at the poolside, his book open on his chest, where it must have landed when he dropped off. He looked around. The sun was much nearer to the horizon than it had been before he dozed off. It was way past mid-day. He looked at his watch. Two-thirty. No wonder he was hungry.

He scanned the poolside for Rupert, who wasn't there. He looked over beside him to talk to Lorne only to find a young bikini-clad woman sunbathing. His gaze lingered a moment on her youthful, smooth brown skin, and then he shook himself. He needed to get up and find something to eat. This girl was young enough to be his son's girlfriend. Or Rupert's. And she was probably just as bouncy as Mandy had been.

Bouncy. He chuckled. Only Rupert would use that adjective to describe a woman.

Where was Rupert anyway? He would find him later, after he had something to eat. They were likely to close the lunch buffet soon so they could get ready for dinner. He wanted proper food, not a poolside burger.

He sat up, relieved to find his legs were still pasty white. No sunburn was always good, particularly as he'd forgotten to bring sunblock. Hopefully Rupert would have some in the room. He slipped his feet into his flip-flops and rose, grabbed his book and traipsed to the buffet restaurant near the water.

The ceiling fans moved the air inside around providing a breeze and he was happy to find only a few people there. It would be easy to find a place to sit near the beach side. He shoved his book into the pocket of his shorts and picked up a plate to add fish, salad, and some vegetables. He paused at the dessert section and looked down at the paunch he had been growing the past couple of months. Pass. He looked longingly at the chocolate cake as he took a few more steps and then retraced those same steps to pick up a plate. He would pass tomorrow. He was, after all, on vacation.

"Hey, you finally woke up." Lorne greeted him as he walked toward a table, startling him. He hadn't seen the man sitting there.

He thought a moment about his book and then sighed. He couldn't really remember where he was in the story, anyway. "Mind if I join you?"

"Please do," Lorne laughed. "Looks like we are just a couple of bachelors right now. When is your friend coming?" The way Lorne said friend made him uncomfortable. Did he think he didn't have a friend?

"Oh, he's in his room. Sleeping, probably. Looked bagged when he got here."

"Oh, he's a guy?"

"Yeah. My step-brother actually, but we were friends long before we were brothers." Why did he feel he had to tell this man this detail? "We've known each other since we were toddlers."

"Oh, a guy's trip." Lorne said. "Do you guys do that often?"

"Not really. Not since…" Since when? His mind cast back to the last time he and Richard had gone on a trip together. "I guess not since we were both married. We used to take trips with our families. We have boys about the same age, but Rupert is recently separated from his wife and asked me to come alone this time."

"That's too bad." Lorne said. "About his marriage, I mean."

"Yes." He picked up his fork and ate a bite of fish, chewing so he couldn't say anymore. He was still not sure what had happened between Lucy and Rupert. They had always seemed so solid. Even more solid than he and Susan were.

"What do you suppose happened?" Lorne asked. "Did he leave her? Or did she leave him?"

Richard chewed more slowly. "Why do you ask?" He said it more sharply than he normally would, but he wasn't comfortable sharing information about his friend's marriage with a virtual stranger.

Lorne startled. "Oh. Didn't mean to offend." He took a swig of his drink and then seemed to ponder the question. "It's just that my wife says she's decided not to come down."

Ah. So that was it. Lorne was having marital problems of his own. Poor guy. It would be hard to have your wife give up on you after a long marriage. He thought of Susan. She wasn't the same woman he married all those years ago. She was a little plumper, a little more set in her ways. But she was also his rock. At least she had been. Lately she was losing patience and seemed to never have time to spend with him. She also rarely smiled anymore.

He missed her smile. He missed her warmth. He missed the Susan she had been before he lost his job, before Brian moved out. When had that been? He counted back in his mind. It had been six years since Brian had finished university and got a job with the government and four years since he had announced he had saved a down-payment and was buying a condominium. Four years since Brian no longer needed his father to help him out. A young man should learn to stand on his own two feet and a parent should be proud when they accomplish it. But still. It would be nice to be needed just a little. If it weren't for the biweekly Sunday dinners that Susan insisted they have, he might never see Brian anymore. The server came by and replenished Lorne's drink, and Richard put down his fork to look the man in the eye.

"You want to tell me what happened?" he asked. He could listen to Lorne. He had a lot of practice listening to other people, though normally they were staff. Or colleagues. Maybe that was what was missing for him? His family hadn't needed him for years, but it hadn't bothered him until his company made him redundant.

Lorne cleared his throat, as though he were trying to clear away tears. Probably was, come to think of it. "My wife says I'm boring. Always working. Never enough time for her."

"But weren't you supposed to be here with her?" This was confusing.

"She texted me a couple of hours ago to ask if I brought the computer." He sighed. "When I said yes, she told me not to expect her company and she might not to be there when I got back."

Hmmm, think. What could he say? "So, she figured you would work your whole vacation because you brought the computer?"

"I guess so." He picked up the fresh drink and took a sip. His eyes were rheumy. How many drinks had he had? "I do work too much, but it's hard to find a project manager you can rely on. Someone who will stay on. I've lost so many in this market."

"What type of projects do you do?" He knew project managers. Hell, he was a project manager. Maybe he could help this guy out and connect him to one of the people he knew in Vancouver.

"IT. It's a competitive business though. Hard to keep people long. They're always being scooped up by someone else."

"I know the feeling," Richard said. "I used to run projects myself. Finding resources, particularly finding talented people who want to stay on, is hard. Most just want to live in the city. Keeping them on the island is difficult."

Lorne looked up at him. "You're in IT?" He was slurring his words now.

"Yeah. But they made my position redundant. Not sure what happened. Thought I'd be there until I retired."

"You wanna move to Vancouver? Maybe you could work for me."

"Not ready to relocate to the city yet." He shivered at the thought of commuting in thick traffic when he had been only ten minutes away at his last job. "But I do have a few contacts there. I can see if anyone knows of someone looking for work."

Lorne nodded, taking another drink. "Yessh. Thanks. Hard to keep people. Espessshly people you can count on. She never understands."

Richard eyed Lorne as the guy picked up his glass again. He should probably stop him. Lorne wasn't looking well. "Hey, why don't I walk you to your room so they can clear up in here? I think they would like to set up for dinner."

Lorne blinked and slowly turned to scan the now empty room. "Sure. Yeah." He placed his hands on the arms of his chair and tried to rise without pushing the chair back first. Failing, he flopped back into his seat. "Just a minute. I gotta rest a sec."

Richard rose and moved behind Lorne's chair, pulled it out and then helped him stand. He bent to pick up his book and shove it into his back pocket again, only realizing then that he hadn't eaten the dessert. Oh well. Maybe tomorrow.

It turned out that Lorne's room and his were in the same wing of the hotel. He got him safely inside and told him he would come back to look in on him when he and Rupert went down for dinner, just to make sure he was okay. Paradise was nice, but it could be lonely if you were here on your own, doubly so as he had expected to be here with his wife. Thinking of wives, he would have to get back to his room and send Brian a text, see if he could look in on his mother and make sure she was okay.

WHEN HE GOT BACK to the room, it was quiet. Too quiet. Where the hell was Rupert? Maybe he passed him on the way in. He stepped out onto the balcony to look at the poolside. Not there. He looked over toward the cafeteria he had just left but no, he wouldn't be there either. It was closed now. Maybe he was still in bed. He'd look, but first he wanted to text Brian.

Richard: Hey Bri. How're you doing?

Brian: Not bad. They're just plowing our street so should be out soon. What about you guys?

Richard stared at the phone a minute. How to word this so he didn't say too much. Brian was still good friends with Joel, Rupert's son. Did Joel know where Rupert was? Hell, he didn't even know where Rupert was right now.

Richard: I'm visiting with Rupert. Can you look in on your mother?

Brian: You left Mom alone in a snowstorm?

Richard: Not on purpose. What kind of guy do you think I am?

Brian: Just a sec…

Richard waited.

Brian: I just checked. Mom's end of town was out of power for most of the morning. But she was at Jack and Sylvia's place. She's fine. Power back on.

Richard: Thanks, bud.

Brian: When are you coming back?

Richard: Two weeks.

Brian: Okay, I'll look in on her. TTYL.

Richard: Thanks. Talk to you later, too.

He set the phone back down on the bedside table and then picked it up again to text Susan. Then he put it down again. She still hadn't responded to his first text, but at least he knew she was okay. He would try again later once he had time to visit with Rupert. Right now, he needed to find the guy.

He walked to Richard's room and listened through the door. It was possible that he was still asleep, though there was no snoring coming from the other room. He edged the door open, knocking softly, and heard a groan from the bed.

"What?"

"Hey, you okay in there?" There was a pause. "Rupert?" What was wrong with him? It wasn't like him to stay in bed like this. The flight and the breakup must have really hit him hard. He heard some shuffling and a muffled "juss a minute," and stood back as the shuffling came closer to the door.

Rupert opened the door and lunged toward the bathroom, staggering as he took the few steps to get there.

"Hey, what's up?" Richard asked, as he followed him into the bathroom and then did a quick one hundred eighty degree turn when Rupert upchucked into the toilet. The room reeked of alcohol, but that made little sense. Rupert didn't drink enough to throw up. Rupert rarely drank at all.

"Shit," Rupert said, swiping at his mouth with his hand before leaning over and emptying more of the contents of his stomach.

"Anything I can do to help?" Richard peeked in and then gagged at the stench of vomit and quickly stood back again.

"No. Go away." Rupert said, glaring at him. "And close the damned door. I don't need an audience."

"Okay, okay." Richard put up his hands to ward off any further discussion. "Just trying to help." He closed the door behind him, hoping that Rupert wouldn't be in there for too long. He went over to the couch and waited. No Rupert. He got up and wandered to where the liquor was on the counter and looked at his watch. It was four o'clock in the afternoon. Not yet cocktail hour, but he had already had a mojito and he was on vacation. Then he looked at the closed door and decided on a soda instead. He wasn't an "if you can't beat 'em, join 'em" kind of guy.

He was sitting on the couch looking out the window at the impossibly blue water when he heard a crash. He set down his soda and went to the door of the bathroom. "Hey, you okay?" Concerned, he tried the door handle and discovered it was unlocked. "Hey, coming in." Still no answer, so he pushed open the door, tentatively at first. Rupert was on the floor, crumpled in front of the toilet, unconscious. "Shit." He rushed toward Rupert calling his name and bent down to shake him awake. Rupert didn't respond. He felt for his pulse and breathed a sigh of relief when he found one. "Rupert?"

His friend finally stirred and came back to consciousness. "Rick. What happened?"

"You passed out. How much did you drink?" Did he have enough in his system to cause alcohol poisoning? Looking at the toilet he decided if it had been the case, it wouldn't be any longer.

"Not a lot."

"Let me get you up. Take you to your room." Richard grabbed his friend by the armpits.

"Sure. Yeah."

As he hoisted Rupert to his feet, he noticed he must have lost thirty pounds in the past few months, making it easier than he expected to help Rupert to his feet where he staggered slightly before regaining his footing.

"Come on." He pulled one of Rupert's arms up around his shoulder and grabbed him around the waist. Rupert came along meekly, docile. And suddenly he was really heavy. Richard turned to discover he had passed out again. "Damn it, Rupert." He said under his breath as he half dragged, and half carried his friend into the bedroom where he winced at the smell of vomit and booze.

Rupert was clearly off the wagon and he wished he'd known or suspected as much. Rupert had been off binge drinking for decades. Something he owed to his now estranged wife, Lucy. She had supported him to stay sober for years. Now that he had left her, he appeared to have returned to habits from his twenties. Why had he left Lucy? Richard still didn't understand and wished Rupert would go back to her. He didn't want to be helping a drunk to bed and lying to his own wife about where he was.

The room was as messy as a room with few contents could be. The bedcovers were strewn on the floor.

Two bottles of liquor were on the table, and three glasses. Why he would need three, Richard couldn't work out, but they littered every surface. An empty gin bottle was on the floor in a pile of vomit. He gagged, held his breath and turned his gaze away from the sickly yellow-green mess. He'd have to clean up. Rupert was in no shape to do it, and he hoped he could do it without puking.

He maneuvered Rupert into bed and covered him with the sheet and blanket, straightening it as best he could before he plunged toward the French doors leading to the balcony and opened them wide to let the fresh sea air wash through the room. Much better.

Turning, he looked at Rupert, his face colorless against the pillow, and stepped forward, holding his breath until he saw Rupert's chest rise and fall. The sight reminded him of when he and Rupert were teenagers, when Rupert first started drinking. How many times had he been there for Rupert to help him sober up? Countless. Enough to turn him off most liquor himself.

He had grown up with Rupert on Granger Island, a small island off the north coast of Vancouver Island where their fathers made their living fishing. His father, Allen, and Rupert's father, George, fished together until the industry began to falter and Richard's mother died in a storm when he was fourteen and away at boarding school. He closed his eyes as he remembered the look on his father's face as he told Richard his mother was gone. It was the same look he saw on Rupert's face three years later when Rupert learned his father had left his mother, Sandy.

Rupert never got over George leaving, and he never understood it. George had been a big man who brought a calm energy to every situation, the anchor for Rupert's family and their whole island community until he left leaving nothing but a note asking for forgiveness, and enough money to get Sandy off the island where they had always lived.

Rupert had blamed himself. If only he had been there fishing instead of in school. If only he could have stopped his father from leaving. If only he had been the son, his father wanted him to be. Richard had tried to convince him that he couldn't have changed it, but Rupert never listened. Not to Richard or anyone else. Not then anyway. Not until years later when Lucy came into his life.

Sandy had turned to Richard's father, Allan, who had left fishing to take up carpentry, a job that would be more financially stable and less dangerous than fishing, and the two had married after they learned of George's death four years later.

Richard watched his friend's chest rise and fall and then went downstairs to the front desk to ask for some cleaning supplies. What a way to spend his first day in Mexico. He would rather shovel snow.

Three days after the storm, Susan could finally drive to her office.

"Thank goodness you're here!" Jennifer said as she walked in.

"What's wrong?"

"It's the venue. The conference center. They don't have our booking. I called to ask for the menus and they said they didn't have our information."

"Who did you speak to?" This couldn't be right. She had spoken to Boris who had agreed to speak to Annette before she left for Australia. Annette had a contact at the venue and had agreed to book it.

Boris. She hadn't followed up because he was her boss and he hadn't said he had any trouble with the booking. It had sounded like a slam dunk that just needed a paper trail. Annette had already negotiated a good rate in exchange for a charity receipt and sponsorship recognition.

"I don't know. The receptionist who answered the phone."

"Let me look into it, okay? Don't panic." Was she reassuring Jennifer or herself?

"Okay." Jennifer looked close to tears. "I just can't believe that so many things can go wrong only a few weeks before an event like this."

"It's not unusual to be tossed a few curve balls. It gives you a challenge to rise to. Is Boris in yet?" Jennifer nodded and Susan walked the few steps down the hall to his door, hoping against hope that Boris had followed through on booking the venue as he said he would. She didn't mind jumping through a few hoops, but she really hated it when she landed knee deep in alligators.

"Come in," Boris said when she knocked. He smiled when he saw her. "Hey, Susan. Good job getting the new keynote at such short notice. She sounds like she'll fit the theme really well." It was nice that he noticed, but it wasn't what she needed right now. She looked at him, his mop of blond hair flopping over his eyes, and had to tamp down a compulsion to wet her hand and slick it back like she might for a child. Boris was only a few years older than Brian, so nearly young enough to be her son. She had to remember that both men were adults and fully capable of doing their jobs. She hated it when people used her age to assume things about her abilities, so she needed to stop making assumptions about Boris.

"Thanks." She accepted the compliment and then plowed forward. "I'm here to check on the venue. Jennifer said that when she called them for menus this morning, they didn't have a record of our booking." She watched as color drained from his face and her heart pounded. Where on earth would she find a decent venue in time?

"I. Um. I."

"Boris. You confirmed the venue, didn't you?" Why hadn't she insisted on a copy of the contract before now? She should never have assumed Boris would follow through. He had been left with too much responsibility too soon.

"Let me call them," he said, his voice shaking.

"We need enough room to bring three hundred people together." Her voice was rising, and she fought to keep herself calm. He already felt bad. No need to make him feel worse. He was doing the best he could considering Annette had abandoned him.

Still, she had asked him to do one thing and he hadn't done it. She closed the door to let him make the calls without her hovering. It wouldn't help either of them. She went back to her office and called Jennifer to join her. "Listen. It sounds like we may need a Plan B. Could you pull up the list of venues we researched before Annette said she had spoken to the conference center?"

Jennifer looked at her, her eyes wide. "Three hundred people at only a few weeks' notice? Where am I going to find that?"

"Pull up the list. Look at the capacity. See if anyone has had a cancellation. Find out the cost. We need to know our options." Jennifer walked out of Susan's office looking grim and Susan went back down the hall to speak to Boris.

His head was in his hands when she pushed the door open and he looked up and shook his head. "Annette was supposed to sign the contract before she left for Australia," he said. "The guy said he hadn't heard from her so he assumed we wouldn't need it. What are we going to do, Susan?" He looked even younger than he had the last time she was in the room. Young and vulnerable and, she needed to remind herself, perfectly capable of helping solve this problem he helped to create. She didn't get his job, but she could do her best to help him learn it before she found a better-paying job herself.

"Jennifer is making some calls to the other venues in town. How about we meet right after lunch to talk about our options?"

"Thanks for helping with this, Susan," Boris said.

She waved his words away with her hand. The last thing she wanted was to discuss this further. "Don't worry about it. Let's just salvage this the best we can and have a solid plan before you have to brief the board." When she called Cecelia, the board president, to ask for an employment reference, she would mention this to her. Much as she didn't think Boris was ready for the job, she knew it wasn't all his fault. They should know what a mess Annette had left them in when she rushed off. She was fed up with the leadership in her organization, but that didn't mean she didn't still believe in the programs and services they provided. Their clients needed them, and they needed leaders who would be there when the chips were down. Not in bloody Australia. She walked back to Jennifer's desk to see how she was getting along and offered to call some of the names off the list. Jennifer's eyes were bleak. This would be a long day.

Susan finished calling the first five venues on her section of the list and was relieved to find she had at least one potential option: the clubhouse at the local golf course had capacity if she could negotiate rooms at a decent rate in a nearby hotel. Jennifer bounced in a few minutes later to say that the hotel downtown that had been under renovation would be finished sooner than expected.

"Let's get Boris to come with us to scout these out. We need to make sure we get one that meets our needs." She would include Boris in far more of the details from here on in. He needed to understand what was happening and why. If he saw the venues, he could show the board he knew what he was about. He needed more guidance, and it was something she could give him while she sought other work and waited for Annette to return.

After lunch the trio visited the two venues and stopped at the local coffee shop, the Bumblebee Bistro, known to locals and "the hive," to talk about their options. She listened to them while they laid out the pros and cons of each venue and coached the pair to identify the key information that Boris would need to take to the board so they could make a decision. She tasked Jennifer with setting up the board meeting. She sat back and watched them work together, pleased that the initial crisis had passed.

"Susan, is that you?" Lucy's voice said from behind her left shoulder. She turned and rose to give her friend a hug, excused herself and walked a few feet from the table to gain some privacy. Not that the duo paid her much mind. They seemed to only have eyes for the work they were doing, and if she wasn't mistaken, each other.

"How have you been?" she asked Lucy. "I haven't seen you in days." In some ways, Susan had been thankful for the snowstorm. That, and the extra time involved in snow removal and catching up on work, had given her a plausible excuse to avoid Lucy. Her friend had been angry with Rupert for months, and Susan found it difficult to listen to the same old refrain week after week.

"I've been taking guitar lessons." Lucy's smile was wider than Susan had ever seen it. Perhaps she was finally moving beyond anger and toward accepting Rupert leaving.

"That's great."

"You have no idea."

Her friend's eyes were sparkling. Sparkling! Was there was more to this than guitar lessons?

"I'd love to hear more about it. Maybe we can get together soon." She glanced over at the pair she'd left at the table, their heads bent together, deep in discussion. She needed to get back to work.

"We could get a coffee after you finish work," Lucy said.

"What about dinner?" Susan suggested, and then nearly bit her tongue.

"Tired of having Richard around already?" her friend teased.

"Oh, he's out of town." Susan remembered where Richard had gone and who he had gone with, and said, "Listen, I should get back to work. How about we meet at the Loft on Main Street around seven?"

"Could we make it the Blue Room? Vince's playing there tonight. You can meet him."

"Vince?"

"My guitar teacher." She giggled.

Susan laughed, relieved they had moved off the subject of Richard. "I can't wait."

Lucy floated out of the café and Susan turned back to the table. It was good to see Lucy happy. It had been a long time. Rupert had a lot to answer for.

SUSAN LEFT work on time for a change, and walked toward where she'd parked her car, past a block lined with women's clothing boutiques that were usually closed by the time she ventured this way. She paused along the way to window shop and in the third window saw a red dress with a skirt full enough to swish around her calves when she walked. Or danced. She could wear it dancing and it would be one more thing she could strike off her bucket list.

She stepped inside the high-end boutique that smelled faintly of lavender. Why had she never been in here before? She looked past the front racks that held tailored suits, silk blouses and sweaters that looked hand crafted by artists, clothes of exceptional quality, until her eyes rested on what she came for. The red dresses were three racks away and when she got to them, she was delighted to find one in her size. She picked up the hanger and held the dress up to admire.

"Excuse me." A saleswoman appeared to her left and Susan jumped. "Oh, I'm so sorry," the woman continued, "I just wanted to let you know that we have a sale on everything on this rack and on those two over there." She pointed to another rack of dress slacks, skirts and jackets.

"Thank you." Susan walked to the other rack and sorted through them, picking out a gray skirt and a pair of blue slacks. These clothes would be more practical than a dress. She could wear them to work and get a lot of use out of them. She sorted through more hangers and picked a white blouse and a navy shell that would go with what she already had in her closet. If she spent money on clothes, she should probably stick with practical items. She felt the weight of the five hangers on her fingers and turned back toward the first rack and hung up the red dress. She could always get one later.

"Can I take these for you?" the saleswoman was at her side again and she turned to hand over the clothes, turning to the rack to look at the red dress one last time.

It wouldn't hurt to try it on, would it? Maybe it wouldn't even look good. Then she could leave it behind and not give it another thought.

"Can I try this one too?" she said to the woman before she could change her mind and was immediately whisked to the back of the store where the changing rooms were.

Once inside, she quickly disrobed and pulled the dress over her head. It floated down over her body like it was made for her. She looked at herself in the mirror and swayed her hips a little. The silky material swished just as she thought it would and the cut was flattering, hiding her extra bulges while accentuating her assets. Her cleavage was on display more than it had been in anything since she was in her thirties, but it was flattering. She stepped out of the room and looked at it in the three-way mirror in the fitting room hallway.

"That looks lovely on you," the saleswoman said.

"Thank you." Susan had to agree with her. It was a flattering cut. Could she buy it? Should she buy it?

She returned to the change room and after admiring herself in the dress a little longer, took it off and hung it on a hook where she could look at it while she tried on the other clothes. The skirt fit well and would be good for an interview and she hoped to go to interviews again soon. She hung it up again and placed it on another hook in the room and looked at the two items, comparing them while trying on the slacks which were too tight in her rear and the blouse which gaped over her bust. The shell fit, but it did nothing for her, so it was down to the two.

She looked at the price tag on the dress and did a quick calculation in her head. The skirt was cheaper, but not by much after the discount. She would buy the practical one. Once she had a new job, she could buy a red dress like this one. Decided, she gathered up the hangers and placed the discards on a rack on the way out.

"Oh, aren't you going to get the red dress?" the woman asked sounding disappointed, as disappointed as Susan was. "It looked fantastic on you."

Susan paused a moment, and then turned toward the rack where she had left the dress, reaching out to feel the silky fabric with her fingers. The woman was right. She looked fantastic in this dress and it might be a long time before she shopped for clothes again now that Richard wasn't working.

"You know, I think I will." She picked it off the rack, added it to the skirt, pulled out her credit card and was soon walking out of the store swinging the bag. She would wear it tonight and get Lucy's opinion, though the only person's opinion she wanted was Richard's and he was thousands of miles away.

*R*ichard read in his room until dinner time and went to see if Rupert was awake yet. He knocked softly and there was no answer and when he pushed open the door, he could see Rupert was fast asleep, curled up around a pillow like he had slept when they were kids. He might not wake up for hours, so Richard went down the hall to see if Lorne was awake and was happy to find him fully recovered from the afternoon's overindulgence.

When Richard and Lorne finished their meal, they adjourned to the lounge in front of the stage to watch the entertainment for the evening. They ordered beer and Richard was relieved to see that Lorne nursed his drink over the next thirty minutes. It looked like he had learned his lesson about drinking too much, too quickly, in the hot weather.

"I spoke to my wife," Lorne finally said, as they waited for the dancers to come onto the stage. Richard felt a cramp in his stomach. He hadn't phoned Susan and the guilt was eating at him.

"Yeah, did it go okay?" he finally asked, knowing he was expected to say something.

"She read me the riot act," he said. "She wants me to put the computer away for ten hours a day, every day, while she's here."

"So, she's coming after all?" Richard was surprised. It had sounded like Lorne was heading for divorce like Rupert had.

"She's coming in six days, the flights were re-booked for then, and I've extended my stay here for another week."

"Well, that's good news," Richard said, then saw the scowl on Lorne's face.

"She said, just because I'm being a jerk doesn't mean she should miss out on a vacation. I suppose if I look at it from her perspective, I promised her a vacation from work and that we would spend time together for a change."

"Uh huh." Richard tried to sound non-committal, took another swig of his beer and stared ahead at the stage, willing the entertainment to begin so he could stop talking about wives and marriages and promises. He had promised Susan that she could retire in a year. She had given up a promotion when she let the board know of her plans and now, instead of moving up in the organization, she was stuck working with a couple of inexperienced newbies. Lorne was still talking, so he pushed Susan to the back of his mind and tried to pay attention.

"I can probably commit to ten hours of not working if I get something done in the morning before she wakes up," Lorne was musing. "And if I keep my head clear," he looked at the drink in front of him, "I can follow up at the end of the day to see what the staff gets done."

"Sounds like you need a system," Richard said. "A way to track the tasks your staff get done and check in on them less frequently. Maybe delegate more."

"What do you mean?" Lorne asked, leaning closer to Richard. "What would that look like?"

The music was starting, and Richard glanced up at the stage. "Why don't we meet tomorrow morning and I can find out more about what your business needs are?" he said to Lorne. "I've been helping people with business solutions for years. If you tell me what your business model is like, I can try to help you figure out a solution. I might at least be able to point you in the right direction."

"You'd do that for me?" Lorne said, grinning from ear to ear.

"Absolutely." He'd have to do something productive with his days if Rupert was going to continue to drink himself into oblivion. He knew from experience that when Rupert wanted to drink, there wasn't much anyone could do to stop him.

"Hey, the show is starting." Lorne said, poking him on the arm. "I've heard this mentalist is good."

Richard spent the next thirty minutes laughing at the way the entertainer fooled them all while telling jokes.

"Didn't I tell you?" Lorne said when the act was done.

"Yeah, he was great." He felt another pain in his stomach, but the pain wasn't from guilt. It was from something else.

"Listen, I'm going to go see about my friend," he said to Lorne. "I'll see you tomorrow."

"Sure. I'm looking forward to our chat tomorrow morning."

"Let's meet for breakfast where we had lunch this afternoon. Around eight, okay?"

He smiled and then race walked to the nearest bathroom, glad to find an empty stall. As he sat, stomach clenching, relieving himself, he wondered what else could go wrong on this trip. So far, he was babysitting two drunks, helping one sort out his marriage, then tomorrow, his business, and now he had obviously eaten or drank something that was off. He wished Susan were here. She would know what to do about all this and would have remembered to bring medicine. But she wasn't here, and neither was her stash of helpful items. He would have to get himself to his room and hope that whatever he had would run through him quickly.

Rupert approached him as he was coming out of the bathroom and heading back to their room. "Hey, there you are. I've been looking everywhere for you."

"I've been watching the show," he said. "And now I'm heading back to the room to sleep. I'm not feeling too good." Another wave of cramps hit his abdomen and he grabbed his stomach.

Concern flashed across Rupert's face and then his eyes lit in amusement. "Got the runs, so you gotta run, eh?"

"Something like that." Richard groaned and dove past Rupert, heading toward their room.

"See you later," Rupert laughed after him. He walked faster, glad that Rupert would be out for a while. The last thing he wanted right now was company.

CHAPTER 9

he Blue Room was a tiny bar on Main
Street, just a block away from the
waterfront where she and Richard often walked on
warm summer evenings. They rarely came downtown
this time of year as they preferred to stay home in the
dark winter evenings and on chilly weekends.

Actually, it was Richard who preferred to stay home.
When he was away on business, she ventured out
with friends for a drink now and then as she was
doing tonight. It was he who preferred to unwind at
home after work, and she had learned to go along
with it. What else had she gone along with all these
years? She glanced down at the high black boots she
rarely wore, opting most days for comfort over

fashion. The boots and the long coat she had worn over her new red dress kept away most of the cold as she walked as briskly as she could along the icy sidewalk. Flatter soles would have been more practical, but she did love the way the dress moved against her legs. She should wear dresses more often.

She finally got to the restaurant. The warmth of the fireplace near the center of the room, and the mellow tones of a saxophone playing jazz, enveloped her as she stepped inside. She looked around to find Lucy as she slipped off her coat. Lucy wasn't there, so she approached the hostess to ask about the reservation and was escorted to a high-backed booth facing the stage, passing several men who turned to watch them as they passed, their eyes she was sure were on the woman in front of her, though it was nice to imagine this dress turning a head or two. She ordered a glass of merlot to sip while she perused the menu. The mushroom risotto sounded good. Decided, she set the menu aside to enjoy the music while she waited.

"Susan?" A man's voice got her attention and she turned to see Sid approaching her table. "I thought it was you," he said as his eyes flitted from her face to her chest and back again. She flushed at the attention. It had been a long time since she had noticed a man noticing her.

"Hello," she said, looking up at Sid whom she had known since they were teens. They had dated a long time ago, before he had slept with and married Beth, her high-school nemesis. After that, she had left town to attend university and had only rarely run across him through Richard's work.

"Are you here alone?" He slipped into her booth without waiting to be invited. She sat back, surprised at his sudden intrusion, and examined him from across the table. He had aged well. He had been an athlete when they were going out and he was still fit. His black hair had only a hint of silver in it, and his brown skin, courtesy of his mother's South Asian heritage, showed few creases from age.

"I'm waiting for a friend," she said, and his eyebrows raised. She wished she had thought to bring a Pashmina with her to cover her shoulders and cleavage. His steady gaze was making her remember the way he had looked at her all those years ago before he broke her heart. She glanced down at the drink in front of her to break her train of thought. The last thing she needed was to be thinking about another man. She looked up again.

"I'm glad I caught you here," he said leaning forward. "I wanted to apologize for not being able to give the keynote for your conference."

She relaxed a bit. This was why he was sitting here. That made sense. "It wasn't your fault," she assured him. "How could you have predicted what would happen?"

He frowned. "Well, I should have expected it after they let Richard and the other managers go in his department." He was looking down when he said it, not meeting her eyes, for which she was grateful. He didn't see her jaw drop. What did he mean when they let Richard go? What was he talking about?

He glanced up to meet her eyes. "How's he doing, by the way? I keep meaning to call him but, well, I feel awkward being the one who had to do the deed."

"Oh, you mean you were the one…." She let her voice trail off, hoping he would finish the sentence for her and leave her absolutely certain of what he was saying.

"Yes, I was the one they had lay everyone off and so I shouldn't have been surprised when they called me into the office last week to lay me off, too."

"That must have been difficult," she said, not knowing what else to say.

"It made it easier that I could offer them a good package, though now I'm wondering what we had to give up for it." He looked miserable. "The pension isn't as secure as we all thought it was, but I guess you knew that already."

"You mean about them not investing it properly?" She took a stab in the dark, trying to sound like she knew what the heck he was talking about, without showing him the panic and dismay that was running through her mind. She took another sip of wine, holding the big bowled glass with two hands to keep them from shaking.

"Yeah. Sounds like the accountant, Louis Taylor, was diverting the pension money to an offshore account before taking off to Mexico or wherever he went."

"The accountant was embezzling." She made it sound like a statement rather than a question. What the hell was going on? Why hadn't Richard said anything?

"Apparently he'd been skimming off the top for ten years before he figured he had enough to retire." He said "retire," with all the derision he could muster. "We were lucky to get the packages we did get."

"Have you heard how much pension is left?" she asked lightly, her heart sinking.

"Well, luckily a lot of it was locked into an investment fund long before they hired the guy, so he could only skim and redirect since he started. We'll find out in the next couple of weeks, when the forensic accountants finish looking into it, how much we'll have. Meanwhile, we're all looking for work again, which is hard when you're over fifty."

"Yes, it hasn't been easy." No wonder Richard was always so distracted and not settling into retirement. He wasn't retiring. He was unemployed. And now he was unemployed in Palm Springs with Rupert. What the hell was going on with him?

"I'm glad I invested nothing with Louis. Some people lost a lot getting into a fund he was promoting."

"Yes, I can imagine that would have been a rude awakening for them." She could be grateful that at least Richard wouldn't have made any crazy investments without talking to her first.

"Anyway, I thought I would stop by and apologize again about the keynote. I hated to let you down, but given the circumstances…"

"It's okay. We've found someone through some connections I have. She'll do an excellent job."

He looked relieved to be completely off the hook. "Tell Richard I said hi," he said, shifting himself toward the edge of the booth to let himself out.

"Hold still!" they both heard a voice say, and they turned to find Lucy with her iPhone pointed at them. "Say cheese!" Before Susan could register what was happening, Lucy had snapped their photo. "Great picture!" she said, looking down at the screen. "Here, hold this." Lucy set her bag and coat down beside Susan. "I'll be right back!" And before either of them could say a thing, Lucy was off again, heading toward the band, iPhone at the ready.

"So sorry about that," Susan said. "She'll be back in a few minutes." He was still sitting there watching her, as though waiting for her to give him permission to leave. "How's Beth?"

"Beth and I are separated," Sid said. "She left about six months ago."

"Oh, I'm so sorry to hear that." The two had been together for over thirty-five years. Here was another example of long-term couples separating. What was this, an epidemic? Was it something in the water?

"It's been coming a long time," he said. "She and I stayed together until the kids left and then, after the grandchildren started coming, it just became apparent that we had nothing left. She wanted to travel. I wanted to garden. It was a mess."

"Hopefully you're adjusting okay."

"I'm fine. In a lot of ways, it was a relief. It was hard to always be waiting for the next blow-up."

"I suppose that would be a relief," she said.

"It's been lonely but I'm doing things I've been putting off. Like starting seeds for the community garden plot. I have a membership there this year."

"Oh, that would be fun," she said. "I'm trying a few new things as well. No grandchildren to keep me busy. Thinking of taking dance lessons."

"Ballroom?" His eyes lit up and she nodded. "Remember having to do that during gym class? You were pretty good if I recall."

"I don't know about that," she shook away his compliment, "but I do remember it being fun. I'd like to try ballroom again."

"I have done nothing like that in a long time. Beth wasn't much of a dancer."

"Richard isn't either." But she didn't want to talk about Richard. She tightened her grip around the base of the wineglass and tried to think of something else to say, to steer the conversation away from that topic.

"Where is Richard tonight?" he said as though just realizing he was absent.

"He's in Palm Springs." She fought to keep her voice steady, to keep the rising anger at bay. Why hadn't he told her he got fired? Why all the secrets? "He's visiting his brother for a couple of weeks. Needed the break."

"Richard's in Palm Springs with Rupert?" Lucy's voice broke into the conversation and Susan turned to see her friend's eyes mirroring the anger she was feeling.

As though sensing trouble, Sid slid out of the booth. "Listen, I should get back to my table. I'll see you soon." She watched him leave. Coward.

Lucy slid into the seat he had just vacated. "Why didn't you tell me he went to see Rupert?"

Susan raised the wineglass again and took another deep sip before facing her friend's wrath. "Because I knew you would react like this," she said, "and you know damned well that Richard and Rupert are brothers. Did you expect them not to see each other?"

Lucy glared at her again and then sighed. "No, I guess not." She set down the glass of wine she had carried over to the table with her. "But I wish we could talk about this stuff."

"It's hard for me, too," she said. "I don't enjoy having to divide loyalty between you and Rupert. I feel like

I'm stuck in the middle. And besides, right now I have other things to worry about."

"I'm sorry. It has been all about me for a long time," Lucy said. "Thanks for putting up with it. Tell me, what's happening that has you worried?"

She should keep it bottled up. She never talked about her marriage to others, but she couldn't help it and Lucy was more than her oldest friend. She was her sister-in-law. Between the time they ordered their meals, and when the food arrived, she had shared with Lucy how things were going. The layoff, the lies, and the horrible fact that she was now terrified she could never afford to retire.

Lucy listened without comment for a long time and then, when the risotto arrived and they had taken their first bites, she said, "Look. This isn't what you want to hear, but I'll say it, anyway."

Susan took another sip of her second glass of wine and waited, fork down, to hear what Lucy had to say.

"When Rupert left, I was devastated."

"I remember," Susan said, and then stopped talking when Lucy held up her hand.

"And I was blindsided because he left me with less than I thought we had, even though I know he didn't take even half of it."

Susan now knew how it felt to be blindsided by the one person she'd always been able to count on. It was like discovering the solid foundation of your house had been devoured by termites.

"He did leave the house and once I sold it, and sent him some money, I knew I'd be okay."

"That's a good thing to learn," Susan said. "I mean, it must have given you some peace of mind knowing that."

"Yes, but I have learned something more important than that since he left. I learned that I'd been living in Rupert's shadow all these years." She paused and looked into space as though searching for something and then focused her gaze back on Susan. "No, I wasn't exactly in his shadow. It was more that living as a couple made me forget who I was as an individual. I did things he wanted to do, you know? And I didn't really push myself to go beyond what was comfortable. After thirty-two years, I was suddenly shoved out on stage without my lines and had to improvise. If that makes sense."

Susan took a bite of the risotto and chewed slowly, thinking of what to say while trying to enjoy the texture and flavors of the food. She would never order risotto here again. Though she was sure most people would find the subtle blend of vermouth and oyster mushrooms very appealing, to her it was tasteless as she considered what Lucy was saying. Improv was an accurate metaphor for what she was experiencing right now.

"So, you're saying I should...? What?"

"I'm saying you might want to consider your Plan B. You know, figure out what you want in the next half of your life. With or without him."

With or without him. Her throat closed and she couldn't speak. Was Lucy saying Richard might not come back? That wasn't possible. She looked across at Lucy who had taken a moment to turn toward the musicians.

Lucy had taken months to deal with Rupert's leaving and though she talked about not having much Susan knew Lucy had a good pension plan and had bought a condo in a nice location. She was still working part time. Lucy wasn't in the same situation as Susan was. And Lucy didn't know how bad it could really get.

Susan knew. It had happened to her Aunt Josephine.

"Oh, they've started," Lucy said, shifting to the end of the booth to watch the dashing young guitar player accompanying a soloist. That must be Vince. She could certainly see the attraction. Vince was fit, tall, broad shouldered. A physique much like a younger Rupert, on a man who looked much different. Rupert was a big man who had grown his muscles through years of physical labor. Vince was thinner, with dark skin, and warm brown eyes. Wavy hair with a curl over his eyes, that he pushed back occasionally. The way Lucy looked at him it was clear she wanted to run her fingers through that dark hair. Susan looked away again and took another sip of her wine.

No. Lucy had no idea how bad things could get for an older woman left alone. She hadn't been there when Susan was twelve and had accompanied her mother across town to check in on her mother's Aunt Josephine. And Lucy hadn't watched her mother's shaking hands knocking on the door, and her frenzied search through her tote bag for the spare key. Her mother had directed Susan to keep knocking until her knuckles hurt.

Her mother finally found the key, scrambled to fit it in the lock and pulled Susan into the darkened entrance way, screaming Josephine's name. "Go look in the living room," her mother ordered as she headed for the little bedroom at the back of the apartment. Susan stepped slowly toward the couch that sat in the middle of the room facing the television, struggling to make out the shapes in the darkened room. Where was the light switch? And what was that smell? She moved slowly, wanting to know and not wanting to know. She moved her hand along the wall at the entrance of the room and found the switch, flicked it on and heard a groan coming from a small mound at the end of the couch. "Turn it off. It hurts my eyes."

She quickly switched it off again and yelled down the hall, "In here, Mom." She'd backed toward the wall as her mother charged past, wanting to sink into the plaster but needing to watch.

"Turn on the light," her mother snapped, kneeling beside the mound that was her aunt. "I can't see anything."

She switched it back on and her mother leaned closer. "Call 911," she said, standing and looking directly at Susan. Susan wavered, taking in the directions. 911. That was who you called for emergencies.

"Never mind," her mother said, bustling to the table at the other end of the couch where the phone stood. "I'll do it myself." She picked up the receiver and began to dial the number. "You go into the kitchen and see what that smell is. Make sure the stove's off." Susan nodded, looking at the groaning mound. "Now, Susan. Go!"

"Yes, Mom." Her mother's raised voice set her going, like the starter pistol at the school track and field events. She was around the corner to the small pocket kitchen in a moment, where she checked the stove was off and listened to her mother's end of the conversation with the paramedics. They were coming. Meanwhile, she looked around the kitchen for the source of the smell, opening cupboard after empty cupboard until she opened the oven. She held her breath and leaned in to look then yelped and jerked back when she saw the maggots wiggling in the meat that had been there far too long.

"Did you find it?" her mother asked from the other room. She was back murmuring to Josephine, trying to keep her calm, which seemed to be working. The groaning had stopped and was now a mere whimper.

"Yes," Susan answered, closing the door to the oven again. "It's rotting meat in the oven," she said, coming around the corner as the phone rang again.

"Answer that and buzz them in," her mother said. "Then go back into the kitchen and put the meat into a trash bag. We'll drop it in the garbage bin on the way to the hospital." Susan grimaced and her mother eyed her sternly. "It's only rotten meat, Susan. Do it now. And check to see if there's anything in the fridge that needs to be thrown out. I doubt she'll be back for a while."

Susan nodded. That look on her mother's face brooked no argument and she didn't dare cross her. She buzzed the paramedics into the building then opened apartment door to let them through.

"In here," her mother called from the living room. The pair rushed to her aunt's side and her mother stood back to watch them and then looked up at Susan, pointed to her and then to the kitchen, spurring Susan into action.

She returned to the kitchen and opened a few more cupboards to look for a garbage bag. The shelves were bare except for a few dishes and jars of fruit and vegetables her mother had brought in the fall. She opened the fridge to find it empty but for a jug of filtered water. What had her aunt been eating? She heard the door close and her mother's steps approaching.

"Hurry up," her mother said entering the room. "They've taken her to the hospital, and I need to go to her so she doesn't worry. She's delusional from lack of water."

"Just looking for a bag to put it in," Susan said, opening the drawers on the other side of the kitchen, sighing with relief when she found a plastic shopping bag that would do the trick. She turned to see her mother standing in front of the open empty cupboards.

"Why didn't she say something?" her mother whispered through tears. "I would have helped."

"I don't know," Susan said, turning toward the oven and opening it.

"Oh, my." Her mother shoved her aside and took the baking tray from the oven and poured the wriggling mess into the bag Susan was holding before popping the tray into the sink and running hot water over it, adding soap to allow it to soak. "We'll come back later to give it a good cleaning."

"What happened? Why doesn't she have food?" Susan asked her mother as they waited for the doctor to give them Aunt Josephine's prognosis.

Her mother pulled her close and lowered her voice, as though afraid someone would overhear. "I can't be sure, but Aunt Josephine never had to handle the money when Uncle John was alive. And I know from my cousin that John made some bad investments and lost quite a bit just before he died."

"Can't she get a job?"

Her mother had looked at her with that tolerant look older people give children who come up with improbable solutions, her face a mixture of sadness and patience. "No. She's well into her seventies now and she's never worked outside the home. I don't think she has enough work experience to find a job."

"Well, I'm always going to have a job," Susan had said, resolving that day to never trust anyone with her money. And she hadn't until she met Richard. She trusted him to never put their future at risk.

But then, she had always thought he would never lie to her either. At least not about the important things like pensions and jobs. She had always thought they would figure out how to navigate the next decades of life the same way they had done the last three. Together.

She picked up her glass. It was empty, so she switched to water. She would have a headache in the morning if she didn't hydrate and she had to finish some of the meal in front of her or she would regret it later.

"Isn't he wonderful?" Lucy turned back to her, eyes still shining. She looked a decade younger.

"He plays very well," Susan answered, suspecting Lucy wasn't talking about Vince's guitar skills. The next act took the stage several minutes later, and Vince strode purposely toward their table. Lucy scooted over to give him room to slide into the booth beside her.

"Vince, I want you to meet Susan," she said, "my sister-in-law."

Susan looked sharply at Lucy. This was the first time in a very long time Lucy had introduced her this way. Usually it was 'my friend' or even 'my best friend.'

"Hey," Vince said, nodding in her direction and smiling. "You enjoying the music?"

"Yes, very much," she said, though in truth, she wasn't even sure what song he had just played, nor how long he had been playing.

"I wanted Lucy to hear the guitar accompany a talented singer, so she could see what it sounded like. She's one of my best students, you know?"

Lucy smiled up at him and said, "Flatterer."

He shook his head. "No, really, I wish every student I had practiced as much as you do. It's great when a student actually tries." He leaned forward to talk to

Susan. "Do you know what she said when we started working together?"

Susan looked between Lucy and Vince. "No, tell me."

"She said, I need to learn this as fast as possible. I don't have much time." He sat back and laughed. "I thought she was telling me she had cancer or something."

Lucy slapped his arm a bit and laughed too. "No silly, I was saying I'm not a teenager and I have a lot to learn to get good at this."

"Anyway, I agreed to teach her, and she's progressing three times faster than any of my young… ahem… other students," he said. "I wish they all took it so seriously."

"Who thought I would be a poster child at my age?" Lucy laughed and they both joined in.

"Can we get you a drink or something to eat?" Susan asked.

"Nah, I don't want to crash your dinner. I have to go back on stage in a few minutes anyway. Just wanted to come and say hi to my girl Lucy here." He reached over and squeezed Lucy's arm and she giggled. Giggled like a schoolgirl with her first crush. The man wasn't much older than Lucy's son.

"See you on Tuesday," he said to Lucy as he got up to leave.

"Yes, you will," Lucy said and then the two of them watched him saunter back to the stage.

Lucy turned to Susan. "Isn't he great? I was so lucky to get him to teach me. His fingers are amazing!"

I bet they are, thought Susan, wondering what those amazing fingers did best. Then she thought of Richard. It had been a long time since he had shown her what his fingers could do, or shown her much affection outside of a peck on the cheek every few days. Lucy was right. She needed a Plan B.

She and Lucy left the restaurant together an hour and two drinks later, and shared a cab home, neither trusting themselves to drive. "Thanks for coming out with me," Lucy said, as she opened the door to climb out in front of her condo complex. "I'll see you for coffee next week sometime, I hope?"

"Absolutely." She was relieved. Now that Lucy knew about Richard, there was no need to avoid her. "How about after work on Wednesday at the hive?"

* * *

WHEN SHE ARRIVED HOME, she paid for the cab and let herself into the cold house, thankful she had remembered to leave a light on over the landing. She walked into the kitchen and sat on a chair to take off her boots. It was silent except for the tick, tick, tick, of the fish clock on the wall above her. Tick. Tick. Tick. It was taunting her. He lied to you. Tick. Tick. Tick. And you fell for it. Tick. Tick. Tick. And he's probably lying about more. Tick. Tick. Tick. While you stay home and work. Tick. Tick. Tick.

Anger raged through her and she stood and dragged the chair to the wall, scraping the floor as she went. Then she climbed onto the chair teetering on her high leather boots, reached up, and grabbed the offensive clock off the wall with both hands, yanking it hard and stepping back, realizing too late that she misjudged her footing. She landed hard at an angle onto the floor, the heel of the boot collapsing under her weight and sending her foot forward while forcing her other leg behind her. On the way down she hit her chin on the edge of the chair seat and landed with two hands still on the clock like a steering wheel. Tick. Tick. Tick. She stared at the clock a moment and then with a roar of frustration flung the offensive thing away. It landed with a satisfying crash.

"Damn you, Richard! Damn you, damn you, damn you!" she yelled, over and over until her throat hurt.

Exhausted, she folded her arms onto the chair seat and rested her head, gathering the strength to pull herself up. Why hadn't he told her about the layoff? Why was he keeping information from her? She thought they had always been a team. Maybe she had been wrong about other things too. Maybe he was having an affair with a younger woman. She pictured Richard and Rupert with two women with long flowing hair, laughing at their every word, and quickly pushed the thought from her mind. She didn't want to think about that, and so far there wasn't any evidence that he was cheating. But he had lied about his job. And he had been distant, barely touching her for weeks.

"Owww," she moaned as she used the chair to pull herself up from the floor. Staggering, she grabbed the table nearby to steady herself. "Owww," she moaned again as she sat on the chair to pull off her boots and then again as she pulled herself to her feet. Tomorrow when the bruises were blooming all over her body, she would really regret this, but right now she took a few satisfied moments to appreciate the silent kitchen before turning off the light and gingerly pulling herself up the stairs to their bedroom.

She took off her dress and examined it, thankful that it hadn't been torn in her mishap. She hung it up and let the fabric slip through her fingers one last time before closing the closet door, putting on her nightgown, and going to the bathroom to brush her teeth and wash off her makeup. The bruise on her chin was coming in strong and she wasn't sure how she would explain it at work. Concealer would hopefully cover it. She looked like she'd been in a brawl.

Clicking off the bathroom light, she walked to the other room, edged herself onto the bed and pulled the extra pillow toward her. It smelled of Richard, so she chucked the pillow across the room. She didn't want to think of him and his lying ways right now. She rolled over onto her back and immediately realized her mistake. The room was spinning. Four glasses of wine was far more than she had drunk in years, and never on a work night. She flipped over on her stomach and there was that scent again. She gingerly worked her way to a sitting position and regained her equilibrium then she stood and struggled to rip the sheets and pillowcases from the bed, threw them into the clothes hamper and shuffled down the hall to get clean ones. Returning to the bedroom, she leaned against the doorframe, before gathering the energy to do more. Why not just curl up on the naked bed under a duvet? What would it hurt? And the mattress looked so inviting right now.

She pulled the duvet and a pillow from the floor. The pillow still had a faint Richard scent, so she pushed it into a pillowcase and smelled it again, happy to find the soft scent of lavender still clung to it from the last time it was washed. Carrying the pillow and pulling the duvet behind her, she crawled back onto the bed, shifting her aching body until she found the least painful position.

Tomorrow would be a new day and she would face it on her terms whether or not Richard came home.

*R*ichard visited the bathroom four times in the night and finally fell asleep near dawn, unsure of whether Rupert had returned. He picked up his smartphone before he got up to see if Susan had texted. Nothing. He lay back and closed his eyes. What was he going to do? He had to get home soon. This trip had been nothing but a mistake.

He scrolled through to see if there were new messages and found none. Was this what his life amounted to now? Looking after drunks, getting sick with no one to comfort him and now no messages from Susan to even see how he was doing?

Turning to his email, he noticed a few notifications that people had posted on Facebook. He rarely looked at Facebook but given it was five in the morning and he was going to have to wait at least another hour before breakfast was available, he had time. If he could even stomach breakfast. Perhaps coffee and dry toast might be best today.

He went to Facebook's login screen. What was the password again? He tried two before finally getting into his account and scrolling through to see what he had missed.

A couple of friends had posted about the cruise they and their wives had taken. Others, who had been laid off, were keeping lower profiles like he was, with posts about birthday parties and an ice fishing trip. Lucy had been busy last night, taking pictures of a band, in particular the guitar player, and some of the audience. He scrolled past a woman in a red dress before scrolling back and enlarging the picture with his thumb and forefinger. What the hell? He stared at his wife showing off more of her cleavage than he had seen in years, sitting with Sid. Sid! What the hell was she doing with Sid? And where did she get that dress?

He looked at her again, a little closer. She wasn't there to have drinks with Sid, was she? No. That made little sense. Lucy wouldn't have posted it if they were trying to hide a date or an affair. Unless…

Unless Lucy forgot he was on Facebook. Or had been drinking. There was a glass of wine in front of Susan. He looked more closely at the photo. Susan looked startled, like she'd been caught off guard. Or was she feeling guilty? And Sid was there, leaning in, tilted toward his wife, like they had been in an intimate conversation. He had never liked that guy and now that he, Richard, was out of town less than a week, Sid was already swooping in. Maybe this wasn't the first time. He lay back and remembered the number of times they had asked him to travel for work, leaving her alone. Lonely. And Sid had been single for months now.

He dialed Susan's number and then groaned and hung up before it could ring. It was six in the morning and there was still the minor matter of Rupert and his secrets to figure out before he spoke to her, otherwise he would sound like a twit. She would ask why he didn't tell her he was going to Mexico, and what would he say? Because Rupert told me not to? Like he was six years old and not nearly sixty? Even if it was the honest reason, he didn't want her to know. She would think he was choosing Rupert over her again, like she always did.

Rolling over, he pushed himself to a sitting position and held onto the bed. His head was still spinning from the illness. He needed water and a shower. Once he felt human again and had some breakfast, he would try texting Susan to see how she was doing. Meanwhile, he would tell her he liked her new red dress and that he wished she had been wearing it for him... instead of wearing it around Sid and looking better than she had looked the day he married her. She looked damned good. His groin warmed, and he quickly tamped down his wayward thoughts. He climbed out of bed and went to take a cold shower. He'd first focus on helping Lorne. Then he could figure out what the hell was going on with Rupert. And then he would get himself home at the end of the week so he could see that dress peeled off her in person.

He emerged from his room at six-thirty, dressed. Rupert was snoring, so he took his phone and a book with him to the breakfast area to wait until they opened the buffet, stopping first to report that he thought he'd been exposed to food poison. As he was leaving the desk Lorne approached him.

"Did you say something about food poisoning? That's probably what was wrong with me last night too. Just glad it wasn't a long bout. Sometimes it can go on for days."

"Well, maybe things will start looking up from here," Richard said, trying to inject a bit of positivity into the morning. "Why don't we get a coffee and talk about your business? May as well do it early." The earlier the better so he could move on to Rupert and find out what the heck was going on.

Three hours later, he had worked with Lorne to identify the gaps in his business process and found several areas that he needed to delegate to other members of his team. They had written it down in a document on the computer Lorne had brought with him, and Lorne had left looking relieved and happy. "I'll show this to my wife tonight over Skype," he said. "She'll see that I am working on delegating and she'll have to forgive me. How can I ever thank you?"

"No need to thank me, Lorne. I was happy to do it, though if you think of anyone who might have some work, I'd appreciate the lead."

"I'll ask around," said Lorne. "And thanks again."

CHAPTER 11

Susan had barely begun to dream when she was jerked awake by the sound of a phone ringing from across the room. Groaning, she forced herself up on her elbow and squinted in the dim light coming from the hallway to see what time it was. Seven in the morning. Who was calling so early?

She rolled over, the pain on her left hip bringing tears to her eyes as she strained to bring her feet to the floor. She pushed her feet into the warm slippers on the side of the bed and sat momentarily dazed. Why were there no sheets on the bed? Right. She remembered now. The phone seemed to be louder now that she was sitting, more insistent, so she forced herself to her feet and carefully stepped to her desk to pick it up.

"I am sooo sorry," Lucy said. "I didn't mean to do it. I don't know what I was thinking."

"Didn't mean to phone me at seven in the morning? It's okay, I should be up by now, anyway."

"Nooo," Lucy wailed. "I'm sorry I posted that picture of you and Sid on Facebook."

"What are you talking about?" Susan reached up to push her hair behind her ear. Lucy was often more dramatic than she needed to be but usually Susan had a cup of coffee and a shower before she had to face her sister-in-law's rambling.

"I got a message from Joel, about the picture I posted on Facebook."

"I still don't know what you're talking about. What did Joel say that has you all upset?" Joel was often melodramatic too, now that she thought of it. Just like his mother.

"He saw that picture I snapped of you and Sid last night. I put it on Facebook."

"Aww Lucy, you know I hate having my picture on Facebook."

"I know. And I'm so sorry. I took it down after I talked to Joel. He saw it and asked me if you were having an affair with Sid."

"What?" She laughed. "Why on earth would he think that?"

"Because of the dress you were wearing. You were drinking wine. I don't know. Do you think there's a chance that Richard saw it?"

"I don't think Richard uses Facebook, and even if he saw it, would it matter?" She sounded bitter even to her own ears. "I don't even know if he's coming back."

"No. That's not true."

"He lied to me about losing his job, Lucy. Who knows what else he's lying about?"

There was a lengthy silence prompting Susan to ask, "Are you still there?"

"Yeah, I'm still here. I was just thinking I hope you don't have to go through what I've gone through these past few months. I wouldn't wish that on anyone."

"Well, if I do have to go through it, I'll know who to go to for advice." She refrained from saying more. She didn't want to assume there were more lies until she found them, but really, what project did Rupert have him working on in Palm Springs? Why wouldn't he say anything about his job? Why didn't he trust her to tell her the truth about such an important thing in his life? Their lives.

And if she couldn't trust him, could she stay with him? They had based their marriage on trust. Without trust, what did they have left?

"I'm here for you, no matter what happens. I just hope you don't have to go through this, Susan." Lucy's voice broke and Susan braced herself to listen to tears, as she had many times in the past six months. She really should have had coffee before dealing with this. Lucy continued; her voice clearer. "If he does leave, I hope you get an answer to why. To what went wrong. Closure." Unlike Lucy, who still did not know why Rupert had left home. According to her friend, one day everything was fine and the next day it was over. Just like that. Maybe Richard could at least find that out for Lucy. Susan would ask him if she thought he would give her an honest answer.

"Well, I'm not there yet. Listen, I should get going. Thanks for warning me about the Facebook post. Can we talk soon?"

"Yes, of course. And again, I'm so sorry, the last thing I want to do is stir up trouble between you and Richard."

She hung up and plugged the phone into the charger before getting ready for work. Her head was pounding from either the fall, or the wine, or both, and her legs ached. She took stock in the mirror. The bruise on her chin was purple and when she raised her nightgown to examine the rest of her injuries more closely, she winced as she looked at her legs. They looked as though she had gone ten rounds in a kick-boxing match. Leaning forward, hands on the counter, she peered more closely at the damage to her face and thought about what she would have to do at work today. Could she delegate most of it to Jennifer?

Yes. If she were to find a new job, she would leave Jennifer to do this by herself. Jennifer would learn faster if she started taking on more of the responsibility now. Besides, she had more important things to do today than explain to everyone why she had a bruised chin.

She took a pain reliever and a shower, dressed in a pair of comfortable sweatpants, and phoned Boris to let him know she would be away that day. Then she put clean sheets on the bed, cleaned up the broken clock in the kitchen (feeling no regret at its silence), had breakfast, and went to find their bank statements and investment portfolio to discover what else Richard was hiding from her.

Three hours later she looked up from the calculator, her heart pounding after confirming her worse fears. Sid had been telling the truth, and Richard had been hiding the fact that he had been drawing down on a lump sum payment he had received four months earlier. There were large payments going to an account she couldn't access. Where had the money gone? She could ask Richard.

She scrolled through the phone and noticed a message from Richard. I like the red dress. So, he had seen Lucy's Facebook post. Normally she would feel good that he had noticed what she was wearing, but right now she couldn't find any pleasure in it, especially when she read the next line. I wish you had worn it for me.

How dare he suggest she had dressed up for Sid? How dare he question her intentions? How dare he… Her anger flowed through her fingers as she banged out her reply: Why didn't you tell me you got fired? She started to add more about the large payments, the debt she suspected, and decided against it. Maybe she shouldn't tell him everything she knew. Maybe she needed to keep back some secrets too. Maybe they wouldn't end up separated but listening to Lucy's woes for the past few months had at least given her an idea of what she would need to do if it happened.

She dialed the bank to confirm the time of the appointment tomorrow with Esther, the loans officer at their local branch whom she had worked with for years, glad she hadn't remembered to cancel it when Richard left. Maybe Esther could help her make sense of this and tell her where the money went. She would sort this out.

Her phone buzzed. Richard. Thank goodness. She looked at the phone messages and her heart sank. Not Richard.

Brian: Hi Mom. Can I come by on Sunday to use your washing machine? Mine's on the fritz again.

Susan: Sure, but I thought you were going skiing with Joel this weekend.

Brian: Joel shifted his hours around so he could go visit Uncle Rupert.

Susan: When is he going there?

Brian: Damn. Don't say anything. He hasn't told his mom yet. Or his dad either.

More secrets to do with Rupert. They used to share everything, but now secrets and lies had worn at the connections in their whole family.

Susan: Do you have time for Sunday dinner?

Brian: How about breakfast? I have plans with Bianca Sunday afternoon.

Bianca was Brian's girlfriend and Susan was pleased Brian found so much time to spend with her. She was good for him.

Susan: Sure. See you around nine?

Brian: Yeah. Nine's good. See you then.

At least she would have the company of one of the men she loved this weekend.

*R*ichard leaned back in his chair and watched Lorne stroll toward the exit. The man seemed happier after he'd helped him, and for his part, Richard had enjoyed the morning. Strategy and coaching were always his favorite part of the work he did, but it had been a very long time since he had showcased his strength.

He pulled his phone out to write a few notes. He could add this information to his resume, maybe focus on finding more work like this. Then he checked his emails to see if Susan had answered his earlier text.

Susan: Why didn't you tell me you got fired?

He swallowed and stared at the screen. She knew. He knew she would find out eventually, but he'd hoped she wouldn't until after he had fixed it. Until after he had found a job.

He thought back to the Facebook post and the stunned look on her face. She hadn't been doing something wrong. She had just found out something that angered her. Damn, he hated Sid. He looked at her text again. Why didn't you tell me you were fired? What could he say to make her understand? He could pretend he hadn't read it yet, but that was just putting off the inevitable. He could try the truth.

Richard: I was embarrassed.

He pressed send and waited.

No answer. She wasn't online.

He needed more information, so he emailed Louis Taylor to see if he was back from vacation. He would be able to tell him more about the pension. He was the company accountant, after all. A few moments after pressing send the email came back undelivered. That was strange. He checked the email address was correct. Yes. He had the right address. Who else would know what was going on?

Richard thumbed through his contacts and found three colleagues he hadn't checked in with for a few weeks. He emailed them for an update and realized he really needed to reconnect with them when he got back.

Maybe they could get together for a beer and a hockey game. He missed them and they would understand what he was going through more than anyone else.

Joe was the first to respond and as he read the words, his chest tightened. Louis Taylor had embezzled from the company and Joe had lost all his investments. The fund Louis had sold them had been a scam.

Susan would never forgive him for this. Borrowing money and getting into debt was the thing she feared most, and he hadn't even consulted her. Louis had convinced him it was a sure thing, that the return on investment would allow Susan to retire early, just as they'd planned. He had just wanted to surprise her. Well, she would be surprised all right. He had to get home. He needed to explain before she found out on her own. Where was Rupert?

He walked to the suite and wrenched open the door, slamming it against the wall inside. Damn that felt good. He stalked into the room.

"Hey buddy, where you been? You feeling better?" Rupert greeted him looking far more cheerful than Richard felt.

"What the hell am I doing here, Rupert? What is so damned important that I have to keep secrets from my wife?"

Rupert stared a moment as though he'd been slapped. The smile slipped from his face.

"You had breakfast?"

Richard stared hard at him, jaw tight, fists clenched. He would hit the guy in a minute.

"Yes. I've had my damned breakfast," he spat out.

Rupert looked over Richard's shoulder and then back at him. "I didn't want to tell you yet. I was going to tell you on Tuesday, but you're right. You should know why I asked you here." He took a deep breath and Richard heard his own teeth grind in the frustration of waiting.

"Out with it," Richard finally said.

"I have prostate cancer."

"Shit." It all made sense now. Prostate cancer was what Rupert's dad died of when he was in his late fifties.

"I came here because I couldn't afford treatment in the states. And I called you because I need someone to be with me when I see the oncologist here this week." Rupert looked haggard now, as though telling him had made it more real. Maybe it had. "I thought I could count on you."

"Man, I'm so sorry." Richard's anger evaporated and he stepped forward to embrace his brother. "Of course, you can count on me." Susan would forgive him for this once he told her.

He just hoped she would forgive him for everything else.

Susan spent the rest of Friday trying to ignore her phone. She searched the internet and made a list of jobs to apply for but found she couldn't refrain from picking her cell up every few minutes to check for messages. She had texted him back after she had received his last message.

Susan: What is there to be embarrassed about? And why did you lie? Is there something else you aren't telling me?

It had been three hours and he hadn't texted her back. She needed to distract herself, so she went for a walk to stretch her muscles that still hurt from her fall in the kitchen, leaving the phone behind.

Breathing in the chilly fresh air felt good. The winter snow was nearly gone now, and spring would be here before she knew it. A time for new beginnings. She needed to take control of something in her life, so she went over the list she'd made in her mind and decided that getting a better-paying job would be her priority. There had been three that had interested her in her search today. One, The Home Connection, was looking for a director. She knew the contact person so send off a friendly email to ask a few questions about the position before updating her resume. Before bed, she looked one last time to see if Richard had replied. Nothing. Yes, tomorrow she would work on her resume.

* * *

SHE UPDATED her resume the following morning and when she sat back to read it over, she felt encouraged. She looked great on paper. Any organization would be lucky to have someone with so much experience. She would definitely hire her. While she was still on her high, she took out the list of jobs she had made the night before and applied for the top three. Hah! She would do this. Getting another job would be easier than she thought. Why hadn't she done this before?

It was time to reward herself and she knew exactly what she had to do. She went outside to get in her car to drive downtown. Damn! Where was the car? Her heart pounded as she thought back to when she had last seen it. Downtown. Near the restaurant. She had taken a cab home the other night. She took out her phone and called the cab company and waited for one to pick her up. This was not her best week.

While she waited, she read emails from work and was glad to see that Jennifer had handled all the tasks she had assigned her. Jennifer was growing in her role and would be ready for promotion soon. She would talk to Annette about considering Jennifer to replace her when she left. The cab still wasn't there, so she turned to her personal emails. There was one from her friend Jill at The Home Connection. Her heart beat faster as she opened and read the email. Jill had received her resume and wanted to know her availability for an interview the following week. Yes. She wanted to scream. Instead, she phoned Lucy.

"I got an interview."

Lucy did the screaming for her. "Awesome!! Let's celebrate. Do you have time for a coffee?"

"I have to get my car first. I left it downtown and forgot about it. And I have an appointment after that for about an hour."

Lucy laughed. "That's not like you forget your car. That's something I would do. Why don't I take you? I can be over in ten minutes."

"I called a cab."

"Cancel it. I'll be there in a few."

She dialed the cab company and canceled the cab and then read the email again. It had been years since she had been to an interview. She would have to get her references in order, think of what type of questions they would ask, and prepare her answers.

No, not just prepare. Over prepare.

She looked in the plate glass window as she waited, and her hand went to her hair. She hadn't changed her style in years. She needed a new haircut and highlights, layers instead of the severe bob she always wore. Something that made her look like she still had some life in her, something to take her a bit further from her comfort zone.

A car pulled into the driveway and she looked up to see Lucy smiling. This was the second time she had seen her happy in the past two days, just like the Lucy she had known for years. It seemed she was finally moving on from Rupert.

They drove to where she had left her car outside the bar and it relieved her to see it sitting there with only a ticket. Things were looking up.

"Thanks for driving me down here. Do you want to meet at the hive?"

"Sure."

"Can we make it two hours?" she asked. "I have an appointment at one that will take me about an hour."

"That will give me time to do some shopping. I want to pick up some music and groceries. I'll see you then," Lucy replied.

Armand's School of Dance was on her way to the bank and she was soon standing outside looking at her reflection in the glass door. She didn't look like a dancer, unlike the woman who was coming up behind her in the reflection and reaching toward the door. She turned to see the woman in person who was long and lithe, even when covered in a heavy winter coat. The woman held the door open. "Are you coming in?"

No, she didn't look like a dancer, but as Sid had reminded her the other night, she had once been pretty good. Besides, it was on her list. "Yes," she followed in the woman's wake and stepped over the threshold.

"Are you here to sign up for classes?" The same woman was now behind the desk, her coat lying on the back of the chair behind her. "We still have a couple of spots for next week's tango lessons. Tuesday and Thursday evenings."

"Can I take them on my own?" she asked. Richard wouldn't be back until the following week and might not want to take the lessons. She hadn't been in the mood to ask him.

"There are a few singles in this class," the woman said. "We can have you partner with one of them. Or the instructors."

"Sign me up," she said and filled out the paperwork. When she finished paying, she asked where she could get a pair of dance shoes. She was directed to the supply store a few doors down the street and after thanking the woman, left to find a pair of silver dancing shoes, like she'd once seen a tango dancer wear. Something else she had always wanted to own but never found a reason to buy.

She got to the store and asked where to find the shoes.

"We only have a few," the salesclerk said. "We usually special order them. Do you want to look at the catalogue?"

"Oh, I was hoping to find some today." Though if they were expensive, maybe she would be better off waiting.

"Well, you're welcome to look at what we have. They're in the back." She pointed to a shelf a few feet away.

"Thanks." Susan walked briskly in the direction the woman had pointed and found all the shoes were on clearance sale. She scanned the shelf and there they were: A pair of silver shoes in her size.

Checking her watch, she calculated she had another twenty minutes before she had to get to the bank that was just a little way up the street so she sat down, shed the shoes and socks she was wearing, pulled on a little nylon socket from a box beside her, slipped on the shoes and fastened the little buckles. She stood and looked at the shoes in the little mirror. They fit perfectly.

This really was a good day.

She quickly paid and hurried to the car. She was making quick progress on her list today and Richard or no Richard, she would enjoy the dance lessons. She opened the trunk of the car and put the shoes inside, a little sad that Richard wouldn't be taking lessons with her. Maybe one day. Meanwhile, she needed to learn steps to a dance she could do without him, just in case. She closed the trunk and hurried to get into the car. She didn't want to think about Richard, particularly as he still hadn't texted her with a reason for his lie.

He was avoiding her, and she didn't know why. She walked down the street from the dance studio to a florist she knew to buy a bouquet of pink and white tulips. The flowers made her smile because they reminded her that spring would be there soon, and spring was a time for hope and new beginnings.

Next she drove to the bank to meet with Esther. After settling into the comfy chair in Esther's office, Esther faced her across the desk and got right to business.

"After you called, I pulled out your file." Esther clicked a few keys to bring up a screen on the computer. "The payment you were wondering about is going toward repayment of the mortgage."

"We don't have a mortgage." There must be some mistake. They had paid off their mortgage five years earlier. She had sent the taxes to the city directly since then.

Esther looked sympathetic or was that pity? "Actually, Richard took out a mortgage about seven months ago." What? She had to be hearing this wrong.

"He took out a mortgage on our jointly owned house? How did he do that?" She rubbed her sweaty hands on her pants to keep them from shaking. This couldn't be happening. Why was this happening? What was Richard up to?

"According to the file he saw one of our other loans officers and borrowed it to pay for renovations to the house. About sixty thousand dollars."

"Sixty thousand dollars?" Susan stared at Esther a moment before realizing her mouth was gaping. She shut it again.

"You didn't know where he got the money to renovate the house?" Esther asked as though she were a dolt.

"There have been no renovations, Esther," Susan said flatly. What the hell was Richard up to? How many more lies was she going to uncover?

"Oh. I see." Esther kept her face neutral in that way people had when they watched others receive unwelcome news. Keeping herself separate, as if feelings of hopelessness were contagious.

"Are there any other loans or investments I should know about?" Susan asked.

Esther looked back at the screen and scrolled through the information there. "No. That's the only loan outside of your car loan which will be paid off in about," she tapped a couple keys, "four months."

"Thanks, Esther. I appreciate this." Susan rose.

Esther smiled sympathetically. "It could be worse. Sixty thousand is a small amount against the equity you have in the house. If you were to sell it, you could pay it off quickly and still have more than enough for a condo or rancher."

If she sold the home they'd built together. The home she had shared with Richard for decades. He was a good father. A good husband. A man she could always trust.

Until now.

He hadn't even had the decency to phone her and explain, as though she were nothing but his roommate.

Or housekeeper.

Was that what their marriage boiled down to now? Just a pair of people passing in the night? Was this what she wanted from the rest of her life? There had to be more than this.

"Was there something else, Susan?" Esther asked, reminding her of the other reason she had kept the appointment.

Susan sat back down again. "Could you tell me what half of my assets amount to?"

"Sure." Esther didn't seem surprised at the question. Did many people Susan's age divide their assets?

After reviewing her information and talking it through with Esther, she felt some relief. Esther had clarified that she wouldn't be starting with nothing if she and Richard separated.

If she got a better job, worked another ten years and if she was very careful, she could avoid the life her aunt had led in those years after her husband died. All she had to do was find a new job that paid more and get a decent price for the house and hope that Richard didn't have any other debts she wasn't aware of.

Esther had also given her the card of a realtor she knew. "I'm not recommending her in my capacity as bank employee, you understand. We aren't supposed to show favoritism."

"I understand. I just want to know what it's worth now and how hard it would be to sell in its current condition."

"Well, this realtor has helped a few women I know in your situation."

Susan looked down at the card, ignoring that statement. She wasn't sure how she felt about being a woman in a common situation. "Her name is really Sheila Sales?"

Esther laughed. "Yes, and her tagline is a bit cheesy, 'Sheila SalesSheila SalasSheila Salas Sells,' but she's good at her job and would be happy to give you an evaluation so you know what your house is worth."

"Thank you, Esther, I really appreciate this."

"Good luck. I hope it all turns out okay."

She met Lucy at the hive and they sat at their favorite table by the window, in an alcove away from other patrons. "Did you get the music you were after?" Susan asked as they sat down. Maybe if she could get Lucy to talk about mundane things, she could forget what she had just learned.

Seeming to sense the tension in her, Lucy replied warily. "Yes. I got some complicated pieces for my next lesson, like Vince recommended. But what about you? You look a bit shell-shocked. Has something happened?"

"He took a mortgage out on the house and didn't tell me about it," she blurted out. Lucy had told her plenty about what she and Rupert had gone through in the past year, but she was still embarrassed about sharing her own dirty laundry. She was the one who helped others. Not the other way around.

"Oh, honey," Lucy said and then reached forward to pat her hand. "What can I do to help?"

She moved her hand away. She didn't need sympathy; she needed answers. "Nothing. I talked to the bank and have a card for a realtor." She smiled through gritted teeth. "Basically, I'm doing what you did six months ago, I guess. If he were here right now, I would wring his neck." How could this happen? She had always thought their marriage was good. How could she have been so stupid?

"I know how hard this is," Lucy said, "and it's good to get an idea of what you have to work with."

"I'm sensing a 'but' coming."

"But my advice is to hear his side of things before you make any rash decisions. He must have a good reason for doing this. It isn't like Richard at all."

"But," Susan countered, "it wasn't like Rupert either. And they are so close. You know how much influence Rupert has over him."

Lucy's face fell. "Yeah, that's true. I don't even know what to say. It all comes back to Rupert doesn't it? I wish I knew what was going on with him."

"I know." They sat for a moment, silently commiserating until the server brought their lattes.

"Hey, what happened to your chin? You look like you got punched."

Susan reached up to touch her face. "Is it really noticeable?"

Lucy tilted her head to get a better look. "No. Not too bad. I just noticed it because we're sitting so close. You've done a pretty good job of covering it up."

"Don't lie to me. I've had enough lies this week to do me for a lifetime."

"No, really, it's hardly noticeable. What happened?"

She told Lucy about the clock escapade in vivid detail and they were soon laughing at what would have made Charlie Chaplin look like an amateur if it had all been on film.

"I can just picture it." Lucy laughed. "I think I would have smashed it long ago. It was a butt ugly thing."

Yes. It was ugly, and she had put up with it for a while. It felt good to get rid of the things she tolerated. What else had she been tolerating in her marriage?

After sharing a few more laughs with Lucy, she drove home, slowing down and laughing again when she saw Angel, Sylvia's little black cat, picking her way through the slush on the sidewalk. The poor animal looked miserable, picking up each paw and shaking it before setting it down and picking up the next, but she would soon be home with her people. She looked up at Jack and Sylvia's place and saw them sitting in the living room in front of the fire; she was knitting, he was reading. The cozy scene made her sad because in all her thoughts of new beginnings, she had been ignoring the reality that new beginnings came after ending old ways and old dreams. She had always imagined she and Richard growing old together, comfortable in each other's company. But that had been before he left, before he had put her in debt, and before the lies.

Her phone beeped and she ignored it while she put away her new shoes, found a vase for the flowers, and cooked herself some dinner. Finally, unable to avoid the phone any longer, she picked it up and searched for a return text from Richard. Nothing.

She needed to ask him more but didn't want to do it in a way that was obvious. Instead, she poured herself a glass of wine and curled up on the couch to watch a murder mystery she normally taped and viewed after Richard was in bed. Richard didn't like the shows she liked, so they would normally watch what he wanted to watch. Why didn't they do what she wanted to do more often? When the show was over and she had finished imagining Richard as the murder victim, she picked up her phone and typed in a request.

I want to get a jump on getting the taxes done this year. Can you tell me where all your receipts are? There. That would give him the perfect opportunity to tell her he had mortgaged their house and what he did with the money. Meanwhile, there was nothing useful to be done this late in the day, so she poured herself a second glass of wine and watched a movie. Two hours of uninterrupted television time was a luxury she rarely enjoyed. She checked her phone before going to bed. She hadn't expected a reply but was disappointed to find she had guessed right.

Before getting into bed, she searched the internet for the number of a family lawyer she knew and added it to her phone contacts. If Richard wasn't coming back right away, she would spend that time gathering all the information she needed, so she was in an offensive position instead of a defensive position, as Lucy had been. If he thought she was too busy to notice what he was up to, he would be sadly mistaken. If she was to face the next years alone, she would do what she must to secure her future.

In the middle of the night she awoke to go to the bathroom, then checked her messages again. Nothing yet. As she was drifting back to sleep, she remembered something that had been nagging at the back of her brain. Sid had told her that Louis Taylor had convinced people to invest with him and he had absconded with that money too.

"Oh, Richard, what have you done?"

For the next few hours she lay staring into the darkness trying to understand why he had done the one thing she had warned him she would never ever forgive after they were married. The only conclusion she could come to was that he was trying to drive her away. Or that he had already run away without bothering to let her know.

She needed to work harder on her Plan B if she was going to come out the other side of this time in her life, and the thought of it put a crack in her heart.

"Mom? I'm here!" Brian's voice was a welcome sound and right on time. She was glad she had raised such a punctual son.

"Come into the kitchen, the breakfast is almost ready." She watched the bubbles pop on the raw side of the pancake she was making and flipped it. "Do you want some coffee?"

"I'll be there in a minute. Just putting the clothes in the wash." A few minutes later he came bounding into the room. "Hmm, blueberry pancakes. Smells great!" he said, as he bent down to hug her. She was still surprised at how tall he was and how much he looked like his father had at his age. He straightened and brushed his dark bangs back from his face. He needed a haircut, but she wouldn't say anything. A nagging mother wasn't welcome at any age.

Instead, she set the table and dished out the food, congratulating herself on her timing. It felt good to have something work according to plan, even if it was only a meal.

"Nice flowers," he said as he sat down to eat. "Where'd you get them?"

"They came from the florist downtown."

"Nice." He looked like he wanted to say more but instead took a bite of food. "This is great, Mom. I can never make pancakes like this."

"Anytime you want to learn, I can teach you," she teased, knowing full well what he really liked about her cooking was that he didn't have to cook it himself.

"What happened to Dad's clock?" he asked, around a mouthful of food and gesturing to the wall with his fork.

She glanced up at the wall, unnecessarily, while she formed the answer. "It came off the wall and broke." Not exactly a lie, but not the entire truth either. She quickly took a sip of coffee and held the large mug in front of her face, knowing it was likely redder than normal. Judging by how his eyes narrowed, he suspected there was more to that story than she had shared. Or perhaps that was just her guilty conscience.

"Too bad," he said. "Dad always loved that clock."

"Yes. Too bad." She took a bite of her breakfast and they ate in silence for a moment. She was about to ask what his plans were this afternoon when he fired another question her way.

"What are you doing to keep busy while Dad's away?"

"I've been working. Looking for a new job. Oh, and I'm starting tango lessons on Tuesday."

"Why are you looking for a job?"

"I decided I need more of a challenge and better pay."

"I thought you would retire with Dad."

So had she, but she wasn't about to share her marital woes with her son, no matter how tempted she was to do so.

"Well, the closer I get to retirement, the more I realize I'm not ready to leave work." As she said it, she realized it was true. Looking for work felt more like an adventure than a chore.

"Oh," he said, taking another bite of food. "I guess that makes sense. That's probably why Dad's been looking for work too."

"I didn't know he told you," she said, trying not to sound bitter at being left out of Richard's circle yet again.

"Well, he didn't exactly tell me. He told Rupert, and Rupert told Joel, and Joel told me."

"I see. That makes sense." Yet another example of Richard sharing things with his stepbrother that he hadn't shared with her. Rupert had always been Richard's priority. Why did she continue to be surprised every time something like this happened?

"Do you want more coffee?" she asked, getting up to pour herself another cup.

"Nah, that's okay. I'm meeting Bianca for lunch in a couple hours. I'll have another one then." She turned back from the coffeepot and caught him snapping a picture of the flowers with his phone. Caught in the act, he blushed and brushed his hand through his hair. "I'm...I'm... gonna send this to Bianca. She'll like them."

"She'd probably like real flowers more than a picture," she said sitting back down and eyeing her son more closely. He was up to something. Brian always stammered and ran his hand through his hair when she caught him in a lie or a half truth. Just like his father.

He stood and took his dish to the sink to scrape off the food in the compost bin and put the dishes in the dishwasher. Then he walked to the fridge to read the card she had posted there so she wouldn't mislay it. "How come you have a realtor's card?" he asked, "You selling the house?"

"What is this? The Spanish Inquisition?" He looked chastened and she felt sorry for him. If he and Joel had been talking, Joel probably told him his fears about her having an affair with Sid. Good grief. That was the last thing she needed, her son worrying about her marriage as much as she was. "Your dad and I have been thinking of downsizing. With the market picking up, I wanted to see what we could get for it. This house is big for just the two of us."

"Yeah, that makes sense." He said it as though he was thinking through what she said and measuring it against other theories he had been considering. It was a good thing he had taken a job as a policy analyst at the government. The job suited him.

A bell sounded from the other room, signaling that the washing machine was done, and Brian bolted from the room to put his clothes in the dryer. Too bad he hadn't been that eager to do his laundry when he lived at home, she mused, as she stirred a teaspoon of sugar into her coffee.

For the first day since his arrival, Richard spent time with Rupert. They went boating, snorkeling, swimming — any activity that ensured they could avoid talking. Rupert hadn't changed in that regard. He never talked about his problems. And Richard didn't know what to say until he had more information. Once they saw the oncologist, he would know better how to help Rupert through this, no matter the prognosis.

Richard also wanted a reason to avoid Susan's latest texts. She knew they had fired him and now she was asking questions about their financial situation. What if she found out about the mortgage? Or learned they had been surviving mostly on her income? He had been using his money to pay down the money he had put into Taylor's investment scheme. She would kill him if she found out, and he wouldn't blame her. He felt stupid for being scammed, but he had trusted the guy. He had once even considered Louis Taylor his friend. Well, some friend he turned out to be.

At the end of their active day, he and Rupert sat in the lounge, exhausted, sipping on another mojito. How many had he had, anyway? It didn't matter. He was feeling a pleasant buzz and all his problems had gone out with the tide until he made the mistake of checking his messages.

Brian: Are you and Mom separated?

Richard: What? No! Why would you ask that?

Brian: Sharing an image. Look at the flowers Mom got.

Richard: Nice flowers.

What was the kid getting at? He tried to focus his attention through the haze of alcohol.

Brian: She said they came from the florist downtown.

Richard: Well, she likes to buy spring flowers when they come out.

Brian: Sharing an image. Well, what about this? This is where your clock used to be.

Richard: What happened to it?

Brian: Mom said it came off the wall and broke.

Came off the wall and broke? He had put that thing up himself. An earthquake couldn't knock that thing off the wall.

Richard: We'll get a new clock then.

Susan never liked that clock, particularly after he had stopped work and she had kept working. She told him a few weeks earlier that the ticking grated on her nerves, like it was counting out the seconds left in her life. He knew it was more that it didn't go with the decor in the kitchen, but it wasn't like her to break a clock. Maybe it had fallen off the wall as she said it had.

Brian: Mom says she's not retiring. She's looking for a new job.

Richard stared at the phone. This was not good. A new job? Was she looking for another job because she didn't think he would find one? Did she think she needed to earn more money? Of course, she was. It was her way of making things go according to plan. He took a deep breath. Why didn't she trust him to take care of this? Why did she always have to jump in and solve things? He needed to do some damage control with Brian.

Richard: Don't worry about it Bri. Your mom is just ready for a new challenge.

Brian: Yeah, that's what she said. Said she decided she wasn't ready to retire.

Yes. That was probably it. She just wanted something new. She hadn't been happy with her job since not getting the promotion.

Brian: Dad, when are you coming back? Are you taking tango lessons with her?

Richard: As soon as I sort out Rupert and his problem.

Yes. That was better than saying 'I have no idea.'

Brian: How come you never told me you were thinking of selling the house?

Wait a minute. What?

Richard:?

Brian: Mom is talking to a realtor about selling the house. Says you want to downsize.

Richard: Oh! That's what you're talking about. Yes. We have talked about downsizing.

He racked his brain for something plausible to say next so the kid wouldn't worry.

Richard: We just want to see what it's worth now that the market is picking up.

Brian: Yeah, that's what she said. OK. TTYL.

Richard: Talk to you later.

What was going on with Susan and why was Brian so concerned? Had he missed something? He scrolled through his text conversation with Brian and reread it. The flowers he could explain, though it wasn't like her to buy such a lavish bouquet. Still, it was winter there and spring flowers often cheered her up this time of year. The clock bothered him more. He had always kept that clock to remind him he had only a few more years until retirement. Maybe she took it off the wall because he retired. She hadn't known otherwise until the other night when she learned the truth from Sid. Still, she had always hated the clock so he could understand that.

Also, a new job. Maybe something happened at work that frustrated her more than normal and she was ready to move on. That made sense, too. She was working with a couple of newbies now that her

Executive Director, Annette Taylor, had gone off to somewhere — Australia? — on some kind of family emergency. That place had never appreciated her talents. He wasn't sure why she had stayed as long as she had.

But tango lessons? She was taking tango lessons? Why hadn't she told him about the tango lessons? The last time she had taken ballroom was when she was in high school, except for the few lessons they had taken together to prepare for their wedding dance. He had hated those lessons. The teacher had harped on about him not holding his frame strong enough. "You need to be stiffer." She would say pushing at his arms and making him hold them up and resist the natural urge to bend them. "Strong so you can guide your lady through the dance and through life." The old battle axe had been a tough teacher, but the entire thing had been hopeless. It had been Susan who had taught him enough that they got through their wedding, but after that she had lost interest in dance. Hadn't she?

She hadn't asked him to take tango lessons, and if she wasn't taking tango with him, then who would be her partner?

Maybe he had missed something about a new job and about tango when he had texted with Susan. He had been sick the other night. He scrolled through the few brief messages he had exchanged with Susan and cringed. He had told her he had arrived, practically accused her of having an affair, and then told her he would have to stay longer. For her part, she wanted to know why he hadn't told her he was fired — a question he had answered badly — and then asked for tax information because he said he wouldn't be back right away. He hadn't sent a response to that question either. He would need to figure out what to say by morning that would keep her from digging further into their finances and keep her from giving up on him.

"Want another drink?" Rupert asked, reminding him he was in a lounge and it was late.

"Yeah," he said. "Make it a double." He wanted to drink enough to forget that his wife was reorganizing her life without him.

"You should probably make it a single," Rupert said. "My appointment tomorrow is at ten and it's nearly one now."

Richard peered at Rupert and shook his head. "No. I want a double." Rupert was the reason he wasn't home with Susan clearing up his mess. Rupert stared at him hard, clearly surprised Richard had stood up to him instead of doing exactly what he wanted him to do. Richard stared back at Rupert, daring him to look away first and then remembered Rupert had cancer, felt like a schmuck and relented. "Forget it. Let's just go back to the room."

They walked back along silent pathways. "Why Mexico?" Richard finally asked when they got to the elevator. He waited a long time and wasn't sure Rupert had heard him. Finally, as the door to the elevator opened, the reply came out of the darkness.

"It's where we were happy," Rupert said. "I wanted to be somewhere where I could afford the treatment and where we had been happy as a family. You remember the times we all came down here. You, me, Lucy and Susan, and the boys?"

"Yeah. Those were good times."

"I figured I could end my life surrounded by good memories of family."

"Why did you leave Lucy?" Richard had wanted to know for months and the mojitos had loosened his tongue enough to finally ask.

"I couldn't face Lucy knowing I was just going to get sicker. I wanted her to remember me like I was."

"So, Miss bouncy was just an excuse to leave?"

Rupert peered at him over his glass. "Yeah, that's right," he said and then took another swig of his drink.

"Well, you're a stronger man than I am," Richard said, thinking of how he had suffered from food poisoning all alone. He couldn't imagine suffering long-term without Susan to help him through. He needed her. He missed her. He really needed to get home before she found out about the money, but how could he leave Rupert to suffer his fate alone?

Susan got to the dance studio early on Tuesday night, giving her time to see the participants in the earlier class leave and to get a feel for who would share her class with her. Couple after couple of various ages came into the room. Where were the other singles she'd been told about? Maybe she would end up dancing with the instructor.

The thought made her uneasy. She had avoided dance lessons for just this reason. She didn't want to be doing something alone that was made for pairs. It reinforced the fact that she was often on her own when Richard traveled, which, up until now, had been fairly often. It wasn't that being on her own was bad. She liked her own company, and she had her work. And Brian. It was only during couples' activities that she felt lonely. So, she had avoided this type of thing until now.

A woman in her early thirties with a bouncing blonde ponytail burst into the room and clapped to get their attention. "Listen up, folks. I'm Felicia and I'll be your dance instructor for the next four weeks and this," she turned to indicate a lithe dark-haired man in his early forties gliding in through the staff door, "is Armand." The participants clapped and Armand executed a graceful bow.

"Now, I understand there are two of you who did not bring a partner. Could you please put up your hands?"

Susan felt her cheeks burn. This was just the thing she tried to avoid, but if she couldn't work things out with Richard, she would have to get used to this feeling of being without another half. Taking a deep breath, she put her hand in the air and Felicia smiled in her direction. "Ah yes, you," she pointed to her, "and you." She pointed to someone behind Susan with the other hand and then pushed her hands together, signaling she wanted them to approach one another. Susan turned to see who they would saddle her with for the next few weeks and looked up to see a familiar grin.

"Sid. What are you doing here?"

"You told me about the ballroom lessons, and I thought, why not give that a try again? It's excellent exercise, I hear. Besides, I thought if you were here, you might need a partner." The skin around his dark eyes crinkled as he smiled down at her. "Until your regular partner returns, of course."

"Well, thank you. I think this will be fun," she said, ignoring the feelings his attention was stoking inside her. In true Sid fashion, he was being presumptuous that she would welcome his company just because her husband was out of town. Or maybe she had inadvertently sent him a signal that this was okay. Did she welcome his attention? It had been a long time since a man, even her husband — no, especially her husband — had sought out her company. She turned to watch the instructors demonstrate the first steps and then turned back to him when it was time to try the dance.

"It will be good to do this with a friend," she finally said, hoping to reinforce to him, and maybe to herself, that that was all this was. But it felt good to have a man to dance with who was light on his feet and wanted to learn. They stumbled through the first steps, remembering them from decades past, and laughed at themselves, slowly getting the rhythm of the dance and by the end of the lesson they had executed some moves correctly.

"You two look like you've danced together before," Felicia said as she approached them. "Very well done."

"Thank you," Susan said, stepping back from Sid who was appraising her, an old knowing look in his eyes. Forgotten embers of a fire that once burned between them crept into her core.

"Would you like to get a coffee after this?" he asked. "We can talk about old times."

She had to do something to douse the embers before they took hold. "Old times before you cheated on me?" she asked, reminding both of them of that long-ago betrayal.

"Something I have regretted for years," he answered, looking down into her eyes.

The invitation was tempting, but she needed to stop fanning the coals. She didn't really need another complication to add to the problems she already had.

"Not tonight," she said, taking a step back. "I… uhm…have some work to do this evening." Which wasn't exactly a lie. She was preparing for her interview on Thursday. "Maybe another time?"

"I look forward to seeing you on Thursday," he said, and the way he said it made her look forward to that day with anticipation. They had been good together once and, other than the fact that he'd left her for another woman, they'd had a lot of fun together. She took a few more steps back before saying goodbye. Then she turned and sauntered from the room, knowing his eyes were on her, and she found she didn't mind one bit.

CHAPTER 16

Richard sat in the waiting room while Rupert was examined and then joined him a few minutes later in the doctor's office. "I need someone to hear what he has to say," Rupert had told him. "Can you write down the important stuff?"

They sat together facing the doctor, Richard's pen poised over the pad of paper he'd brought, waiting for the verdict. Rupert was gray from worry, but when Richard reached over to put a hand on his shoulder to comfort him, he flinched and pulled away. Okay. He didn't want any comfort right now. Just write the facts.

"Well, it's good that you came when you did," the doctor began. "We have caught it early."

Richard sat forward to listen harder. This was good news, wasn't it? Maybe it wasn't as bad as Rupert thought it was. Rupert said nothing and so Richard asked what he would want to know if it were him. He had been up since five a.m. preparing for this, asking Dr. Google any question he could think of.

"What does it mean that you caught it early?" Richard asked the doctor. The doctor looked at Rupert, who continued to stare straight ahead, at a point over the doctor's left shoulder as he answered Richard's question.

"When it's caught early, the prognosis is very good. Particularly as you are still young."

Rupert still sat silent, his hands clenched around the arms of the chair, knuckles white, as Richard continued to speak for him, and the doctor continued to answer as though it were Rupert asking the questions. He had never seen Rupert like this before. The gregarious, outgoing man he had always known was gone. The friend he had turned to in times of trouble, and who protected him from bullies when they were kids, was absent. The man who, when he was younger, had a physique like Hercules and could face anything, was not the same man who sat in the chair beside him.

"What are his options?" Richard asked. "Does he need surgery? Or hormone therapy or chemo?" He had looked this all up on Google the first night Rupert had told him about the cancer.

"I want to do more specialized tests," the doctor said, "but most likely, I'll suggest Internal Radiation Therapy. Very non-invasive."

"And what is the prognosis with that?" he asked.

"With the right diet, exercise, et cetera, the prognosis is very good for someone with your symptoms."

"So, his chances are good at beating this?"

"Your chances are excellent," the doctor told Rupert. "Most men who we catch this early and treat are cancer-free for many years."

"His father died of prostate cancer. Does that mean that his chances are worse?"

The oncologist's eyes softened as he looked at Rupert, perhaps understanding the source of his obvious stress. "Rupert, there has been much progress made with this disease in recent years. This is your battle, not your father's."

Rupert didn't respond and when Richard turned to look at him, he could see his friend's back pressed against the chair. He was stiff, unmoving and silent, knuckles still clutching the chair. "That's great news, eh, buddy?"

He remembered the two of them coming across a wounded crow one day. Its wing was broken, and it had tried to escape, pecking at them even as they splinted the break. Rupert reminded him of the bird and Richard hoped he wouldn't get pecked or punched as he reached out and put his hand on his arm. Rupert sat stock still, but a tear leaked out of the corner of his eye.

"Thank you, doctor." Richard said. "My brother and I are grateful for your help today."

The doctor gave them a slip of paper and told them to ask the receptionist to book an appointment for the tests before the end of the following week.

"I'll see you next Friday to go over the results and the following week we can begin treatment," he said.

Richard rose and urged Rupert to stand. "We'll see you next Friday," Richard said, relieved to know that Rupert would likely be okay.

The cab ride back to the hotel was silent. Rupert still wasn't saying anything, so Richard took out his phone to text a message to Susan.

Looks like I may need to stay longer. I'll tell you how long when I know.

He pressed send as soon as they got within Wi-Fi range and then followed Rupert, who still hadn't said anything, back to the room.

"I need some time alone," said Rupert. "I need to process this."

"You're not hungry?"

"No. You go have lunch. I'll eat later."

"I need to know something first," Richard said. Something had been bothering him ever since the visit with the doctor.

"Can't it wait?"

"No. I want to know what your family doctor told you back in Canada. You seemed surprised today."

"He told me I was being referred to an oncologist. He suspected prostate cancer but wanted to have it confirmed."

"What did the oncologist say?"

"Can we talk about this later?" Rupert looked exhausted.

"Did you even see an oncologist before today?" There was no need for his brother to answer him. He could tell by the look on his face he hadn't. "Why not? What were you thinking?"

"I never told you I found my father before he died, did I?" He walked to the couch and sat down, placing his head in his hands, leaving Richard stunned.

"Are you kidding? When?" Richard found his feet and joined Rupert on the couch. "What happened?"

"He was bad off, in palliative care in a hospital in Calgary when I found him. And mad." He turned toward Richard. "You remember his temper? He was always calm until he lost it, and then, watch out."

"Yeah, I remember. I was terrified of him then."

"We were all terrified of him when he lost it. Luckily, it didn't happen often." He paused, lost in an old memory before he focussed his eyes back on Richard. "Anyway, after he yelled at me for hunting him down, which took me four months to do, he accepted that I was there. He was dying and didn't have as much strength to push me away. After a few of days of me visiting, he gave up trying."

"Was that where you went when I was in grade twelve? You were gone for months that year."

"Yeah, that's right. I stayed there, my car at a campsite, and visited him every day, sitting with him, listening, trying to understand why he left us. He finally told me it was because he didn't want to see our pain. He wanted Mom to be angry with him instead of sad."

"Well, he certainly achieved that. She was angry with him for years."

"He also thought it would help push her toward Alan. He believed they would be good together and be able to keep us all together after he was gone."

"They do seem happy," Richard said.

"They are. He was right about that, and he was right about sparing Mom having to see him in pain. It was awful to watch. I didn't want my family to see me like that. I've played that visit over and over in my mind for years. It was the reason I started drinking the first time." He raised his arm and pointed to the minibar. "And this time."

"Why didn't you say something?"

"You know us Cowen men. We have to keep all the terrible stuff bottled up inside. Protect the family." He laughed bitterly.

"So then why did you call me?" Richard asked.

"I guess I figured, of all the people I knew, you would be the one most able to take it. You're a lot like your dad. Alan always makes me feel safe and took care of people. I didn't realize how lonely it would be, or how terrifying. You saw me today. I'm a wreck."

"You're also a moron. Do you know how much trouble you've caused Lucy and Joel and me?"

"I know." He stood up and walked toward his room. "I have no idea how I'll fix it, but right now I need a nap."

CHAPTER 17

Susan got up the courage to phone Cecelia Chan, the board president, on her lunch break on Wednesday to ask her for a reference. After so many years with the organization it felt like a betrayal to be leaving, although she knew others wouldn't feel that way. Susan had seen many employees come and go over the years, launching their career with Family Services and going off to get better-paying jobs elsewhere. Loyalty wasn't as valued as it once had been, and she had to get over the guilt she was feeling.

Cecelia was gracious during the conversation. "Absolutely, I'll give you a reference. You've been such a valuable employee over the years. But I don't understand; I thought you were planning to retire."

"So did I, but the closer I got to retirement, the more I realized I'm not ready. I want a challenge and this job I'm interviewing for is for a director's position, overseeing several programs. Something I think I'm ready for."

"I agree, you're definitely ready for more challenge. You have been under-utilized for years. I wish I'd known you weren't retiring. I would have offered you the director's job here."

"I didn't realize how much I wanted to continue working until after Boris started, and by then it was too late. But Boris is learning quickly. He's a hard worker and wants to be successful in the job."

"Yes, I noticed in the past week or so that he seems to be coming into his own. If I didn't know any better, I would think he had been coached," she laughed.

"He's a fast learner. Sometimes it just takes someone expecting you to step up to help you do it."

"Sometimes," Cecelia agreed. "And sometimes you just need a little help from a friend. Thanks for helping Boris learn his role, Susan. I wish you luck, but we will miss you."

She hung up the phone and smiled to herself. That hadn't gone as badly as she thought it would, so before she lost her nerve, she immediately looked at her list of contacts and phoned two others she hoped would be her references. Then she went back to work while going over possible interview questions in her head. She had her first interview in the morning and needed to be prepared.

Susan arrived at work late on Thursday, still on a high from her interview. It had been a long time since she'd talked about her accomplishments and the conversation had gone well. The panel had seemed thrilled to hear about her work and the job sounded perfect. She would have a director's position, a five-person team, and new subject matter. After working in family services for nearly thirty years, it would be a welcome change to work in an organization that helped to rehouse people who were living on the streets. It would be a steep learning curve, but she was up for it.

Boris looked up when she came in. "I'm glad you're here," he said. "We have some auditors in today and they need access to all our files. I thought you could help pull the ones related to the conference and answer any questions they have about program expenses."

"Sure. Not a problem."

"I hope not. I haven't gone through an audit like this before."

"You've been through a year end, haven't you?"

"Yes, but this feels different."

"It's just because you're in a different position this year."

"Maybe." He didn't seem convinced.

"I'll get the files that show the records, but if you need more specifics, you'll have to ask Bonnie. She's the accountant."

"Yes. I have her involved already."

"Well, you're in excellent hands, then," she said.

"I know. It just feels like they're being a lot more thorough than other years. When you find the file, can you give it to Bonnie? It will save me a few steps."

She found Bonnie in the kitchen getting a cup of coffee. "I heard auditors are here."

Bonnie looked up at her as though she were a rabbit caught in a whippet's sight, then said breezily, "Yeah, you know. They do this every year."

"I know. Boris said you were looking for this." She handed Bonnie the file.

"Thanks," Bonnie said, and she skittered down the hall with the file in one hand and coffee in another. Susan checked if there was a decaf pot and thought Bonnie should probably stop drinking coffee after noon. It seemed to be affecting her.

Susan poured herself a glass of water and went back down the hall to her desk to check on the enrollment numbers for the conference. They would need to put out another round of advertisements by the look of things. If they didn't get more delegates, they wouldn't make enough money to break even. She needed to find another target audience to market the conference to.

She would ask Sid that evening. He had been in business for a long time. He might have some ideas and it would give them something neutral to talk about during the lesson.

Before she left to go to the studio, she checked her messages to see if Richard had connected with her. No contact. What was he up to?

* * *

"YOU LOOK LOVELY," Sid said when Susan arrived at the studio wearing a simple black shift. She had accessorized with silver drop earrings and a pendent

Richard had given her for their last anniversary. It felt good to dress up a little, to put on more make-up than she used at work, to go dancing, and she especially liked her new haircut.

"Thank you," she said. "I bought new dance shoes and thought this would go better than the jeans I wore on Tuesday."

"Well, you clean up good."

It felt nice that he'd noticed the effort she put into her appearance tonight. Richard rarely noticed her anymore unless she cooked his favorite meal, or she stood between him and the television.

The lesson started and as they were learning the steps, she asked him for some marketing ideas.

"I think you have to target a wider audience. You have more capacity this year, and an excellent line-up of speakers. Why not target youth workers and schools? A lot of the speakers are talking about the youth theme."

"We haven't used that angle. Thank you." She looked at their feet for a moment, to make sure she had the steps right. When she had picked up the rhythm, she looked up again. "How's your job search coming along?"

"I had an interview today for a director's position. It's an organization working to house people who are homeless."

She squeaked as she stumbled, and he caught her. "Sorry, these new shoes are trickier to dance in than I thought," she said, covering up for her shock that they had been competing for the same job. "Congratulations on getting the interview."

"I think it would be a great opportunity. I've always wanted to work in the non-profit world."

She didn't know how to respond, so she pretended to focus on her steps, counting them out loud under her breath. She knew they'd interviewed others for the job, but she didn't think it would be someone she knew, let alone Sid, and now she couldn't help comparing herself to him. Sid had been in business all his life and had done a lot for charities and community causes. She had experience working for non-profits and knew the challenges they faced with their constant need for volunteers and fundraising, but she hadn't held positions beyond middle management up until now. She thought the interview had gone so well, but now she wasn't so sure.

"Let me take you for coffee after class," Sid said. "It would be nice to talk about old times."

"That would be nice," she said, "but I think I'll go home. I've got a lot on the go tomorrow." What she wanted to do was go home, alone, so she could have a good cry. She was feeling old, unwanted and lonely and she wouldn't be very good company.

"Just for half an hour?" he asked, and she nodded, distracted by her negative self-talk. Sid had far more leadership experience. What had she been thinking trying to get into a new line of work at her age?

She stumbled through the rest of the class, cursing herself for wearing the heels. She needed to learn the steps without them first. Next week she would wear flats. The music ended and she walked to the back of the room to get her coat off the coat rack. Sid walked beside her and took it out of her hands, holding it up for her, to help her into it.

"Thank you," she said when she turned and closed the buttons. He was standing close. Very close. It was a little hard to breathe.

"You're welcome," he said, not stepping back. "Is Luigi's okay?"

"Luigi's?" She was having trouble concentrating. What was he saying?

"For coffee. It's just down the street."

"Oh, I should really…"

"Come on," he broke in, "you said you'd come for half an hour. Don't back out on me now. Luigi's has a fantastic chocolate cheesecake I've been craving all week."

She wavered, musing over what he'd said. Chocolate cheesecake and one coffee. That was harmless enough. Even Richard wouldn't be able to fault her for that. Besides, he was probably spending time with Rupert's friends. Rupert's very young friends who were probably parading around in bikinis in the hot sun. That was far worse in her mind.

"Dark chocolate or white chocolate?" she asked.

"Both," he grinned.

"Well, I can't say no to that."

He pulled his coat off the rack and shrugged into it and then took her elbow and guided her out of the building. She looked at where his hand was and tried to remember the last time she and Richard had gone out for cheesecake and coffee, or the last time he had touched her elbow like this. It had been long ago, probably before Brian left home. When had they stopped doing the little things that kept a marriage alive?

And was there anything left to bring back to life?

Luigi's was a tiny bistro only steps away from where she'd parked her car, a restaurant she had noticed many times but never entered. Now she wondered why. It had a pleasant atmosphere with plush seating, high-backed booths, low lighting and a two-sided fireplace that made the entire place feel cozy and intimate.

Sid guided her to a booth near the window and ordered two lattes and a piece of cheesecake. "Two forks please," he said to the server and then turned to her. "They are huge pieces."

"Good call. I don't think I could eat an entire piece of cheesecake tonight." Her words were affirming but his actions made her slightly uncomfortable. He was acting proprietary again.

"I'm enjoying the lessons," he said. "I'm glad you're my partner. You make it more fun." He was staring at her the way he had when they were younger. Like she was a piece of chocolate cheesecake and he wanted to devour her. Luckily the real cheesecake arrived at the table just then, along with the lattes, breaking his gaze.

"Thanks, I guess if we didn't have each other we'd be dancing with the instructors." She laughed a little at her joke and reached for her cup. It was a deep cup filled to the brim so she would have to stay the whole half hour she promised or risk being rude.

"I'm not surprised that you are picking it up quickly," he said. "You were a great dancer in high-school."

"That was a very long time ago." She shouldn't have said yes to coming here. "I'm a completely different person than I was back then." She paused and took a bite of the cheesecake onto her fork. The faster they finished it, the faster she could go home. "Oh," she gasped as she tasted the dessert, "you weren't kidding."

His eyes lit up at her pleasure. "Right? The best you've ever had, eh?"

"Definitely," she said, putting down her fork and picking up the latte. She would have to pace herself with this. It was rich and decadent and wonderful.

"And you're the best I've ever had," he said as she took a sip of her drink.

She gulped it down to avoid spitting it up all over him. "What?" She couldn't have heard him correctly.

"I've been thinking about us. We were great together. And when we're dancing, it's like... it's like... we've always been together."

She put down her cup and looked him straight in the eye, wanting to make sure he was paying attention when she said what she had to say. "Sid. There is no us. I'm married. Married. We're just dance partners who happen to share a very, very distant past."

"Did I misunderstand? I heard from a friend that Richard left."

"He's visiting his brother in the States. He'll be back in a week."

"No. That's not what I heard. I heard he left." He seemed convinced.

"Who have you been talking to?"

"One of the guys we used to work with. Richard went to the States to work on a project. Said he didn't think he would be back for a while."

She sat back and looked at him, thinking over what he had just said. "Yes, he has gone to the States to work on a project. His brother needed help." She said it slowly, enunciating the words, "and he's expected back next week." She watched his face, hoping realization would dawn on him and he would understand that he had misinterpreted what he'd been told.

"That wasn't the impression I got. I'm sorry." He didn't sound sorry. "I think you may have misunderstood Richard. I heard he went to be with his brother. The same one who left his wife for a mistress."

"Same brother, but the mistress isn't there." Richard had been adamant about that fact and Richard never lied to her. At least the old Richard had never lied. Not about important things. But now... Maybe Sid was right. Maybe she had misinterpreted the situation. "Sid, I have to go. I've got a lot of work to do tomorrow." She took out her wallet and put down enough money for her half of the order and slid out of the booth.

"I'm sorry Sue, I thought that was why you were taking tango lessons alone. I didn't know that you thought he was coming back."

She pulled on her coat and glared at him. "He's coming home, Sid. He's coming home in a week." She turned on her heel and left the restaurant, stopping at the car to fumble in her purse for her keys. She heard footsteps behind her.

"Sue." He put his hand on her shoulder and turned her toward him. "I'm sorry. I shouldn't have said it like that."

"Take your hand off me," she said, jaw set, keys now clutched in her hand the way that she had learned to clutch them as a girl. She could do some damage with these keys if he didn't walk away.

"I'm sorry." He said, dropping his hand immediately. "I guess I was projecting my situation onto you. Beth just left one day, and I haven't seen her since."

"Well, I guess that's understandable." She felt herself relenting, putting this man's needs before her own. Had she always done that? "But you and Richard are different people and Beth and I are different people. If he said he'll be back, he'll be back."

"Yeah, I understand," said Sid. "But if you ever need my help, you know where to find me."

"Thanks, Sid. I should be okay." She waited until he backed up and walked a few yards away before she turned to open her car door. She put on her seatbelt and watched him walk away, realizing only then that she was breathing harder than if she'd run five miles. She pulled her phone out of her purse to check her text messages and found one from Richard. Looks like I may need to stay longer. I'll tell you how long when I know.

She looked down the sidewalk. Was Sid right? Was her marriage over and she just didn't want to admit it?

Richard left Rupert to ruminate and went for a walk to wear off his anger. This whole trip had been completely unnecessary. If Rupert had bothered to go to the specialist and learn about his prognosis, he would have saved Lucy and Joel a world of pain.

He stopped and had some lunch and then wandered over to the stage to listen to some music. He needed to go home as soon as possible, but he had given Rupert his word that he would stay as long as he needed him. But didn't he owe Susan the same courtesy? Was Susan right? Did he always choose Rupert's needs over hers? He was here and not at home, which would probably lead her to believe that. He wondered if Rupert would let him tell her about his diagnosis or if he wanted to be the one to tell Lucy?

A group of people were gathering on the floor in front of the stage for some kind of activity. He ordered a drink from one of the passing servers and sat down to watch.

A vivacious woman swirled onto the stage, ebony hair piled high on her head, wearing a joyful multi-colored skirt. He sipped the drink he'd ordered and watched the band set up. The woman clapped her hands together. "Hello everybody, my name is Elena. Today we are learning the most sensuous of dances. The tango." Richard choked on his drink, which drew her attention.

"Senior, join us," Elena said, approaching him and extending her arm. He shook his head no and she continued to move closer. "It is important that every man knows the tango." There were titters among a few of the guests, and he soon found himself drawn to his feet, walking toward the dance floor. "You will be my partner," she said, bringing him to the front of the class. All eyes were on them as she used him to demonstrate the way to hold a partner. "You must hold the frame, like so. I will demonstrate the man's part first." She took him in her arms, and he followed along, listening intently so as not to embarrass himself in front of everyone. If Susan were here, he would be at the back at the bar right now, watching her participate.

"And as you dance, you use the weight of your arms to guide your partner. Like so."

She pushed him a little with stiff arms and he found himself following her lead. So, this was how it should feel.

"Now you try," Elena said.

He raised his arms again, held her as directed and used the weight of his arms to direct her as he stepped forward and she effortlessly matched his step and floated backward. This wasn't so bad.

"Very good," said Elena, then she stopped, dropped his arms and turned to the rest of the class. "Now everyone, hold your partners and you try."

The rest of the class dutifully followed instructions and he watched Elena go around the room to help the others before returning to him for the next part of the lesson.

As the class ended Elena clapped her hands again to get their attention. "Tomorrow we learn a more complicated sequence. Be here at one thirty."

He nodded and found himself looking forward to it. Perhaps if he had had her as his first dance teacher, he would have wanted to do this more often. Elena made it easy.

Lorne was sitting in the lounge with a pretty auburn-haired woman wearing a purple sundress and a broad smile. "Looking good out there, Rick," he called from across the room.

"Thanks," Richard said, approaching them to say hello.

"Hey, I want to introduce you to my wife, Theodora."

"Call me Teddy," she said. "I'm so pleased to meet you. I can't thank you enough for helping Lorne come up with a plan to reorganize the company."

"I've been using that new software you told me about," said Lorne. "It's a great way to keep track of things at a glance, and everyone on the team is using it now."

"I'm glad it's working out," said Richard. "And I am glad to meet you, Teddy. Lorne was really looking forward to you joining him."

She grinned and squeezed Lorne's arm. "I'm so glad I came."

"Can I get your contact information?" Lorne asked. "I told a friend about you and he wants to meet you. He owns a consulting firm in Vancouver and hires business coaches and project managers."

"In Vancouver?"

"He has contacts all over the place. He wants to talk to you if you're interested. Here." Lorne reached into his pocket and handed Richard a sheet of paper. "His contact information is here along with ours. Please call him. I kind of gave him my word you would."

Richard took the sheet of paper and opened it. Salim Malik. He couldn't believe it. Malik Consulting services was huge in his business. "Got a pen?" he asked as he tore a strip from the bottom half of the paper.

"I do." Teddy reached into her purse and looked into his eyes as she handed him a pen. "I hope you do contact him. Your work with Lorne has helped save our marriage."

Saved their marriage? Now he just needed to work on his own. He had an impulse to phone Susan, just to hear her voice.

"Thank you for this," he said to the pair, as he handed Lorne his information and Teddy the pen. "If there's anything more I can do to help you, don't hesitate to contact me."

"I'm hoping to see much more of you," Lorne said. "We'll be over to the Island this summer to go fishing. Teddy's a first-rate angler." He smiled at his wife and she reached out to grasp his hand.

"Well, let us know when you're coming. I would love for you to meet Susan. And if you need a place to stay, we have a guest room that always needs more company." At least he hoped he had a guest room. And a house. And a wife. He wanted to talk to Susan, but first he had to check in on Rupert.

* * *

"How're you doing?" Richard got to the room to find Rupert sitting on the couch swirling a drink, staring at a show being broadcast in Spanish. Rupert didn't answer, so he tried again. Maybe he didn't hear him the first time.

"What's up?" Still nothing. This silence was really testing his patience. Why didn't he answer? He couldn't help Rupert if he didn't know what to help with, he thought, then realized that the voice in his head sounded like Susan's. She'd asked questions like this for the past few months and he had done the same thing, been silent and retreated into himself, trying to solve his problems without her. He could see now how frustrating that must have been.

"I think I got some work," Richard said, trying to open a conversation. "A guy wants me to talk to him about business coaching. Got any advice?"

Rupert turned toward him. "You don't need advice from me. I'm a screw-up."

"No. Just an idiot," Richard said lightly, expecting Rupert to fight back. He had always called Rupert an idiot when he wanted to get a rise out of him, but today he got nothing. He sat down and reached to put a hand on Rupert's shoulder. Rupert jerked away.

"I screwed up my entire life," he finally said. "I walked away from the best thing that ever happened to me. I don't know what to do."

Richard stood and took the drink from his hand. "Well, first you're going to quit drinking this crap." He poured the drink down the little sink near the bar fridge.

"I never deserved her."

"No. Probably not. But she loves you anyway."

"She'll never forgive me for this. I betrayed her. I cheated with a girl half her age and I didn't even enjoy it. I'm an ass."

"Yeah. You cheated and you're an ass, but have you ever even told Lucy you have cancer? And that you're sorry?"

"No."

"And that your affair was for what? A few months at most?"

"Not months. Hours. I've been staying in a buddy's trailer in one of those adult-only retirement places for the past six months, until he came down and needed the trailer back."

"Doing what?"

"Online investments. Drinking. Trying to figure out how to leave a better legacy for Joel and Lucy."

"Investments?" he shivered. Investments were what would sink his marriage once Susan found out.

"I'm doing pretty well at that, at least. Learned a lot. Making enough to put some money aside, which is good. Being a plumber is too hard on my knees these days. I can't do much of that anymore, even if I hadn't sold my business."

"Okay… have you been in touch with your family at all?"

"Joel texted me this morning. He's in Palm Springs. Came to surprise me."

"Shit. Did you tell him where you are?"

"Yeah. Of course. Got my buddy to drive him back to the airport. He's on his way home but he's pissed with me. Really pissed."

"Did you tell him about the cancer?"

"No! I didn't want him to hear by text. I'm not that much of an ass."

Richard's cell vibrated in his pocket. "What time did he contact you?"

"Maybe half an hour ago."

"Shit. You could have warned me." He pulled the phone out of his pocket and scrolled to see the latest text from Brian.

Brian: What are you doing in Mexico?

Richard: Long story.

Brian: I've got time.

Richard: Not my story to tell.

Brian: WTF does that mean?

Richard: Here with Rupert. He needed me.

Brian: typing… typing… typing.

Richard: Please don't say anything to your mother. Will explain soon.

Brian: Okay. I won't say anything.

Thank God for that, Richard thought. Susan would never trust him again if she knew he was in Mexico and he wouldn't blame her. If she pulled something like this... Well, she wouldn't pull something like this. This was on him.

Brian: But I think Joel told Aunt Lucy already. She had to send him the money to get home. You better have a way to fix this.

"Damn," he said. "Rupert, what the hell have you got me into now?"

"What do you mean?"

"Joel told his mother. She had to lend him the money to change his ticket and get home. Lucy will tell Susan. You and I will be roommates forever and you're not my first choice."

Rupert looked stricken. "I hadn't considered how this would affect you. I'm sorry. But Susan will be okay.

She'll understand why you came and had to stay longer once I explain why I needed to leave the States. I couldn't get medical coverage for a pre-existing condition and if I have to die somewhere, I would rather do it here where we used to spend our vacations."

"Rupert, Susan's not going to understand. You're not the only one who's screwing up their marriage." He proceeded to tell Rupert that he had lied to Susan about the layoff, the pension, the mortgage, and being swindled.

"Why didn't you tell her you were laid off?"

"I was embarrassed. I didn't want her to know how much I screwed up by taking out the mortgage. I wanted to fix it and then tell her about it. As it is, she thinks she always has to fix everything herself."

"Well…" Rupert seemed hesitant.

"Well, what?" Richard glared at Rupert and motioned for him to continue speaking. "Out with it."

"I can understand her thinking that."

"What's that supposed to mean?" This was the last thing he expected Rupert to say.

"She's kind of been left to take care of things on her own, a lot." His eyes widened when Richard glared at him, but he kept going. "I mean, you traveled so much to see clients. She used to call me when she had a question about house stuff, and I've referred her to people I know quite a few times over the years. And Lucy told me you expect her to do most of the housework."

Was that true? Was that why she never asked him for help? He thought back to their most recent conversation. She had been angry with him before he told her he was going to see Rupert. Something about garbage cans and chicken. He slapped his forehead with his hand. She had been asking him for help. He just didn't recognize it. "And now it's worse. I lied about where I am and why I'm here and she's got to be wondering what's going on. She had already said I was going to Palm Springs to have an affair with a young thing like you did."

"But you and Susan are solid. You'll get through this."

"She's so pissed she's looking at selling the house."

"Damn," Rupert said. "We might be roommates for life."

They sat side by side on the couch, watching the images flicker on the TV screen that made little sense as neither of them understood Spanish. Finally,

Rupert reached for the remote and clicked off the television. "Let's go get some dinner. I've got an idea of how I can at least help you with your cash flow problems."

Richard stood slowly. His marriage was in the crapper but maybe if he could get home and had some money to help get them out of this bind he was creating, maybe, just maybe, she would eventually forgive him. He would call Susan later once he found out more about Rupert's plan.

CHAPTER 19

On Saturday, Susan woke early and spent the entire day getting the house ready for the realtor's visit. Getting an idea of what the house would sell for was just research, she told herself. It would help her figure out what she was up against and plan for her future.

Sheila Sales arrived on her doorstep at two in the afternoon, her purse over her arm in the same manner that Queen Elizabeth II carried hers, and Susan nearly laughed out loud at the outrageously garish outfit that somehow looked great on her. As Susan gave Sheila the tour of the house, she could observe the realtor. She was a no-nonsense woman in her mid-forties who had earned herself an excellent reputation and an award for Realtor of the Year more than once.

Sheila asked excellent questions as they walked through the house and knew the answers to everything Susan wanted to know. She told Susan what to do if she were to spend money on improvements before she sold. Minor things, like patching chipped paint, would be the easiest things to do. Or she could spend money on a kitchen renovation. "Although, this being a sellers' market, I personally wouldn't waste money on that," Sheila said. Which was a good thing, Susan thought, considering the money Richard had borrowed to do renovations was gone. She dismissed that thought to listen more closely to Sheila, noting the areas she needed to fix and what would be best to clear out before she sold.

"My team works with a staging company to help show the house to its best advantage," Sheila said, "and also a company that can help with organization. Many of my clients have found it hard to know where to start if they're downsizing, and they can give you as little or as much help as you need."

"I see," said Susan. "I didn't know there was so much involved in selling a house these days."

"Oh, yes, but my team and I are a well-oiled machine. We make it as easy as possible. Do you know when you would like to list?"

"I'm just beginning to consider this," she told Sheila, "and will need to discuss it with my husband. He's away on a family thing right now." She saw a flicker of a smile flash across Sheila's face and wondered how many times she had heard this excuse for a man's absence. Was it a euphemism for separation in her line of work?

"Yes, yes. Take all the time you need. Selling the family home is a big decision, especially when you have lived here for so long. Meanwhile, I have looked at other houses in this area, seen what they've sold for and prepared this package for you." She held out a folder with the company logo on it. "I'd like to go over it with you, if I may?"

They sat at the kitchen table and Sheila showed her the listings and the amount that she could likely get for her house. It was well over what they had paid twenty-five years earlier. It was far more than even Esther, at the bank, had estimated. Selling this house could solve all their money challenges.

"We don't have many listings but there are quite a large number of buyers. I have at least four I can think of for whom this house would be perfect. It is in a great location near both levels of schools. And as I said before, it's a seller's market so if you are interested, I would recommend listing sooner than later."

"This is wonderful information to have. Thank you for doing all this work."

"Have you found a place where you'd like to move? Would it be in town? If you tell me what you are looking for, I can take you out to look at the areas, do a few walk-throughs."

"I haven't really thought about that yet," she said. What kind of place would she want to live in?

"I have put a few listings of condos and townhouses in the back of the folder, and there are more on my website." She pointed to the website address on the cover of the folder. "If you go there, you'll find all my latest listings. I can also send listings to you by email if you give me your email address. It will give you an idea of what things are going for."

Susan wrote her email address on a piece of paper and handed it to Sheila. It wouldn't hurt to know what was out there.

"Thank you, Sheila, you have given me a lot to think about. I will talk to my husband when he gets back and we'll decide how to move forward from here." She saw the woman out and watched her drive away before closing the door and returning to the table.

She opened the folder again and did some quick calculations on the inside flap of the folder. Even after paying off the mortgage, they could easily afford a new condo, or even one of the townhouses she saw in the selection Sheila left. The balance of the money could be invested — wisely this time — and would be enough to keep them in their old age.

Or they could afford a good down payment on two condos. If she worked a few more years, she would be fine on her own. And if Richard found work, so would he.

She looked through the listings at the back of the folder and placed stars against a couple that she liked. They were small, but if she were living on her own, she wouldn't need much room. She could call Sheila next week if Richard still wasn't back and take a look at some, just to see what was available.

She walked through the house, turning off the lights and writing down the things to do to get the house ready. She placed the list and folder on her desk in her office, leafing through the pages again, still finding it hard to believe there was so much equity in the house.

Tomorrow she would go to the hardware store and get some paint and a few supplies. Even if she didn't sell for a while, some of the rooms could use a touch up to brighten up the place. She would start with the kitchen and paint over the spot where the clock once was.

* * *

AFTER SPENDING the day shopping for paint and then putting on the first coat of a fresh off-white that went well in the kitchen, Susan was sitting down to some warmed-up casserole when she got a text from Lucy. Can you come over? It's urgent that we talk.

Susan: What's up?

Was there news about Richard?

Lucy: It's better we talk in person.

Susan: I'll be there in a half hour.

When she pulled up to Lucy's house, Joel and Brian's cars were in the driveway, so she parked on the street. What were the boys doing here?

"What happened?" she asked when she walked into the kitchen to find Lucy close to tears.

"I'm just so mad, I could scream," Lucy said.

"What's wrong?" Susan asked., She really didn't have time for drama today. She was tired from painting.

"His own son. He didn't tell his own son," Lucy was muttering. Susan turned to Brian and raised her eyebrows in question.

"Dad and Rupert aren't in Palm Springs," Brian said. "They're in Cancun."

"Mexico? How do you know they're in Mexico?"

Brian cleared his throat. "Joel went down to Palm Springs to visit Uncle Rupert, as a surprise, remember? I told you last week."

"Yes, I remember."

"Anyway, when he got to the address Rupert gave him a few months ago, Rupert wasn't there. Hadn't been there for over a week."

It was more than a week since Richard left. Did that mean he had flown directly to Mexico? He'd lied again! She wanted to punch something.

"Joel talked to Rupert's friend, who had just arrived. He owns the mobile home. Apparently, the guy's a snowbird but had to have a hip replaced last year so couldn't travel to his place in the States until now."

Joel broke in to pick up the story. "So, I talked to a few neighbors to find out if they knew where Dad went, or if they knew anything about him. From what

I can figure out, he kept to himself a lot, didn't mix with anyone except to say hello a few times."

"What about his girlfriend?" Susan asked, looking apologetically at Lucy who had was listening intently.

"No one ever saw him with a woman. He's been living in that retirement community alone, from what I can tell," Joel said.

"What on earth has he been doing down there, then?" Lucy asked.

"According to the neighbors, he's just been holed up at that trailer, leaving once a week to get some groceries and alcohol."

"Alcohol?" Lucy frowned. "But he hasn't had more than the occasional drink since before you were born. Are you sure?"

"That's what one of the neighbors said," Joel answered.

"Tell them the rest," Brian urged, and Joel reached into his messenger bag to pull out a bundle of envelopes. "This is his mail, his friend asked me to get it to Dad."

Lucy grabbed the letters from him and began to leaf through them. "They're all just bills and bank statements except this one." Joel reached over and pulled one of the envelopes from the pile and handed it to her. She looked at it more closely and froze. "Oh no."

"What is it?" Susan asked.

"It's from an oncologist's office in Vancouver." Lucy's tears welled up in her eyes. "Does this mean he has cancer?"

Susan reached over and grasped Lucy's hands. "You don't know that. Maybe it's just a referral for tests or something."

Lucy turned toward her. "No Susan. It all makes sense now. Don't you see?"

"What makes sense?"

"I think this is why he left."

"That would explain it," Susan grasped what Lucy was talking about.

"What do you mean?" Joel said. "Dad doesn't have cancer. He'd have said something. Open the letter."

"No. It's not my letter to open," Lucy said. "And he wouldn't necessarily have said anything to us Joel."

"But if he had cancer, why wouldn't he stay home. You're a practical nurse. Why wouldn't he let you take care of him?"

"May I?" Susan looked at Lucy for permission to share what she knew, and Lucy nodded. "I think there's some family history you boys need to know. It might explain why Rupert left the way he did."

The boys leaned in to listen and she turned to Brian first.

"You know that your dad and Rupert are step-brothers."

"Yeah, but what's that got to do with Dad going to Mexico because of cancer?" Joel asked.

"When Rupert and Richard were little, they lived with their parents on Granger Island where they were fishers. When the boys got to eighth grade, they had to go to a boarding school, here on Vancouver Island."

"Yeah, Dad told me about that once," said Brian.

"Rupert went over a year earlier than your father because he was older and when Richard went to school, Rupert used to protect him from bullies. I think that's why the two are so close. It must have been lonely for them."

"Of course," Lucy said. "You know, even after all these years, I hadn't made that connection. Rupert doesn't talk about his childhood much."

"Anyway," Susan continued, "when Richard was in eighth grade his mother died in a storm. His father was devastated and just couldn't stay on the island in that isolation anymore. So, he sold his fishing license — they were worth a lot of money then — and came to live on Vancouver Island. He went back to school and got some training in carpentry and moved into building and renovations."

Brian reached over and squeezed Susan's hand. "I can't imagine losing a mother at that age. Poor Dad."

"Yes, from what I know, it was a real shock, which is why your grandfather moved to Vancouver Island. He wanted to be closer to where Richard was going to school, and he got a large enough place that both the boys could live with him instead of in the dormitory."

"So that's when Rupert began living with them. I always thought it was after his father left," Lucy said. "Go on." They were all now listening intently and so Susan continued.

"Three years later, Rupert's father left his mother. He came back from a trip to Vancouver Island to get some supplies and the next day she woke up to find a package of information about accounts, a copy of his will, and enough money to start over without him. She didn't know until years later why he left. All she got was a letter saying goodbye, saying that this was for the best because he didn't want her to suffer."

"So that's when Gramma Sandy went to live with Grandpa?" Brian asked.

"Yes, that's right. She didn't know where else to go, and Richard's dad took her in until she could get back on her feet, but they ended up falling in love, marrying, and raising the boys together," Susan said.

"Didn't want her to suffer what?" Joel asked.

"They never talked about it," Susan said. "But I do know Rupert's father died of prostate cancer. They learned of it five years later."

"And his father was the kind of man who didn't want to be seen as weak," Lucy said.

"Like Dad," Joel added.

"Do you think that's why he left?" Lucy asked. "He's always said we shouldn't have to put up with him. He was acting so strangely the few months before he went. He sold his business, gave away everything Joel didn't want."

Susan looked at her and thought over what she had learned in the past six months about Rupert leaving. "I thought he had just left to have an affair, but now, I don't know. Maybe he left to save you from seeing him sick."

"He's a nitwit," Lucy said. "Doesn't he think I've seen sick people before?" Her voice was rising, and she continued. "Joel, find out where your father's staying. I'm going to see him."

"I'll come with you," he said.

She turned to him, eyes flashing. "I need to go myself first and see what's happening. If he's really sick, I'll send you a ticket. Besides, you have work this week, and I need you to look after the dog for a few days."

"I can look after the dog," Brian offered.

"I appreciate that, Brian." Lucy scraped her chair back and stood up. "But this is something I need to do on my own. Now. Off you go home. You all have work in the morning, and I need to pack and get a ticket."

"I should come too," Susan said as she stood up, "and talk to Richard in person."

Lucy shook her head. "Let me go as a scout. I'll call you as soon as I see the lay of the land." She reached over to Susan. "I need to do this on my own, Sue, and I need you to be here for Joel, in case it's bad news and he needs someone."

Susan didn't say anything for a few minutes. She didn't want to stay behind and hold down the fort. That was what she always did. But she also didn't want to run after Richard to try to fix things, when it was he who had lied. "Okay. I'll wait to hear from you." But she would go home right after this to surf the net for tickets and make a list of what she could offload to Jennifer and Boris, in case she needed to take off with little notice.

"Goodbye, Mom." Joel hugged his mom at the front door to take their leave. "Call me when you see Dad and don't sugar-coat it. I need to know how he's doing."

"I promise I won't sugar-coat it."

"Bye Auntie Lucy," Brian hugged his aunt. "Bye Mom."

"Thank you for telling us what was happening, you guys," said Susan. "Secrets just make things worse."

She hugged Lucy and said into her ear, "Can you tell Richard to call me?"

Lucy squeezed her tight. "I'll let you know when I get there, Sue. I'm hoping to bring those nitwits home."

Susan drove home via Starbucks and picked up a decaf latte. As she sat in the drive-through line, she mulled over the conversation they'd had at Lucy's. If Rupert had cancer, that would explain why Richard went to Mexico. It could even explain why he hadn't told her where he was. But it didn't explain the other lies and deception related to the mortgage, unless he had borrowed money for Rupert's treatment.

Should she go with Lucy? She hoped her friend wasn't headed for even more heartbreak, but she would respect her decision and would stay here to support Joel and Brian in case the prognosis was bad. Besides, she thought as she paid for her drink, she didn't even know if Richard would want her there. She hadn't heard from him, and he hadn't answered her texts. Was his trip to be with Rupert just a bulletproof excuse to get away from her? No one would blame him for having to be with his sick brother, no matter how long it took. Even she couldn't blame him for choosing Rupert over her in this instance. So why then hadn't he explained it to her?

She drove home and decided on her next course of action. She would stay here, continue to gather information, and plan for her future. If Richard wanted to talk to her, he had her number.

Rupert spent the next few days teaching Richard everything he knew about investing: how to pick a good stock, how to buy, and how to sell. On Monday at lunch, he finished showing him the basics.

"Now it's up to you," Rupert said. "It's taken me a lot of time and practice, but I've learned how do this."

"I'm afraid to invest much," Richard said. "Once Susan hears about what I've done, I may not have anything to invest with."

"Start by pretending you've bought them and then track how they do. Figure out what works and what doesn't. Learn from what the experts in the field do. Then start investing actual money."

"That makes sense. How much time do you spend on this in a day?"

"Now? Anywhere between fifteen minutes and two hours. Depends on how much research I have to do. But when I started, I was putting in four or five hours a day."

"Probably time better spent than what I've been doing," Richard said. "Which is a big fat nothing. No wonder Susan's getting ready to end this."

"How are the dance lessons coming along?" Rupert asked, taking a long sip from his third drink.

"I'm actually enjoying them. Once you know the steps and what to do, it's fun. I can see why Susan enjoys dancing." Rupert needed to cool it with the alcohol.

"Maybe you two can join that ballroom dance club back home."

"Maybe…but meanwhile. Let's see what the doctor says, eh?" How could he go home with Rupert still drinking? Sometimes it seemed Rupert was accepting his diagnosis and then he would disappear into his room to drink again.

"I'll get the treatment options on Friday, then I'll know more about what I need to do, and you can get back home," Rupert said. "Thanks for coming down here. I feel hopeful for the first time in over a year."

"It's actually been good for me, too. I've made a couple of business contacts and it's been good to spend time alone with you. We haven't done this in ages."

"Yeah, we'll have to go fishing one of these days."

Richard grinned. Maybe this was a sign Rupert was coming around. He was thinking about future opportunities which meant he was starting to accept that he had a future.

Music started playing in the lounge and Richard looked at his watch. "It's time for my lesson."

"Okay, I'll see you back in the room."

RICHARD PRACTICED the steps of the tango feeling far more confident in his ability to lead his partner. Several more couples had joined the lessons in recent days, and the class had attracted a growing audience, something he imagined was bound to happen once guests had been at the resort for a few days. One could only sit by the poolside for so long before needing something else to do.

Today, the class broke up and disappeared into the thinning crowd, as the spectators drifted off to watch a volleyball competition on the beach.

He walked toward the bar to order a glass of water and was stopped by a familiar voice behind him.

"Hello, Richard."

He turned to see Lucy standing there, a suitcase on wheels beside her. He looked behind her to see if Susan was there and was disappointed.

"Lucy, what are you doing here?"

"I came to see how Rupert is. Can you take me to his room please?" Her eyes were glittering in anger and he knew that she knew why they were there.

"How did you know?"

"Joel. He went to see his father in Palm Springs and found a letter from an oncologist's office and no father. How bad is it?"

"You should ask him."

"I'm asking you. Don't lie to me. I need to know what I'm up against before I see him."

He wasn't sure how to answer her. He didn't want to betray Rupert's trust, but he knew determination when he saw it. Besides, maybe he could get some tit for tat and learn what was happening with Susan. He asked her to sit.

"How bad is it?" she asked.

"It's in the first stage. So really treatable."

"That idiot," she said, looking clearly agitated now. "I've been thinking about this on the plane all the way down. Running this around my head. You know what I think?"

"No. But I get the idea you're going to tell me."

"I think he found out he had cancer, panicked, left me before he could even figure out how bad it was or what his options were, and has been hiding in Palm Springs for six months avoiding the whole thing."

"There's something else," he said. "He's been drinking again. I think he's terrified."

"Why the hell don't you two just communicate with your wives?" she said vehemently. "Take me to his room. I'm going to hash this out with Rupert once and for all. How dare he just ghost me like that?"

Richard sat back, afraid she might hit him in her anger, although he was just an innocent bystander.

"And after I've hashed things out with Rupert, I'll stay here until he gets his treatment or whatever else he needs. And you," she pointed at him, glaring so hard he pressed his back even further into the chair. He had never seen her so angry. Lucy was usually the fun flakey one. "You," she continued, "will find the next flight home and fix your marriage. How dare you put Susan through this?"

"Susan and I are fine," he said defending them. They may be a little off the rails, but they would patch things up. He just needed to come clean about the money and the job. She would understand. But he didn't like the way Lucy was looking at him.

"You're as much of an idiot as your brother," she said. "She knows you mortgaged the house. She knows you lied about retiring and now she knows you're in Mexico instead of Palm Springs, where you said you were. Richard, did you know she's looking for a new job? Is talking to a realtor? Has been talking to the bank? Is getting a lawyer?"

A lawyer? Why was she talking to a lawyer?

"I get here and you're doing the tango with a woman who could be a sex goddess and back home your wife is doing the tango with another man."

"What other man?"

"Sid Jones. They're in the same dance class. And Richard, she is loving the dance lessons."

"Is there more than dancing going on?" He had to know.

"I don't think so." Lucy shook her head. "At least, not yet. But you need to go home, and I need to see that big oaf I married and talk some sense into him."

"I'll take you to the room. Come on." He should probably warn Rupert that Lucy was here but there was no time and as far as he was concerned, she had the right to confront him. She had stood by Rupert through a lot over the years, which couldn't have been easy.

They entered the room and Rupert wasn't in the seating area, but he'd been spending most of his time in his room these past few days. Drinking and wallowing. Richard pointed to the bedroom door and Lucy slammed it open.

"What the hell, Ricky?" he could hear a sleepy Rupert say. "Don't you knock?" And then, "Lucy? Is that you? What are you doing here?" He heard Rupert's heavy steps walking toward the door. "You look really good."

"Well, you look like crap," she said to him before slamming the door behind her.

Richard retreated to his bedroom to grab his computer. He would take Lucy's advice. He needed to go home and see Susan before she finished creating her new life without room for him.

THE PLANE LANDED AT FIVE-THIRTY, just as the sun was moving lower on the horizon, and he took a cab straight home to surprise her and to share the news that he had an interview the following afternoon. When he arrived, her car wasn't in the driveway. She would still be at work. That would give him time to unpack and get a shower.

Out on the curb the garbage can was sitting, waiting for someone to bring it in. A simple job that he always fobbed off when he could. He put the suitcase down and went to the curb to grab the can and roll it back to where it was kept. She was right; it was only a few yards.

"Hey, welcome back!" Jack said from across their shared fence where he was pruning hydrangeas, getting them ready for spring. "How was your trip?"

"Good. But it's nice to be home." He grasped the handle of his luggage and started up the drive and stopped, remembering something. "Thanks for digging us out of the snowstorm the other day."

"We should thank Susan," Jack said, bending down to pick up the black cat that had been winding around his legs. "She came over and helped Sylvia serve breakfast to the entire neighborhood. It was quite the gathering."

"I'm sorry I missed it."

"Well, Sylvia and I have been talking. Maybe we could have a neighborhood picnic this summer. It was nice to visit with everyone. Rarely get time to even see a neighbor, much less talk to them."

"Count us in," he said.

"Oh good. I'm glad you aren't moving far. We were hoping you would stay in town."

Moving? He must have looked startled because Jack added. "Saw the realtor pull up a few days ago. Couldn't miss that pink car of hers. And Sylvia said Susan was thinking about what to do in retirement. We just assumed you were downsizing."

"Right!" said Richard, smiling as though his life depended on it. "We are certainly considering it, but we plan to stay here in Sunshine Bay. Listen, I'll talk to you soon, okay? I need to get unpacked and organized before she gets home."

"Sounds good," Jack said, petting the cat before setting it down and returning to his work.

The house was quiet and smelled like paint. He walked through the house to find out where the smell was coming from and discovered it was the kitchen. The walls were a nice off-white that made the room look larger and brighter than it had been before. He looked up where the clock had once been and found the wall empty. At least she hadn't replaced it with another yet.

He wandered through a few more rooms, remembering the good times they had had here. Brian's old room, where Brian used to keep all his gadgets, was empty now. Maybe he could turn it into an office and start a consulting firm. He could find work similar to what he had done for Lorne last week, if tomorrow's meeting with Salim Malik didn't pan out. He looked around at the walls and imagined where he would put shelving, a desk, and a computer. This was the first time in years that he felt excited about work. Susan was right to rip down the clock. It was only reminding them both that they were waiting until they retired to enjoy their lives, instead of just living.

The door to her office was open and he wandered inside, glancing at her calendar. Dance lessons at

Armand's Tuesday and Thursday at seven, was written on the top of the calendar in big letters. So that's where she would be tonight. Dancing.

There was a folder from a real estate firm on the desk with a 'to do' list on top. Things to do in the rooms to get the house ready for sale, starting with painting the kitchen. His hand shook a little when he flipped open the folder to read the evaluation. Wow. The house was worth more than he had imagined. There were listings at the back, and he noticed that there were stars beside a few one-bedroom condos. One bedroom wouldn't be large enough for both of them, especially if they both needed office space.

The inside flap had some figures on it, the amount of the house, how much it would be to move, how much they could invest if they bought a smaller place, and there was also a second scenario. What they would each get if they lived separately.

His stomach lurched. She was leaving him. She was really leaving him. Lucy was right. He looked at his watch. Six-thirty. She wouldn't have time to come home before her lesson and he needed to see her.

Now.

CHAPTER 21

Susan wasn't looking forward to seeing Sid tonight, much less dancing with him. She knew he had seen them going for coffee as a date and when she looked back on it; she supposed it was. Was that why she had felt so uncomfortable sharing the cake with him? Had she been cheating on Richard?

It hadn't felt that way at the time, but looking back on it, she had accepted his invitation because she was angry at Richard, hurt by his betrayals, and feeling sorry for herself. She had accepted it because she wanted to be noticed and was enjoying the attention. She had accepted it for all the wrong reasons, and she owed an apology to Sid.

* * *

"HELLO," Sid said, when he saw her. "I'm glad you came back. I was afraid I'd ruined the lessons for you."

"Hi," she said, sitting down on a chair at the side of the room to put on her dancing shoes. She had worn flats with the turtleneck sweater dress today but wanted to try dancing in the shoes again.

"Listen, I want to apologize for Thursday night. I was way out of line," he said.

That was true, but she had also contributed to the misunderstanding. "I'm sorry if I led you on," she said, placing both feet on the floor and looking up at him. "It wasn't my intention."

"Can we agree to let bygones be bygones?" he asked. "I really want us to stay friends."

"As long as you recognize that's all we'll ever be," she said.

"You and I had passion once."

"Yes, we did." She heard clapping then and turned toward the instructor who was starting the class. "But passion can be overrated."

"Well," Sid said holding up his arms and smiling down at her, "we still have the tango."

She laughed up at him and stepped into his arms, glad that they still had their friendship.

At the end of the lesson, after they had mastered the steps in the new sequence they were learning, they walked together to get their coats. "Oh," he said, watching her change her shoes. "I forgot to tell you. I got a job."

"Where?" She stood and he held out her coat for her again as he had done the week before. "At the homeless program you were telling me about?" It felt better accepting his help to put on her coat this time. It wasn't fraught with sexual tension. They were going to be okay.

She turned back toward him, smiling hard, happy that he got a job offer while feeling a twinge of disappointment. There would be other opportunities, but that job really spoke to her.

"No. Even better," he said, buttoning up his coat. "I got an offer from the city. To oversee their Human Resource department and the volunteers for the community garden."

"That's wonderful news," she reached up and hugged him, happy for him and happy that she still had a chance at the other job. "I feel like we should celebrate this. Can I buy you a cheesecake? As a friend?"

He grinned. "Yes. I'd like that."

They walked toward Luigi's and sat by the window.

"Now, tell me all about this new job. I want to hear everything."

CHAPTER 22

Richard seethed as he watched the pair from the doorway of the dance class. They had been dancing well, like a couple that had been dancing together for longer than a few lessons. She fit into Sid's arms perfectly and Sid—damn he hated that guy—Sid was being all gallant and wonderful. Smiling at her as she changed her shoes, holding her coat out for her. She hated it when Richard did that. Didn't she? When had he ever actually held out her coat for her?

Never mind. It didn't matter.

Wait a minute. Now she was hugging him, and she seemed really pleased about it. What had he said to her? Was he hugging her back too hard? Now where were they going?

He stepped into the recess of the next doorway and watched them leave, chattering like a pair of squirrels. What did they have to talk about? Why didn't she talk to him like that anymore? He followed them to make sure she got into her car and drove home, but she didn't. Instead she walked into a restaurant with him. Luigi's. Since when did she go there?

Standing across the street behind one of the old oaks that lined the street, he watched them take a seat beside the window and continue talking and laughing while they waited for their drinks. Then he saw the server bring them two pieces of cake.

He stepped a bit closer to watch them. She looked beautiful tonight. She'd cut her hair and was exuding confidence. She took a bite of the chocolate confection and her face was in rapture. He wanted to run inside and pull her out of that chair. Take her home.

There was a crack of thunder in the distance and he pulled his coat closer around him. He missed Mexico already. The wind picked up and another crack of thunder released the rain. What had gone wrong in his life that his wife was inside enjoying a sensuous dessert with another man while he stood out on the pavement like an abandoned hound dog getting soaked to the skin?

He stood looking until he saw them finish up their drinks and dessert. He stepped back across the street behind the tree, shivering and feeling foolish but not wanting to leave until she got to her car. Alone.

When he saw Sid walking away, swaggering like a man who had just won a prize, he bolted to his car and drove home. She had a lot to answer for looking so happy without him.

A lot to answer for.

CHAPTER 23

Susan arrived home to a roar of anger coming from a half-drowned man who looked a lot like her husband.

"What were you doing with Sid?" the man said. "What the hell were you doing with him while I was away?"

She leaned back against the door she had just closed behind her, trying to understand what was happening, what he was saying and why he was so angry.

"What are you talking about?"

"Why are you taking dance lessons with him?"

"I'm not." Seeing he was about to erupt again, she quickly added, "At least not in the way you're thinking."

"How do you know what I'm thinking?"

"He happened to be in the same class, and we were the only two people without partners. We're just friends!"

"Then what were you doing hugging him?"

"Have you been spying on me?" she asked, incredulous that this was what she was facing tonight. That after all his lies, he was angry about her going to a dance lesson.

"You weren't home when I got here so I went downtown to surprise you. I was the one who got the surprise." He was yelling at her. Richard never screamed and it really wasn't a good look on him. She stood against the door, watching him as though she weren't really there, assessing the situation as though it were a puzzle to be solved.

His face was mottled and half sun-burned, his hair looked like it could use a cut and he had a vein popping out on his forehead. She didn't dare go closer.

"You've been busy since I left, haven't you!" He was still screaming. "What were you planning to do? Sell the house? Leave me on the street?"

Ah. He had seen the realtor's information. That was what was making him mad. She waited for him to come back to reason. Hopefully it wouldn't take long because otherwise she would say some choice things too.

"Well?" He paused for breath. "How could you embarrass me like that?"

"I beg your pardon?" she said, tamping down her anger. "How exactly have I embarrassed you?"

"I got home and the neighbor," he pointed toward Jack and Sylvia's house, "asked me if I was moving."

"And?"

He sputtered. "And then I went to see you at your dance lessons, and you were flirting with another man!"

"I wasn't flirting. I was dancing and congratulating my friend."

"And going out for a piece of cake that…that…"

"That what?"

"That made you look like you were…"

"What?"

"Never mind. It was embarrassing." He was still simmering in anger.

"As embarrassing as learning from someone else that you were fired? Or that you mortgaged our house? Or that you were in bloody Mexico?"

He stopped yelling, startled into silence. "Well I…I…"

"You what?" she asked slowly. "Thought I was too stupid to figure it out? Or did you think I would just blindly trust you and not question what was going on right under my nose? You think you were embarrassed, Richard? Embarrassment is a small thing. I was betrayed by the man I thought loved me."

"I didn't betray you," he said, scoffing.

"You lied. You took out money and put me into debt. And you invested in a scam." She walked past him and up the stairs, stopping to take a suitcase from the hall closet before continuing to the bedroom.

"What are you doing?" he yelled.

"What does it look like I'm doing?" she asked, pulling clothes out of her drawer and the closet, throwing them into the case and then walking to the bathroom to get her toiletries.

"Why are you packing?"

"Because I'm leaving." She turned towards him. "It's my turn to take a break from you."

He reached toward the case and tried to keep her from closing it.

"Get away from me," she snarled with such force he stepped back in alarm and she took the opportunity to close the lid.

"Where are you going? To Sid?"

"It's none of your business," she said. "Just like it was none of my business that you went to Mexico." She stood and scanned the room to see what else she would want to take for a few days then picked up the suitcase. He stood aside as she went down the stairs to her office to grab her work bag.

"Sue, come on. Let's talk about it."

"No." She shifted her work bag and purse onto her left shoulder and made sure she had her keys before leaving. She didn't want to make a dramatic exit and have to come back for her car keys. "I have been beside myself for weeks trying to figure out what's wrong with you. Then I learned you've been lying to me for months. You borrowed that money seven months ago, Richard. Seven months!"

"Haven't you ever made a mistake?"

"Yes, Richard. I make mistakes all the time." He was right that spending time with Sid had been a mistake. In her loneliness she had been tempted but she'd moved past it. Richard didn't have to know that, though. "I just don't lie about them to the person who is supposed to be my life partner."

Or did she? Wasn't hiding something the same as a lie? Now wasn't she a liar too?

And a hypocrite.

She needed to leave and think this through. Figure out how to get past this. But not here and not now.

"Look, I'm sorry," Richard said.

Sorry wasn't good enough tonight. If he hadn't left and if he hadn't kept secrets from her, none of this would have happened. She lowered her voice and hissed. "And I would never, ever, make a financial decision like you did without talking to you first. You know exactly how I feel about that. I can never trust you after this."

"I'm sorry." He held out his hands to her and she just shook her head.

"So am I." She opened the door and stepped into the night.

"Where are you going to go in the pouring rain?"

"Away from you," she yelled, opening the car door and putting her bags on the back seat.

"We need to talk about this."

"Goodnight, Richard." She climbed into the front seat and drove away from the house not daring to look back for fear of losing her composure.

He hadn't once said he still loved her.

What the hell just happened? Richard closed the door against the driving rain. He walked into the kitchen and looked in the fridge for a beer, cracked open a can and sat in the living room staring at the television screen.

He played the scene over and over in his mind. He was in the right here. She had been out with another man, eating cake and looking good. She hadn't looked like that for him in years. For Sid, she had her hair redone and taken up dancing. She had even hugged Sid which was something she hadn't done with him in weeks. No, probably months. Now she was off at Sid's house doing who knew what. He would never forgive her for this. Never.

He turned on the television, clicked from one channel to another and turned it off again. Might as well get some sleep. Tomorrow he had to go to Vancouver to meet with Salim Malik. His harbor to harbor flight left at noon and he had to get a haircut before he left.

If she wanted to start her life without him, then he could do the same.

* * *

RICHARD WOKE up to an empty bed and a headache. He hadn't slept most of the night, imagining what Sid was doing with Susan and planning what he was going to do to Sid. He was out the door by seven and drove the twenty minutes to Sid's house. When he pulled into the driveway, he noticed her car wasn't there. She must have left for work early. No matter. Sid would be there. He was unemployed, too.

He banged on the door and waited. No response so he banged again.

"What?" He heard a voice from above him. Looking up, he saw Sid leaning out of the window, his chest bare, looking ten years younger than he really was. How was he going to compete with his guy?

"Where's Susan?" he yelled.

"No idea."

"You were with her last night."

Sid looked up and down the street. "I'm coming down. Just a minute." He ducked back into the house and closed the window.

The door opened a few minutes later and Sid stood there, shirt half done up, looking concerned.

"Where is Susan? She was with you last night."

"Yeah. We have dance class together."

"And?"

"Not sure what you're asking, Rick. Susan went home last night after we had a coffee. Is she okay?"

"So, you're telling me she never came here last night?"

"Nope. Why would she?"

What could he say? He had been certain she was here. Certain she had run to Sid. He'd got it wrong. No wonder she'd left.

He had to find her and get her to come home.

"Listen, Rick. I don't know what's going on with you two, but take my advice. I'm heading for divorce and it's damn hard. So, do yourself a favor. When you find her, do whatever you need to do to keep her. She's a good person and you two are good together."

"Thanks," he muttered and got in his car. Maybe Sid wasn't so bad after all.

"Hey," Sid yelled, and then walked over to talk to him. He rolled down the window to hear what he had to say. "When you do see her, can you tell her I'm not going to be at dance lessons tomorrow night? I have a work thing."

He nodded, though his mind was now reeling, trying to figure out where she was. What if she had been in an accident last night? The storm had been pretty bad. But the police would have showed up by now if that had happened. She was probably with Brian.

He drove to Brian's building and was about to push the buzzer when Brian came through the front door.

"Hey Dad. Good to see you." Brian put down his laptop bag and hugged him. It felt good, that connection.

"Is your mother here?"

"No. She's probably at work."

"So, she didn't stay here last night?"

"No." Brian's forehead wrinkled. "Didn't she come home?"

Richard shook his head. "Thanks, I'll find her at work."

"Dad, should I be worried about you two?"

"No. We're good. She's just mad that I didn't tell her I was in Mexico."

"Sure, okay." The kid didn't sound very convinced. "Good luck."

"Thanks." When he got to her office, he was relieved to find her car there. At least he knew she hadn't had an accident. Where had she stayed?

He would ask her when he saw her. First, he had to get a haircut, so he drove to the barber and waited in line for Max, the guy he always used. Then, freshly cut and shaved, he went home to get ready for his flight. He had to be at the seaplane terminal before eleven so he could be at the restaurant where he was meeting Salim before one. He needed this job. Maybe if he had a good job, Susan would forgive him and come home.

He thought of what Sid had said to him about divorce and shivered. He didn't want to lose her. He had to find a way to earn her trust again.

When Susan arrived at work that morning, there was a frenzy in the air. What was going on? It was only eight o'clock and she really wasn't up to facing chaos this morning. She'd had little sleep. Lucy's dog, Mason, had whined for hours from fear of the thunderstorm. No wonder Joel was so happy to see her when she arrived at Lucy's apartment and immediately escaped for his apartment when she agreed to dog sit for the next couple of days.

Jennifer was rushing past holding a coffee pot and she stopped her in mid-stride. "What's happening?"

"Emergency board meeting," Jennifer whispered. "Boris thinks it's about the audit. There's something wrong with the books."

"What would be wrong?"

"Annette's married to Louis Taylor."

Louis Taylor, where had she heard that name before? "You know…" Jennifer whispered, "the guy who embezzled?"

"Oh." She remembered now. "But Annette wouldn't embezzle. She's not the type."

"Then why has she gone rushing off on a…" she used air quotes, "family emergency?"

"Maybe because she had a family emergency?" Susan knew that Jennifer overreacted sometimes, though she could see where the idea was coming from. Annette left around the same time that Louis did. She had a sinking feeling in her stomach. Did this mean program cuts? Or layoffs?

"Then why is the board here? And why did they ask me to give them a list of personnel? They want to talk to us. They never want to talk to us."

The door to the boardroom opened and Jake, a board member, stepped out. "Oh, there you are, Jennifer. We're ready for the coffee now." Jennifer nodded and scurried through the door.

Susan went to her office and closed the door to the madness beyond. If they needed her, they would call her. Meanwhile, she would focus on helping the situation and keeping her mind off Richard. She needed to get that marketing information to Boris; if they could fill the conference, that might contribute enough revenue to make a difference to whatever shortfall there was. Was that why Annette wanted to double the attendees? Though she hadn't seemed like the type to embezzle from a non-profit. People were surprising her this month, though. People she knew — or thought she knew — far better than Annette.

Just after ten, her phone rang. It was the human resources manager from the organization she had interviewed with last week, and she braced herself.

"We'd like to offer you the position," the woman said.

"Thank you," she blurted into the phone, hoping she sounded excited and not flabbergasted.

"I'll send you the details of the offer by email. Once you get it and look it over, we would appreciate your decision and written reply by the end of the week."

"I look forward to it," she said, keeping her voice calm. They were sending her an offer!

"If you have questions, please call me. My number will be on the bottom of the email."

And with that, the woman hung up. She got the job! She got the job! She wanted to get up and dance, but given where she was, and what was happening outside her office; she would celebrate later. Instead, she printed off the marketing and communications plan and took it with her to Boris's office.

"Hi," he said, motioning for her to close the door. "I guess you're here about the meeting. Before you ask, I don't know what's going on. I looked at the books and I saw nothing amiss, but then they called in the forensic accountants. She could have been keeping a second set of books."

Susan held up her hand. "Boris, I'm not here to gossip. I'm here with a marketing plan to increase the registration to the conference. The numbers are so low we may only break even at this point."

"Oh," he said, the wrinkle in his brow receding. "Let's see."

"Also, I'm not sure why you believe Annette did anything wrong."

"Her husband did it and now she's gone. You know the saying, where there's smoke there's fire."

"But you just said yourself that you found nothing wrong with the books. It was my experience with Annette that she was trying to build our revenue up so we could expand programs. That's why she wanted the conference to be so big this year."

He shrugged.

"As a leader, you need to be the one to keep your cool in a crisis," she said. "People look up to you. You can't be listening to rumors and making decisions based on innuendo and false information."

He scowled. "Susan, have you forgotten that I'm your boss?"

"No. Otherwise I wouldn't be saying anything to you." She sat down and leaned toward him. "Boris, you've done an excellent job until now. People trust you. They look up to you. You need to be the one to calm them down and I need to know you can do that when I leave."

"Leave? Where are you going?"

"That was the other reason I'm here. I wanted to tell you I've been looking for other work. In fact, I just learned I am getting an offer today."

"Wow," he said, drawing his hand over his face. "Okay. How much notice can you give us?"

"I need to go over the offer first. I haven't accepted it yet. But they need someone to start as soon as possible. So, if I go, I would guess two or three weeks?"

He swallowed hard. "Well, I'll miss you. You've been a real rock the past few months. I'm not sure what I would have done without your support."

"I'll miss this place too. It's like my second home."

He cleared his throat and glanced down at the documents she had brought in with her. "Well, why don't we see if we can fill the conference? Do you want to walk me through what you have here?"

They discussed the plan and she was pleased to see that Boris had some ideas to add. He really was growing into the position.

"I'll make these changes and print out ten copies for the board," she said as she was leaving the office. "Maybe since they're all here, they can approve the extra expenditures today?"

"Good idea," he said and turned back to the work on his desk, looking much calmer than he had when she had walked in. Maybe all he needed was a reminder that he was no longer a worker, but the person in charge.

She walked back to her office and saw someone step out of the boardroom and call in Jennifer, who walked in, a worried look on her face. As Susan sat down to make the changes she and Boris had discussed, she hoped Boris and Jennifer were just overreacting. There was no evidence that Annette had taken money, not that Susan was aware of. But then what was going on in there?

She didn't have long to wait to find out. When Jennifer came out, she came to her office right away. "They want to see you," she said. "It was a weird conversation, Susan. They were asking me about my qualifications, what I did, who I worked with. It felt like I had to defend my work. What's going on?"

"I guess I'll find out," Susan said, gathering the fresh set of plans from her office printer to take with her. "Don't borrow trouble, Jennifer. We have enough with just getting the conference filled." She walked calmly toward the boardroom. She had nothing to worry about. She wouldn't even work here soon.

"Thanks for joining us," Cecelia said as she entered the room. "We have something to discuss with you."

Susan set the stack of papers she brought beside her. Boris wasn't here. What was this about?

"Susan, we have just learned that Annette won't be coming back from Australia. Her family emergency is more indefinite than she expected."

"Oh, I see." Should she ask if the rumors were true? Did they suspect someone of helping Annette take money? She needed to calm down and take her own advice. Listen for the facts and not make any rash judgements.

"So, her position is now open," Cecelia said. "And we would like to offer it to you."

"Me?" She couldn't be an executive director.

"Yes. We've been discussing our options and we think that there is a staff person ready to step into your current position who would give you the support you need to take this organization to the next level. Annette had a vision for us and as she is not here to pursue it, we would like to have someone step in who could help us accomplish it."

Cecelia slipped a piece of paper toward her. "We've put the offer in writing, and we'd like you to take some time to think it over. Call me if you have any questions. I know you have a big decision to make here, and I want to give you time to go through all the options."

"Thank you." She looked around the room at familiar faces. "I really appreciate this."

"Take the rest of the day off," Cecelia said. "I know you have other options, and I hope you decide to stay, but you should take the time you need to be sure. We'd like a decision by Friday."

Susan thanked them all again, picked up her pile of papers and walked to Boris's office to let him know she hadn't presented the marketing plan to the board and she was taking the rest of the day off.

Boris got up and came around the desk. "Look, Susan, I know you talked to Cecelia and that you have a big decision to make," he said, "and that a fresh opportunity is… well, exciting, and novel. But Susan, you have a passion for this work we do. And yes, probably you will have a passion for the other work too, in time. But they may not need you as much as we do."

"Thanks, Boris. I'll consider that when I'm making my decision. Also, I may need more time off than today. I have some personal business that may require I take a week or more."

"Sure. Take all the time you need." He took the documents she handed him.

Before she left the room, she said, "You and Jennifer and the rest of this team will survive without me, whether I'm gone for a few days or…" She swallowed, as it hit her, the enormity of what it would feel like to leave this place she had helped to develop. "Longer."

He flushed and then said, "Thanks, Susan. I really appreciate you." He paused and looked her in the eye. "I think we could really do a lot of good here." Then he waved his hand. "But I don't want to say more. You need to make this decision for yourself."

"Thanks, Boris," she said. "I hope to see you in the morning."

Susan left work and drove out of town to a deserted beach, her favorite place to walk and think when she had important decisions to make.

She walked along the shore breathing in the fresh salt air that was thankfully upwind from the noisy colony of sea lions gathered on the rocks just offshore. Susan took out her phone and snapped a few pictures and was sorry she couldn't share the experience with Richard. It had been a few years since they had come out during the herring run that brought these majestic creatures north this time of year.

A pair of seagulls floated down to land on the sand not far away and she continued her ramble along the shore. There must be someone she could call who knew about career strategy and businesses. Someone who could help her decide. Someone like… She thought for a few minutes and realized the only person she wanted to call about this was Richard. He was her go-to person about important life decisions like this, but after last night, how could she?

She took out her phone to check messages and think about who else she could call. Lucy would be helpful, but Lucy was in Mexico handling her own problems. It amazed her that even after all those months and all that pain, Lucy still had hope that they could work out their differences and that she could find it in herself to consider forgiving Rupert.

The ocean was calm today, the storm from last night completely forgotten. She bent down and picked up five flat stones and threw them the way her father had taught her, delighted when one skipped three times.

Should she give Richard another opportunity to explain himself? Another opportunity to make it right? And ask him to forgive her for being tempted to stray?

His words echoed in her memory: Haven't you ever made mistakes, Susan?

She pulled out her phone and sent him a text: I have a work dilemma I need some advice on.

Richard: Sure.

She sat down on a nearby log and gazed into the sea for a few moments. He had answered her immediately, and she hadn't realized how much she had longed to know he was there. Right there. At the other end of the line. Reliable.

Susan: I have two options and I need to make a choice soon.

Richard: Okay. What are they? Give me the pros and cons.

Susan: First option: A new place, new people, new topics to talk about; opportunity to build new relationships.

Richard: And the second?

Susan: A place and people I'm familiar with, familiar things to talk about but a renewed vision that I can help grow. There would be some adapting either way.

Richard: Which one do you have a passion for?

Susan: Well… I could have a passion for both over time, I think.

Richard: Are there any other benefits to either?

Susan: Both are an opportunity to grow, but the second is a lot more responsibility.

Richard: Which one do you think you could invest in for the next few years?

Susan: They are both fantastic offers.

Richard: Okay, take out a coin and flip it. Heads, option one and tails, option two.

Susan: You want me to do this on a coin toss?

Richard: Trust me.

Trust him. Did she trust him? He had lied to her. He had made her feel like an idiot for not telling her what was happening. He knew about business though, so she took a quarter out of her wallet and tossed it.

Richard: Did you do it?

Susan: Yes. Heads. I guess I go with option one.

Richard: Not so fast. First, think about how you feel about that option. Any regrets? Do you wish it had come up tails?

She considered the question and smiled. Everything was suddenly clear.

Susan: Thanks, Richard. I know what to do now. You should be a business coach. You would do well.

Richard: What did you decide? To go with the new or stay with the old?

Susan didn't answer him. She had to make a phone call. She knew what she wanted. She had known for weeks. It was time for something different in her life, and this was the opportunity she had been looking for. First, she needed to make a few phone calls, ask a few more questions. Be sure.

*R*ichard looked out the window of the cab that was taking him to the interview and then back down at his phone. Why didn't she answer his last question?

He needed to hear her voice, understand what she would do next. Be there at least by phone, to celebrate her decision with her. He dialed the phone and got a busy tone. Who was she talking to? Who would she have phoned instead of him to tell of her decision?

He had always been the first person she called. The first person she shared with. Until recently. Until he betrayed her trust by not telling her about his job and the bad investment he made.

Until he'd hurt her.

Why hadn't he trusted her enough to share his problems with her?

Because he hadn't wanted her to know he let her down. He hadn't wanted her to know that he had failed her. And he wanted to fix it himself instead of relying on her to save him.

The cab was slowing and pulling over to the curb. He had arrived at the restaurant where the meeting was being held. Time to put his game face on and meet his potential new boss.

Before he climbed out of the cab, he sent one last text.

Would you like to meet for a drink this evening? I'm in Vancouver at a meeting, but I will be home by six.

Susan: Not tonight. I'm tired. I've had a lot to think about. And I have to look after Marvin. He's been alone all day.

Richard: Marvin?

Who was Marvin?

Susan: Lucy's dog.

He relaxed his shoulders. She had stayed at Lucy's place last night then. She hadn't been cheating. Now all he needed to do was convince her he could fix his mistake and that he wouldn't betray her again.

Richard: Why not bring him home with you? We can talk there.

Susan: No. If I come home, it will be to stay.

If? If she comes home? She had to come home.

Richard: What would make you come home?

Susan: I need to know that we have a future together.

Richard: We can move past this.

Susan: I need time to think. Let's talk Friday after work.

Richard: What about tomorrow?

Susan: I have dance lessons tomorrow.

Richard started to text that Sid wouldn't be there, but the cab driver turned to look at him, reminding him they had arrived. Instead, he typed out—See you Friday—then paid the driver, stepped out onto the curb and walked down the sidewalk, pausing in front of the restaurant to take a deep breath.

This meeting needed to go well.

His future depended on it.

Susan put the phone in her purse and strolled down the beach. She had to tell him she had considered cheating, however briefly it had been. She had thought about being intimate with someone else. She couldn't leave that secret between them or it would fester.

But it was more than that. She wouldn't have been tempted if he hadn't shut her out, insisted on doing things without consulting her. Maybe they needed counseling to get past this.

A pair of kayakers paddled parallel to the shore, close enough that she could hear them laughing, and she stopped to pick up a few more stones to throw.

It wasn't just the lies, though.

She skipped a stone over the water.

It was that they did nothing fun together.

She threw another stone.

They had drifted apart and were living separate lives. She had become the caretaker of the house, the main breadwinner. He…? Well, she didn't know what he was up to, and that was the problem.

She didn't even know why he was in Vancouver today. Or who he was meeting with. If it was an interview, would it mean he was moving there? If he did, would he want to take her with him?

Would she even want to go?

She fished the quarter out of her pocket. Heads she would work on her marriage. Tails she would move on. She shook her head and put the coin back without flipping it.

She knew they could make it work if he met her halfway.

And if he could forgive her.

Richard picked up a burger on the way home from the seaplane terminal, then detoured to the beach to avoid going home to their empty house. The meeting with Salim didn't go well. Though Salim seemed to be happy enough to meet with him, it felt more like a favor to Lorne than any genuine interest in his talents. He would have to find another way to get work.

He stayed in the driver's seat and unwrapped his burger. As he ate, he watched the sun slip closer to the sea and looked over at the empty passenger seat next to him. He missed her and he needed to work to get her back. He got out of the car and leaned against the hood to finish his burger, trying to forget that he was alone.

Rupert's words echoed in his memory as he chewed his dinner. Rupert had said, "She thinks she always has to fix everything herself," and apparently Lucy agreed with him.

Were they right? Did he leave Susan to fix everything? Did he take Susan for granted? He squashed the burger wrapping and bag into a ball and tossed it into a nearby garbage bin.

Sitting here freezing wouldn't get her back. He was going to do what Lucy was doing — fight for his marriage. He had to fix the mess he made. Without a job or job prospects, he would do the next best thing and fix some of the things in the house.

When he got home, he walked directly to her office to find the list of repairs she left there and decided to start with finishing the second coat of paint in the kitchen.

Three hours later, he slowly climbed the stairs to the bedroom, tired but feeling good that he had successfully completed something. If he worked hard, he could make a good dent in her list by Friday. And fixing the home they had built together might bring him a step closer to fixing their marriage. Besides, it would be nice to have something concrete to spend his time on while he decided what to do next.

No, he corrected himself, while they decided what to do next. It was important to include her in whatever decision he made. No, he corrected himself again, he needed to do more than include her in things. He had to show her he could be her partner and meet her halfway. Only then would she see a future together.

Only then would she come home.

It was nearly time for the lesson to start, and Susan looked toward the doorway one more time. Where was Sid? It wasn't like him to be late like this. She hoped he was okay. She bent over her shoes and did them up then walked over the corner of the room they usually occupied during the lesson.

She glanced at the doorway again. She was seeing things, surely. She tried closing her eyes, but when she opened them again; it wasn't Sid leaning against the doorframe, watching her. It was Richard.

He had a new haircut and he was wearing pressed slacks, a dress shirt, and a cardigan. The man who had been wallowing in their house for weeks was gone and it seemed the old Richard was back. He was watching her with intense eyes, the way he did when they were at parties or events, mingling with others. He would catch her eye that way from across a room and her knees would melt a little, knowing he was the one who would take her home. He hadn't looked at her like that in a very long time.

Richard pushed away from the door frame and his gaze held hers as he approached, as though there were no other people in the room. He circled the room, a panther coming for his prey, and when his steps brought him closer, she reached out to grasp the back of a nearby chair to steady herself.

"Hello," he said, when he stopped in front of her, his voice husky with emotion. He was within arm's reach. If she stepped closer, he could envelope her in his arms the way he had for most of her life. "I came by because I forgot to tell you I saw Sid yesterday. He asked me to tell you he couldn't make it tonight. A work thing, I think."

"That's too bad," she said, licking her lips and trying to swallow. "I guess I'll have to dance with Armand."

"Or you could accept me as your partner."

She shook her head uncertainly. "I don't think they'll let you."

"Don't worry, I explained the situation at the desk. Told them I was thinking of joining the next round of lessons."

"Oh." She looked at him from under her lashes. "You might want to bring a partner. Singles are thin on the ground in this dance school."

"Well…" He reached toward her and took her hand, the warmth from his crept up her arm. She gripped the chair with the other hand. "I had hoped you'd be my partner."

"You hate to dance." She hadn't seen this side of Richard in a long time. His voice was low, intimate, and his eyes were dark, warm and welcoming. In the background she could hear Felicity clapping her hands, signalling the beginning of class and then the first few notes of a tango sprang from the speakers at the front of the room.

"I used to." He pulled on her hand and she stepped toward him. "But recently I've realized the benefits of a good tango."

He took her in his arms, holding the frame better than Sid had. When had he learned to do that? He led her through the steps, and she followed effortlessly, looking into his eyes whenever the dance allowed. His eyes were alight. He was having fun.

They were having fun together.

The dance ended and she felt a loss when he stepped back.

"I've really missed you," he said.

"I've missed you too."

"I was wondering if I could borrow you after this to get your opinion on something."

He wanted her opinion on something? "Of course."

"You sure you don't have to get back to Marvin?"

"He's had his walk. He'll be fine for a few hours."

"Good," he said. "Now, I think the instructor is trying to teach us something. We better pay attention. I don't want to get into her bad books on my first day."

She laughed, and they spent an enjoyable hour together stumbling and learning the new sequence together until they were in sync, moving around the floor effortlessly.

As the class was ending, Felicity caught up to them at the coat rack. "Bravo, you mastered those steps beautifully. Come to our intermediate class next month. I think you're ready."

"Thanks, we'll discuss it," Richard said as he reached for Susan's coat and held it for her to slip into.

Susan hesitated before turning to accept his help with her coat and then put her arms into the sleeves. "Yes, we had a lot of fun tonight."

"Fantastic," Felicity said. "Hope to see you soon then." Then she glided off to talk to some of the other students.

They left the dance school and both drove to Lucy's house where she got into his car, wondering where he was taking her. A restaurant? To the beach for a walk? When he parked in front of the hardware store, she turned towards him. "What are we doing here?"

"New kitchen taps is one item on your list of repairs. I wanted to ask you what type I should get to replace them."

"You're working on the repair list?" He was just full of surprises today.

"Yes. I know I haven't been doing my share around the house for a long time. It's time I made it up to you."

"Oh." She couldn't think of what else to say just then. He was here, he had come dancing with her, and now he was working on the house, but would he want to stay once she told him she'd been tempted to stray?

He unbuckled his seatbelt and turned to open his door. "Come on. They close in an hour and there's something else I want to show you, too."

"Wait."

He turned back towards her. "What's wrong?"

"I need to tell you something." She swallowed hard. "I'm not sure that you're going to want to go shopping with me after I'm finished."

His jaw tightened. "Go on."

"When you were away, I..." She swallowed again. "I was lonely and feeling, well, angry with you for not telling me where you were, or about the money."

"I'm sorry about the money, Sue. I feel stupid and you won't be able to blame me more than I blame myself for mucking up our finances."

"It's not the money."

"I know. I betrayed your trust. And I know it will take a long time to get you to trust me again, but I'm willing to work at it. Together."

"I know you'll fix it," she said. "I know I can learn to trust you again. I'm just not sure if you'll be able to forgive me."

"What are you talking about?" The light from the streetlamp that lit the store parking lot highlighted the crease in his forehead.

"When you were gone, I started to think of what my life would be like without you." She watched the crease in his forehead deepen, so she quickly added, "I've been spending a lot of time with Lucy and when I found out you hadn't been honest with me, I assumed…"

"I'm sorry," he said, and she held up her hand to stop his words.

"I went out for coffee with Sid and well… He thought it was a date." He glowered and she rushed on. "Nothing happened. He didn't try anything. Nothing like that."

"Then what's wrong?"

"Nothing happened. But, well… it felt good that he noticed me, and I was tempted—only for a few seconds, really—to let him think he was right. That it was a date."

"I see." His forehead was still creased.

"I'm sorry, and nothing happened, but I've never before…"

"You've never before been in a situation where you didn't trust me to be here for you," he said, reaching toward her and pulling her close. "I'm sorry, Sue, I didn't mean to put you in that position. I was sure that the investment would pay off like Louis promised. If it had all worked, we could both retire early. Travel. Do all the things you said you wanted. But I failed you, and then I tried to cover it up."

"I know," she shifted in her seat trying to lessen the space between them in spite of the bucket seats. "But…"

"Sue, I know you. You would never have considered cheating if I hadn't given you cause to question my intentions." He pulled her closer. "I love you, Sue. Please come home."

"I love you, too," she said. "I want to come home. I just need to know things will change, that you'll talk to me. That you'll include me."

"I've had a lot of time to think while I was away, and I realize I don't want to help you with all the work around the house."

"What?" What did that mean?

He held up his hand before she could protest further. "Just a second. Let me explain what I mean."

"Okay," she said, shifting back in her chair to listen.

"We fell into a pattern, Sue. I realize that now. You were responsible for getting things done and I helped out when I could." He shrugged a little before continuing. "Or, let's face it, I helped when I wanted to help. If I didn't do it, I knew you would pick up the slack. You always do."

"I probably should have asked for more help," she said and he shook his head before continuing.

"No, this isn't all on you. I realize that what we need to do is talk about sharing the work more equally, especially now that you are the only one working. I promise I'll be the one to pick up the slack now. It's my turn."

"I'd like us to discuss it all," she said. "I would appreciate the help…sorry…I'd appreciate sharing the responsibility."

"And I want us to start doing some of those things we always said we would do after we retired."

"I'd like that too," she said leaning toward him again. Darned these bucket seats. Right now, she just wanted to go home where there was no more distance between them.

"I love you so much, you don't know how much I have regretted what I did. I never wanted to let you down."

"I know." She put her arms up around his neck and pulled his mouth down on hers. He brought her as tight against him as the gap between the seats would allow and they stayed that way, kissing like they had in college; long and thorough and she didn't want it to end. The sound of a squeaky shopping cart brought them back to the present, reminding them of where they were.

"The store's closing soon," he said. "I can change the taps tomorrow if you let me know which ones you like. I've narrowed it down to three."

"Okay," she said, reluctantly turning to get out of the car. "But let's be quick. I want another kiss like that."

"You've got it," he said. "You might even get two." He came around to her side of the car and grabbed her hand, pulling her toward the store. "Let's be quick. We have some catching up to do."

The taps were at the back of the store and he quickly showed her the three he thought would go with their décor and that were of similar shape and color as others in the house. "I like this one," she said, pointing to the middle one. "It has a spray nozzle for the dishes."

"That's the one, then," he said, locating a boxed set on the shelf below. "Now, I have one more thing I need your opinion on before we go." He took her hand and led her to the other side of the store to a wall covered with clocks. "I heard from Brian that the other clock got broken."

"About that…" she said, feeling contrite. "I helped the clock fall off the wall."

"It's okay. I figured as much. When I look at these, I can see your point, that it was quite ugly."

"I'm sorry, though. I know how much you loved it."

"I love you more." He took her hand and led her a few steps down the aisle. "Now, I found a couple that I like and I want to show them to you." He pointed out three and again she pointed to the one in the middle.

"That one. I like that one the best."

"Good," he said. "That's my favorite too. Now let's get out of here."

When they pulled up to Lucy's apartment he asked, "Are you sure you won't come home tonight? You could bring Marvin with you."

"No, I would have to pack and figure out his food. It's easier to stay. Joel said he would take him for the weekend. Besides, I have to work in the morning."

He gazed into her eyes with that intensity again. She swayed and her arms sneaked up around his neck once more as though of their own volition, then pulled him close and kissed him. She had a lot of thinking to do tonight, decisions to make, but…

"Why don't you stay here?" she asked when they broke off their kiss. "I need some help to decide which job to take by tomorrow and I need, no, I want you to help me."

"Lead the way." He grabbed her hand and she led him toward the apartment.

*R*ichard stretched his arms over his head and watched Susan rush around the room, getting ready for work. He had missed watching her in her morning routine.

"You know where the dog's leash is?" she asked for the second time. "And I'm leaving the key on the counter. You'll need it to get up and down the elevator."

"Marvin and I will be fine. Don't worry."

She paused in the middle of the room, counting a mental list off on her fingers.

"If you forgot anything let me know and I'll bring it. Now go. You'll be late."

She spun around to face him, a smile broad on her face. "I did forget something." She walked over to him to give him a kiss goodbye.

He reached up and pulled her closer, then pushed her away again. "You better go now, or you'll really be late."

"Oh, you." She batted his arm and giggled, and it was the most beautiful sound in the world.

"Don't forget, I'm taking you to dinner tonight. Maybe you can wear your red dress. I'd love to see it on you."

"I hope you'll like it in person as much as you liked the photo." She giggled and kissed him one more time before turning to leave. Then she turned and looked back at him. "I'll see you at home tonight. I can't wait to see the new taps."

"Your wish is my command," he said, and she laughed. He vowed then to make it his life's mission to make sure she laughed more often from now on.

CHAPTER 31

"They're here, Mom!" Brian yelled from the living room.

"Coming!" Susan wiped her hands on a dishtowel and rushed toward the door, pausing to yell up the stairs. "Richard! They're early!"

Richard was out of the bedroom and downstairs in a few moments, and he held her hand as they went to greet their guests. When they opened the door, Lucy and Rupert stood side by side, his arm draped over her shoulder and she was leaning into him. It looked to her like they had come through their troubles even stronger than before.

"Welcome back," Susan said, pulling them both through the door and giving Lucy a hug. "We've missed you."

"Rupert, good to see you." Richard pounded his brother on the back. "You're just in time for dinner. Susan made her prime rib."

"It smells fantastic. I can't wait."

"Can we get you a drink?" Susan asked, and seeing Lucy's nearly imperceptible shake of her head, continued, "Coffee? Tea? I've got some sparkling water."

"Herbal tea, peppermint if you have it," Rupert answered. "I've been learning to appreciate the simpler things in life."

"I'll have the same," Lucy said, smiling up at Rupert. Yes, it seemed things were mending in their relationship and Susan couldn't be happier.

"Peppermint tea it is," Susan said. "Have a seat, I'll be out in a few minutes."

"I'll help." Lucy followed her into the kitchen. "I want to catch up on what's been going on with you. How's Richard's job hunt coming along?"

Susan turned on the kettle. "He's started his own company as a business coach. With the connections he had from his last employer and the new ones he made while he was taking his courses, he's doing really well."

"That's excellent news," Lucy said. "I'm so happy for you."

"He's much happier and he doesn't have to travel nearly as much as he did before."

She took the mugs from the cupboard then opened another cupboard to get the tea bags.

"And you? What did you end up doing? I know you were looking for work when I left."

"A lot has happened in the past three months." Susan turned to lean against the counter to talk to Lucy while the water boiled. "I stayed where I was with an organization that appreciates me and I'm glad I did. It's giving me more time to develop my team so that when I do retire, I know the organization will be in good hands." The kettle shut off and she poured the water into the mugs, then arranged a tray with mugs and appetizers. Dinner would be about forty more minutes and they might be hungry in the meantime.

"How about you?"

"We're good," Lucy said, reaching to grab an appetizer and popping the stuffed mushroom into her mouth. "These are good. What's in them?"

"Shrimp. I'll give you the recipe if you like. Meanwhile, tell me, is he back to stay?"

"He is, and we're looking for a bigger condo now that he's making a steady income from his investments. We need a place that's soundproof because he's learning the piano. Can you imagine?"

"That's fantastic," Susan said as she picked up the tray and Lucy took another mushroom. "We should get in there before they think we've left, and before you eat all the mushrooms."

Lucy followed her and then stopped when she saw the new kitchen clock on the wall. "I love it," she said, laughing. "Where on earth did you find it?"

"Richard found it and I agreed that it would be the perfect fit. Come on." She picked up the tray and followed Lucy back into the living room, stopping to grin at the clock. The vintage scene of the sun sinking into the ocean was a bit silly, but it was better than the old fish clock. Besides, it wasn't the picture that drew them to the clock. It was the words at the bottom that had spoken to them.

Our Time.

And indeed, it was.

ABOUT THE AUTHOR

Many writers have a core story or theme they return to throughout their writing life. For Jeanine, it is her believe in the powers of friendship, love and community. It is through coming together that we hold pain and loneliness at bay and create everyday miracles.

Jeanine lives in the suburbs of Vancouver, British Columbia, Canada, just across the water from the fictional community of Sunshine Bay where many of her characters live.

Jeanine is currently working on her next book.